TOP
MARKS
FOR
MURDER

Also available by Robin Stevens:

MURDER MOST UNLADYLIKE
ARSENIC FOR TEA
FIRST CLASS MURDER
JOLLY FOUL PLAY
MISTLETOE AND MURDER
A SPOONFUL OF MURDER
DEATH IN THE SPOTLIGHT

Tuck-box-sized mysteries:

CREAM BUNS AND CRIME
THE CASE OF THE MISSING TREASURE

Based on an idea and characters
by Siobhan Dowd:

THE GUGGENHEIM MYSTERY

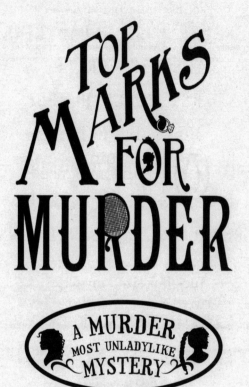

TOP MARKS FOR MURDER

A MURDER MOST UNLADYLIKE MYSTERY

ROBIN STEVENS

PUFFIN

PUFFIN BOOKS

UK | USA | Canada | Ireland | Australia
India | New Zealand | South Africa

Puffin Books is part of the Penguin Random House group of companies
whose addresses can be found at global.penguinrandomhouse.com.

www.penguin.co.uk
www.puffin.co.uk
www.ladybird.co.uk

First published 2019

001

The featured poem is 'Terence, this is stupid stuff', poem LXII of *A Shropshire Lad*
by A. E. Housman, first published by Treubner in 1896

Set in 11/16 pt New Baskerville Std
Typeset by Jouve (UK), Milton Keynes
Printed and bound in Great Britain by Clays Ltd, Elcograf S.p.A.

A CIP catalogue record for this book is available from the British Library

ISBN: 978–0–241–34838–3

All correspondence to:
Puffin Books
Penguin Random House Children's
80 Strand, London WC2R 0RL

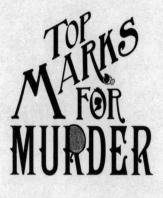

TOP MARKS FOR MURDER

Being an account of

The Case of the Anniversary Weekend Murder,
an investigation by the Wells and Wong Detective Society.

Written by Hazel Wong
(Detective Society Vice-President and Secretary),
aged almost 15.

Begun Saturday 4th July 1936.

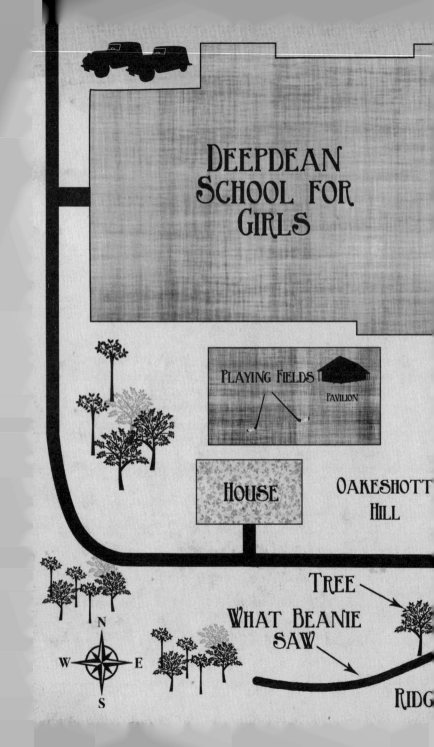

DEEPDEAN
SCHOOL FOR
GIRLS

PLAYING FIELDS

PAVILION

HOUSE

OAKESHOTT
HILL

TREE

WHAT BEANIE
SAW

N
W E
S

RIDG

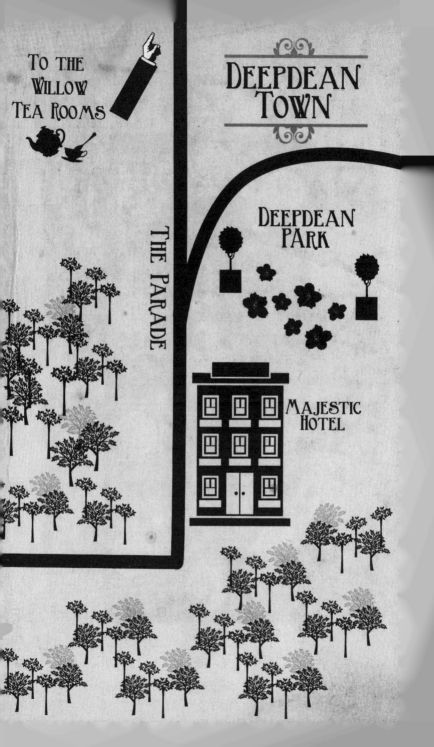

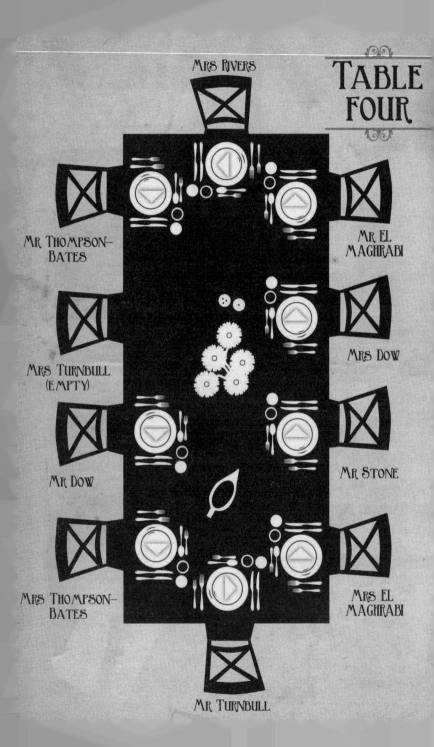

DEEPDEAN SCHOOL

THE STAFF

Miss Barnard, 'Barny' – *Headmistress*
Miss Lappet – *History and Latin mistress*
Mr MacLean – *Reverend*
Mademoiselle Renauld, 'Mamzelle' – *French mistress*
Miss Runcible – *Science mistress*
Miss Morris – *Music and Art mistress*
Miss Dodgson – *English mistress*
Miss Talent – *Games mistress*
Mrs Minn, 'Minny' – *Nurse*
Matron – *Matron*

THE GIRLS

Daisy Wells – *Fourth Former and President of the Wells & Wong Detective Society*
Hazel Wong – *Fourth Former and Vice-President and Secretary of the Wells & Wong Detective Society*
Lavinia Temple – *Fourth Former and Detective Society Member*

Rebecca 'Beanie' Martineau – *Fourth Former and Detective Society Member*

Kitty Freebody – *Fourth Former and Detective Society Member*

BIG GIRLS

Pippa Daventry
Alice Murgatroyd
Astrid Frith
Emmeline Moss
Jennifer Stone

FOURTH FORMERS

Clementine Delacroix
Sophie Croke-Finchley
Rose Pritchett
Jose Pritchett
Amina El Maghrabi

THIRD FORMERS

Lallie Thompson-Bates
Binny Freebody
Ella Turnbull
Martha Grey
Alma Collingwood
The Marys

YOU ARE CORDIALLY INVITED TO

DEEPDEAN'S
FIFTIETH ANNIVERSARY WEEKEND
celebrating the illustrious past, present and future
of Deepdean School for Girls

FRIDAY 3–MONDAY 6 JULY 1936

❀ Concert 7 p.m. Friday ❀ Exhibition Matches 2 p.m. Saturday ❀
❀ Gala Dinner 7 p.m. Saturday ❀ Chapel 10 a.m. Sunday morning ❀
❀ Garden Party 2 p.m. Sunday ❀ Commemorative Play 7 p.m. Sunday ❀
❀ Leaving Prayers 9 a.m. Monday morning ❀

❀ by invitation only ❀

RSVP:
Deepdean Headmistress's Office,
Oakeshott Hill Road,
Deepdean

Suggested accommodation:
The Majestic Hotel,
The Parade,
Deepdean

Motorcars may be parked on Oakeshott Road

Pupils will be allowed to leave school with parents or guardians on Saturday between the hours of
10 a.m. and 2 p.m. Please note that the Anniversary is not a full exeat, nor a holiday
– pupils may NOT leave the school grounds outside these hours, and may not be removed
from House overnight. We appreciate your observance of the school rules.

1

I am writing in this new casebook because death has come to Deepdean once again.

I am not quite sure why I am so surprised – but I am. Perhaps it is because lightning (lightning, in this case, being dead bodies) is not meant to strike twice, let alone several times, in the same place. Perhaps it is because the murder has happened at a time when we have all been ordered to be on our best behaviour, in starched and pressed dresses, as good and polite and law-abiding as schoolgirls can be.

And, although in the world outside I had begun to feel quite grown up and bold, it is funny how easy it was to fall back into school life once we returned to Deepdean. Over the last two days, it has almost been an effort to behave like a detective again, rather than just a schoolgirl, and I can see that Daisy has struggled with that as well – although she knows even more than I do

3

that this weekend we *must* detect. This case matters terribly, and if we do not solve it the consequences will be dreadful. We may even lose Deepdean, the home we all share.

Of course, Deepdean has been in danger before, and we have always saved it, but now I really do worry that this mystery may be too much for the school. How can it stay open, now that it is the location of a *third* crime – and what will Daisy and I do if it does not?

This case has twisted itself into the most confusing thread Daisy and I have ever had to unravel. I feel as though *anything* might happen next.

While these thoughts are whirling about in my head, and while the answer to the mystery dances frustratingly out of my reach, I shall try to explain how everything happened, and how this case began when our friend Beanie told us that she had seen a murder.

2

I ought to say what has happened since our last murder investigation in London – which was really only two months ago, although it seems longer. I thought it might feel odd to be back at Deepdean after all the wild and grown-up adventuring we have done this year, but instead I feel as though we never left, not *really*. Daisy and I are Deepdean schoolgirls, and – no matter where we go – this school is in our blood and bones, the one constant place in all the wandering we do.

I had barely finished writing up the story of the murder at the Rue Theatre, and everything that happened with George and Alexander and Uncle Felix and Aunt Lucy and Bridget, when it was time to wave goodbye to them all and rush through the smoke of Paddington Station to catch the Deepdean train.

A car met us at Deepdean station, and when it pulled up outside House on the afternoon of Sunday

31st May, everywhere else in the world vanished like a dream. It could not possibly be true that just the week before we had been actresses, solving a terrible crime. As Daisy and I stepped through the front door into the dingy entrance hall, I knew that *this* was the only reality – the big clock and the dinner gong and the chipped, ugly staircase going up to the dorm rooms, every mark and dent and rip in the wallpaper familiar.

'Good old Deepdean,' said Daisy grandly, staring about at it. 'Home at last!'

I stood next to Daisy and felt both too big and too small, delighted and bewildered all at once – and then I heard a chorus of shrieks, and Kitty, Beanie and Lavinia, our dorm mates, friends and fellow Detective Society members, came rattling down the staircase and flung themselves on us. After that, all I felt was overjoyed.

'HAZEL! DAISY! YOU'RE BACK!' Beanie shouted in our ears, and then we were squeezed in an enormous six-armed hug. They smelled of soap and pencils (Beanie) and grass (Lavinia) and perfume (Kitty, contraband), and I breathed in happily.

'We missed you, we missed you, we missed you!' Beanie shrieked, jumping up and down and jostling the rest of us. 'We've been watching from upstairs, waiting for you to arrive!'

'It's not been much fun without you,' agreed Lavinia. She said it grudgingly, but Kitty pinched her and she blushed, so I could see she meant it.

'Oh, there's so much to tell you!' cried Kitty. 'Come upstairs, come on, come on!'

Matron came out of her office and glared at us in a welcome-back way, as we left our bags for the maids and rushed up the stairs to our familiar dorm. Except—

'We moved the beds round while you were gone,' explained Kitty. 'It's fearfully cold by the window, you know, and since you weren't here to feel it—'

'We can move back!' said Beanie anxiously. 'We're sorry!'

'No, don't do that,' I said. 'We'll be all right, won't we, Daisy?'

'I suppose,' said Daisy, shrugging.

Kitty gasped, and looked from me to Daisy and back again. Beanie was wide-eyed. Lavinia suddenly grinned.

'You've changed, Hazel,' she said. 'Look at you, telling Daisy what to do!'

'I have not!' I said, blushing, because I thought she might be right.

'Hazel and I haven't changed!' said Daisy. 'That's nonsense. I simply happen to agree with her assessment on this occasion. YOU, on the other hand – *look* at the three of you! Look at Beanie!'

'Um,' said Beanie, wriggling uncomfortably. 'It isn't my fault, it just *happened*.'

'Beanie *grew*,' said Kitty gleefully. 'She's not tiny any more! We're still calling her Beanie, though, but now it's short for Beanpole.'

It was true. Beanie's hair was still done up in the same straggly plait, and her large eyes peered out of her face in the same shy way, but in the five months since we had seen her last she had shot up like a plant. She was now quite as tall as Kitty, but much thinner, and she stood as though she did not know what to do with all her arms and legs.

'*And* Lavinia has bosoms.'

'SO?' said Lavinia furiously, crossing her arms over her now rather pronounced chest. 'I hate them.'

'*She's on the tennis team too*,' mouthed Kitty behind her. 'She's *fearfully* good at sport all of a sudden, but she *hates* it when we tell her!'

'Oh, Lavinia!' I cried. This was not the Lavinia I knew, the one who hid in goal next to me so we did not have to bother with hockey practice – but I could see that Lavinia was pleased with herself, and I was pleased for her.

'Fancy!' cried Daisy, with a funny look on her face. 'Lavinia, a tennis ace!'

'Well, Kitty's got a boyfriend!' Lavinia shot back.

Kitty simpered. 'I met him at a dance during the Easter hols!' she said. 'His name is Hugo. *Don't* tell Binny.'

8

'How *is* Binny?' I asked. Kitty's little sister is in the third form, a year below us, and she played a large part in one of our cases last autumn.

Kitty scowled. 'Hideous,' she said. 'She's become quite obsessed with the new girl in the other fourth-form dorm – all the third formers are. They can't talk about anything else. Her name is Amina, and she's terribly glamorous. I wish my hair looked like hers!'

'She's very beautiful,' agreed Beanie, sighing. 'Everyone says so, even the mistresses. She can get away with anything she likes.'

Daisy sat down on the nearest bed, looking odder than ever. 'New girl!' she said weakly. '*Glamorous!* But – see here, why didn't you tell us about all this before?'

'We didn't think you'd care,' said Lavinia with a shrug. 'You'll see her later, anyway. *I* don't think she's worth much.'

'Nonsense,' said Kitty. 'She's wonderful. All the shrimps have pashes on her.'

'Well!' cried Daisy, cutting Kitty off and standing up suddenly. 'That's quite enough news. Stop it, please.'

'But Amina—' Kitty began.

'No more about her!' said Daisy. 'It's unnecessary. There *may* be a new girl, and *you* may all have changed, but *I* am just the same as I ever was, and so, thank goodness, is Deepdean School. I am back, and that is that. And I have changed my mind about the beds. Move them back, if you please.'

And I understood then what Daisy's expression meant. Despite what she had said to the others, she *has* changed this year, in ways that she is not entirely ready to face up to. Nothing is the same as it was – not me, not her family, and not Daisy herself – and I realized then that she had desperately hoped to find Deepdean just as she had remembered it.

But unfortunately for Daisy, she found the rest of Deepdean just as changed as Kitty, Beanie and Lavinia.

3

Since January, without her there at school to keep it up, the myth of Daisy Wells had faltered, its light dimmed – and it was not easy for her to restore its glow now that someone else had stepped into the light.

It was just as Kitty, Beanie and Lavinia had said. In the middle of the spring term, while Daisy and I were away solving a terrible crime in Hong Kong, Amina El Maghrabi had arrived in the fourth form at Deepdean, from Hampden School for Ladies in Cairo.

Before Amina appeared at dinner that evening, Daisy and I had heard that she was a princess; the daughter of a sheik; betrothed to the new king of Egypt; the best equestrienne Deepdean had ever seen; and the rightful owner of the Koh-i-Noor diamond.

'It's all nonsense!' hissed Daisy. 'Most of that can't possibly be true – after all, there aren't any sheiks in

Egypt, and the Koh-i-Noor is most likely from India. Where did you hear this from?'

The replies were confused but adoring – but one thing was certain: Amina had captured every imagination, in much the same way as the Honourable Daisy Wells had done when I first arrived at Deepdean.

When Amina came through the Dining Room doors, arm in arm with Clementine from the other dorm, I thought she really did look like a fairy-tale princess from one of the stories my maid Su Li had told me when I was little. She had smooth pale brown skin and a glossy head of dark hair, a proud look on her pretty face, and feet as small as Cinderella's. Deepdean's baggy grey uniform hung beautifully on her.

I could see immediately that she was the sort of person that people make up myths about.

'She was ten minutes late to every lesson for the first two weeks she was at Deepdean, and during those weeks she managed to convince all the mistresses that she had never learned to tell time,' whispered Kitty. 'She's terribly wicked, but no one minds.'

'Hush!' said Daisy, a furious frown on her face.

As I watched, Binny Freebody, Kitty's little sister, went hurrying up to Amina and whispered something in her ear. Amina beamed and blew Binny a kiss (Binny went purple with joy), and then she turned and gestured.

Up popped the Marys, holding out their hands – and Amina handed them her hat, scarf and school bag.

'She's *you*!' I whispered to Daisy. 'She's making them carry her things just like *you* used to do!'

I admit, the sight of Amina had startled me. I am used to being the one girl at Deepdean who does not look like all the rest – and used to being gently looked down on for it. But here was darker-skinned Amina making all the pale English misses fawn around her. Was it simply because she looked as though she expected nothing less?

'She is not anything like me!' Daisy hissed back. 'Only *I* am me. There is only one Daisy Wells. These foolish third formers will come back to the person they *truly* adore soon enough.'

'Why should they?' asked Lavinia, rather rudely.

'Because ... because people ought to have some respect!' said Daisy furiously. 'It's not as though I'd *died*, is it? Everyone knew I was coming back! They'll remember me, you'll see.'

But her voice sounded rather thin and unsure.

'Clementine and Rose and Jose tried to bully her at first,' said Kitty, from next to me. 'You know, Daisy, to pull the trunk trick you did on Hazel. But she refused to get in, and then she ordered a hamper full of tuck from Fortnum's and only gave it to Sophie because she'd been nice all along, and then everyone was nice to her.'

'I admit, that is brilliant,' said Daisy, her eyes narrowed as she studied Amina. 'Hazel – I don't like this girl in the slightest.'

Binny and the other third formers came to find Daisy just before Prep.

'We got your note,' said Binny to Daisy, standing up straight and crossing her arms, while the Marys, Martha and Alma all arranged themselves behind her looking nervous but defiant. 'And we don't care. We'll do what we like – and Amina is far nicer to us than you ever were!'

'Nonsense! What about – what about *loyalty*?' asked Daisy.

'Loyalty!' cried Binny. 'When you used us for information all last year, but never let us into your *secret* society?'

Daisy was so angry her eyes were flashing blue. 'Why, you – traitor! All of you!'

'Sorry,' said Marie.

'We still like you,' said Marion.

'But we don't want to carry your coat any more,' said Maria. 'We're carrying Amina's instead.'

They turned and walked away together. Kitty shouted, 'YOU'RE A RAT, BINNY!' after them, but it sounded hollow.

'It's the Marys that hurt the most,' said Daisy, and she spent Prep slumped at her desk, staring miserably into space.

The next day she discovered that her place on the equestrian team had been given to Amina, and there were no more parts for the Anniversary play. She pretended to everyone else that she did not mind about it, but privately she slipped into a funk so black that I did not know quite what to do with her.

I had never seen Daisy like this before, for even when other dreadful things were happening to her, she knew in her heart that she had Deepdean. Now that she could not rule over Deepdean any more, it was as though a crucial part of her was missing.

4

I had to do something. I worried away at the problem for the next day, and then the answer came to me in a flash. It was a plan I could have never imagined carrying out last year, but, like everyone else at Deepdean, I have changed. I am more than the Hazel Wong I used to be.

After Prep was over that evening, during the muddle of toothbrushes, I climbed up through House and knocked on the very highest door. It opened, and there, in her pyjamas, was the Head Girl.

'What do you want?' she asked.

'I'd like your help,' I said, trying not to quail, for she looked very cross. 'We – Daisy Wells and I, I mean – we helped you two terms ago, didn't we?'

'I suppose you did,' said the Head Girl. 'Go on.'

'Can you make sure that Daisy is put back on the equestrian team, and gets a part in the play?' I asked. 'She's . . . upset that she's been taken off the team, and she's a good actress, I promise she is. She won't let the school down.'

The Head Girl frowned. 'She had better not,' she said. 'You know it's a special one this year, for the Anniversary. It's a walking play, where the cast moves around the school and the audience follows. We can't have anything but the best.'

'Daisy's the best at anything she tries, you know that!' I said. 'She won't let you down, honour bright. And she's a real actress – she was in *Romeo and Juliet* at the Rue last month. In London!'

The Head Girl sighed and shrugged. 'All right, then,' she said. 'I'll have words.'

'But please don't tell *anyone* that I asked you!' I said hurriedly. 'She can't know.'

'Go away, Wong,' said the Head Girl, shutting the door on me – but I thought she said it good-naturedly, and, sure enough, the very next day it was discovered that Daisy had only been missed off the equestrian team list by mistake, and one more role was needed in the Anniversary play. A character called the Spirit of the School would watch over the proceedings as the company moved around the school and would bless the actors at the end.

'The prefects asked me specially!' Daisy told me blissfully. 'They said they couldn't do it without me, so of course I accepted.'

'I'm glad,' I said, straight-faced.

'Thank you, Hazel Wong,' said Daisy, with a wink. 'Don't lie, I know it was you really.' Then her face fell. 'All the same – oh, bother, but it shouldn't have to be up to *you*! They ought to simply change the rules for me. That's how it's always been! This school has gone dreadfully downhill.'

'You're not the King, Daisy Wells,' said Kitty, coming to sit on Daisy's bed. 'You just have to get used to being like the rest of us.'

'But I'm *not* like the rest of you,' said Daisy. She said it so emptily that it made my heart hurt.

'Humph!' said Kitty, and she jumped onto Daisy's thin pillow, which made a crackling sound. Daisy went stiff all over and shoved Kitty away.

'Ow!' said Kitty. 'Just because you can't bear to hear the truth! What are you hiding under your pillow, anyway?'

'Nothing!' said Daisy. 'Nothing at all.'

'Show me or I'll find out anyway, Daisy Wells,' said Kitty, poking her.

'It's the programme from my play, if you must know,' said Daisy, teeth gritted, '*Romeo and Juliet*. I am using it to inspire me in my role as the Spirit of the School. That's why it has to stay under my pillow at all times and if you move it I shall hurt you very badly.'

I tensed myself too, ready for Kitty to prod at that quite obvious falsehood. But then . . .

18

'That photo's new,' said Kitty, leaning over to look at the snap that was on my bedside table.

'It's of us with George and Alexander,' I said quickly. 'Uncle Felix took it just before we came back to school.'

Kitty peered at it, and I looked too. Daisy and I were standing together on the London pavement with our arms round each other, the two boys behind us with their hands on our shoulders. We were all four squinting into the sunshine.

'Isn't Alexander handsome!' Kitty cried. I blushed without meaning to. '*So* tall. Ooh, *Hazel*! If I wasn't absolutely loyal to my boyfriend Hugo . . .'

'Hmm,' said Lavinia, leaning over both of us. 'The blond one's all right, but *he's* more handsome.' She pointed at George.

'No he isn't!' I said, rather surprised, for I had never considered George that way. 'He's . . . he's just George.'

'They're both just *boys*,' said Daisy, shrugging. 'There's nothing else to say about them.'

At that moment, Beanie came running into the dorm, startling us all. 'I've just got a letter from Daddy!' she cried. 'He's coming to the Anniversary, and he's bringing Mummy!'

5

After that, the Anniversary weekend was all anyone could think about – and it is funny now to remember how excited everyone was. This year is the fiftieth anniversary of Deepdean's opening, and so a long weekend of celebrations had been planned. The Anniversary was to begin with a music concert on Friday evening in which both current and old girls would perform, and then there were exhibition matches on Saturday, a gala dinner for Big Girls and parents on Saturday night, chapel on Sunday morning, the garden party on Sunday afternoon, the play on Sunday evening, and finally, to mark the end of the school year, Leaving Prayers on Monday morning.

Most parents were coming down on Thursday evening or on Friday and staying until Monday. As well as Beanie's parents, Kitty's were coming, and Lavinia's father with his fiancée as well as her mother, who he was divorcing. Even Clementine's father had promised to make an appearance – and it was rumoured that Amina's people were coming all the way from Egypt.

In fact, Daisy and I were the only fourth formers set to be entirely on our own. I tried not to mind about that and to remember what my father had said during his last telephone call.

'You must understand, Hazel,' he had said to me down the crackling phone line. 'The journey from Hong Kong would take far too long. You must be brave about this.'

'Yes, Father,' I said, thinking I had already been brave enough for a whole lifetime.

'I will come for the Christmas holidays, I promise you,' said my father. 'And IF Rose and May are VERY GOOD, they MIGHT be able to come with me.'

I heard Hong-Kong-faraway shrieks behind his voice, and I knew that my little sisters were in his study with him.

I tried to be excited, but Christmas seemed oceans away, just like my family.

'Buck up,' said Daisy, who was being very don't-care about it. 'Who needs parents, anyway? *I'm* here, that ought to be enough for you.' But I know Daisy too well by now to be tricked by her poses. I knew that she had telephoned London and come out of Matron's office with her shoulders slumped. Uncle Felix and Aunt Lucy were both too busy with work to be able to come down, and Bertie was busy at Cambridge, and that cut Daisy deeply.

'You're lucky!' grumbled Lavinia. 'It's far worse to have your people here embarrassing you. It's going to be *awful*. My parents, in the same room – ugh! They hate each other. And my father's bringing Patricia. If he makes me call her *Mother*, I think I might kill him.'

'I'm sorry,' said Beanie, patting her, 'but Patricia is nice, isn't she?'

Lavinia glared at her. 'I hate her, and I hate my father, and I hate my mother. Ugh, I want to run away all over again.'

Beanie looked quite shocked.

'Hey, Beanie,' said Kitty, poking her. 'Cheer up. Your mum's coming to the Anniversary, remember?'

'She *is*!' said Beanie, and her eyes lit up. We all knew that Beanie's mother had not been well. It was the reason why Beanie had had to stay with Kitty last Christmas – but Mrs Martineau must be better now.

Excitement buzzed about the school. The Games mistress, Miss Talent, was choosing girls for the exhibition matches and the English mistress, Miss Dodgson, was leading play rehearsals. ('She's hopeless,' said Daisy, 'not a patch on Inigo.') The Music and Art mistress, Miss Morris, was choosing performers for the concert, including

Sophie Croke-Finchley from the other fourth-form dorm, who was to play a piano solo. The thumping noises she produced as she played through her piece in the House common room became a constant noise in my head that I would find myself humming at odd moments. We practised walking and curtseying in Deportment, and the Big Girls were gathered in a room and quietly reminded of the niceties of dinner etiquette: holding their forks and knives correctly, passing the salt and pepper to the left at the same time and conversing in a manner both polite and amusing. ('As if they wouldn't already know all that!' said Daisy scornfully. 'We're Deepdean girls, not animals!')

Miss Runcible, the Science mistress, stopped her lessons on solutes and distillation and had the third and fourth forms making fireworks for the display to be held at the end of the garden party on Sunday night. (This made me nervous – Deepdean does not have a good history with fireworks.) And everyone, from the Big Girls to the shrimps, began whispering about the end-of-year pranks. There is a tradition of playing them at Deepdean – but it could not be decided whether we ought to hold off, because of the Anniversary, or make them even more impressive than usual.

'I heard the fifth formers are going to dye the Deepdean pond green during the Anniversary,' said Kitty.

'No, the third formers are going to blow up Miss Barnard's lectern,' said Lavinia.

'That's not a prank, that's a crime,' said Kitty scornfully. 'They'd never.'

'I think Amina and the other fourth-form dorm are plotting something,' said Kitty. 'I saw them all giggling together yesterday. And it'll be spectacular, if Amina's part of it! She's so clever.'

'Oh, do stop talking about Amina!' snapped Daisy. 'Pranks are stupid and childish and we ought to ignore them.'

'*Jealous*,' Lavinia mouthed at Kitty, and Kitty nodded.

'I am going up to the dorm,' said Daisy, her nose in the air. 'Hazel, come with me. The rest of you are *not invited*.'

I could see that, for all my hard work, her mood had not really lightened at all – nor would it, while Amina was at Deepdean. She was a constant reminder that Daisy's grip on the school had loosened. At that moment, I wished that Amina had never come to Deepdean.

But what I could not know was just how important Amina and her family would be during the Anniversary weekend – and to the mystery.

June flew past my head like a rounders ball, in a whirl of lessons and activities and Saturday afternoons in Deepdean town, in Beanie losing Chutney the dormouse and then finding her again (heart-stoppingly) in Matron's study, in Daisy and Beanie preparing for the roles they had been given in the play, and Lavinia for her exhibition tennis match.

We had our last exams, and that was another whirl, a rather more sickening one, in which I realized that the lessons we had been getting from Aunt Lucy in London were not at all the sort of lessons we needed now we were back at school. I had to stop hiding my swottiness in a frantic rush to find out which kings had fought which battles and where Patagonia was, and even Daisy was seen reading a book that was not a murder mystery.

And then it was July, the day the Anniversary celebrations began, and the sun was out and the trees of Oakeshott Woods behind House were green and rustling, and Beanie turned to us and said:

'I – I think I've just seen a murder.'

6

It was Friday morning, the third of July, and the five members of the Detective Society were up in our dorm after breakfast. There were four minutes left until the first school bell, so we were busy piling books into our school bags and doing up our ties and chattering. Daisy, of course, was entirely ready, so she was lying on her bed with her hands pillowed behind her, staring thoughtfully at the cracks on the dorm ceiling. I was still making my bed, folding the scratchy blanket carefully over the neat sheets. Kitty was trying to get her hair to curl and Lavinia was struggling with her tie in front of the small mirror.

Beanie had been standing by the open window, warm summer-morning air breathing over her, staring out at the green tangle of Oakeshott Woods as if in a dream – and then she turned round and made her announcement. She said it quietly, in rather an awed voice, as though she could not believe the words she was saying.

We all stopped talking and stared at her.

'WHAT did you say?' asked Daisy, sitting bolt upright with a bounce.

Beanie was frozen, her fingertips clutching the window frame, and then she gasped, and shook herself, and pointed her finger out at the woods. 'Come and look! Come and look!' she cried. 'Oh, quickly! There he is, on the ridge, next to that tree with a bare branch!'

We all rushed over and crowded round her at the window, staring out at the woods. Our House is on Oakeshott Hill, above Deepdean School, and our dorm faces away from the school buildings, towards the main wood itself. The road from school to House is on our right, and it winds back down again towards Deepdean town on our left, and so in front of our eyes was nothing but green leaves and blue sky, and the next high hill with trees standing up at the top of its ridge.

'Where is he? Where?' asked Daisy frantically, turning her head from side to side as though there might be a murderer behind each tree.

'He's *gone*!' said Beanie with a little gasp. 'He must have ducked down after her – but *he* was there, and *she* was there, and then he put out his arms and— *Oh!* He choked her to death, I *saw* it!'

She was shaking, I could see. Kitty put her arms round her in a comforting way, but Beanie stood rigid, breathing in short little pants.

Daisy looked at me, swift and sharp. I knew what she meant – that she believed Beanie. It is true that Beanie does not lie, at least not on purpose. If she says something, it is at least true to *her*. And if Beanie had seen a crime . . . then this was a moment for the Detective Society.

'Come away from the window, everyone,' said Daisy, in her Detective Society President voice. Her eyes were suddenly brighter than they had been all term. 'Except you, Lavinia. You stand guard and watch, in case anything else occurs or *he* appears again. Beanie, explain yourself at once. Hazel, you take notes.'

'It was awful!' Beanie kept on saying. 'Awful!'

'Yes, all right, *what* was?' asked Daisy fiercely, as I rushed to my tuck box and pulled out a new casebook, my hands trembling just a little. I opened it to its first page and looked up at Beanie, my pencil hovering over the paper. 'Time is of the essence,' Daisy continued. 'You'll forget if you don't tell us quickly!'

'Start at the beginning, Beanie,' I said, trying to sound reassuring (for Daisy, of course, is not reassuring in the slightest). 'It's all right. What happened?'

Beanie chewed on the end of her plait and furrowed her brow. There was a long pause. At last she took a gasping breath and began.

'We'd just come up from breakfast. Lavinia went to the mirror to put her tie on straight, and, Hazel, you were making your bed, and I was looking for my Maths book. Only I couldn't find it, so I went to the window to look out at the woods and see if I could remember where it was. Then I began to think about *Mummy* seeing the woods this weekend and how much she'll like them, and so I leaned out on the sill and I sort of stared into the distance and—'

At this, Lavinia made a grumbling sound, and Kitty said, 'She's *getting* to it, aren't you, Beanpole?'

'Oh yes, sorry,' said Beanie. 'Anyway, you know how sometimes when you're staring at nothing much your eyes sort of focus without you noticing? I did that, with that ridge across from House. I suddenly realized that I was watching two people, a lady and a man.'

'What did they look like?' I asked.

'Ordinary-ish,' said Beanie. 'It's too far away to see details, but they were wearing summer coats – you know, just like any grown-up.'

Daisy, who had been sitting on her hands in an effort to remain calm, leaped to her feet. 'Detective Martineau!' she cried. 'Have I taught you nothing? This is absolutely diabolical observation. Were they tall? Short? Fair or dark? Fat or thin?'

'They had hats on!' said Beanie, shrinking into herself. 'And— Oh, I don't know. The man was a bit taller than the woman, I think. I didn't really think anything about them – they just looked like parents, like grown-ups. *You* know. I thought they were a couple, from the way they were standing talking together. Their heads were sort of bent together. But then they began to argue.

'I couldn't hear what they were saying, but they were waving their arms about, so I could tell it was *bad*. And then the man pulled the lady to him, and he put his hands around her neck and he *squeezed*. The lady was shoving at his shoulders, but it didn't work, and she suddenly went all *limp* and fell down so I couldn't see her any more, and he let go of her, and that's when I turned round and said . . . what I said, and when I turned back he was *gone*! That poor lady!'

Beanie gave a sobbing gulp, and Kitty put her arms round her.

'It's all right, Beans,' she said. 'You're safe, and he shan't hurt you.'

'But what if he *saw* me!' cried Beanie.

'I shouldn't think he did,' said Daisy. 'And if he did, what would he have seen from that distance? A girl with brown hair in a Deepdean uniform. That could be anyone!'

'I'm sure he *didn't* see you, Beanie,' I said, to try to calm the situation. 'But—'

'But,' Daisy jumped in, 'I must say that your story seems credible enough to investigate. And investigate we *must*. Detective Martineau, it is entirely possible that you have been witness to a murder!'

7

At that very moment the bell for school rang, shrill and metallic. Doors banged open all around us and footsteps began to pound down the stairs. We were out of time.

'Oh *no*!' said Beanie. 'I'm sorry.'

'Never mind bells,' said Daisy. 'Never mind school! A crime has been committed, and the most pressing thing is this: we *must* get up to that ridge. We must observe the scene as soon as we can!'

'All right, but when do you suggest we do that?' asked Kitty sceptically. 'We don't have Games today, and tonight's the beginning of the Anniversary. And none of *that* takes place in the woods! Shouldn't we call the police?'

'Stop thinking about timetables!' said Daisy, wrinkling her nose. 'And no, this is not time for the police. We need to make sure that Beanie saw what she says she did before we tell anyone else. We must get up to that hill despite lessons – and I believe I have the answer.'

'Daisy!' I said, catching her meaning. 'No, not—'

'Yes, we are going to miss lunch today,' said Daisy firmly. 'Ignore Hazel, she is not thinking like a detective any more than Kitty is. We must find a way of escaping House to get to the woods. We can ask the third— Oh, bother those turncoats! Never mind. Oh! I know! Watson, bring my bag – I must run down to Matron's office. I'll catch up with you at the House door!'

She spun on her heel and bolted out of the room, her golden hair flaring out behind her.

'What d'you think she's going to do?' asked Kitty.

'Something stupid,' said Lavinia with a shrug. 'Come on, let's go.'

I shouldered Daisy's bag as well as my own, staggering rather under the weight of them as I followed the other three out of the dorm. As I went, I looked back once more, out of the window at the empty ridge.

I felt . . . uncertain, somehow. I could see how frightened Beanie was. She believed what she had told us. Could it *really* be true, though? Daisy seemed to think so. She was utterly ready to detect . . . but, after a month of being miserable, Daisy needed something like this.

This term, at Deepdean, everyone was in the middle of their own stories, and Daisy and I were nothing more than bit parts. I had learned to fit in before, so adjusting was not too hard for me. But nothing in Daisy's life so far had prepared her to be ordinary, to find herself in the shadow of other girls. Now that Beanie believed she had seen a murder, though, Daisy could be a detective again. She could be daring and important and *extra*ordinary. In an odd sort of way, what was dangerous to anyone else in the world brought comfort, and even a strange kind of safety, to Daisy Wells.

Would Beanie be proven right when we went up to the ridge?

1

I dreamed through Science (luckily, Amina was telling the whole form about all the kings she had met, and *that* made Miss Runcible too giddy to teach us), and at last it was bunbreak. We queued for biscuits first – gingernuts make any mystery better – but because I had been slow putting my books into my bag, Daisy and I were rather behind the rest of the Detective Society in the queue.

Daisy was sighing and wriggling, darting pointed glances back at me and forward to the biscuit table.

'You can go on!' I said at last.

'I can't,' said Daisy. 'I've lost pushing-in privileges. And, well, if I pushed in, what about you?'

I hooked my arm through hers and squeezed gladly.

'What I mean is,' said Daisy in my ear, 'that as soon as we get our biscuits, we'll have to go and meet the others by the pond. They're there already – look. And I wanted to have a word with just you first.'

I looked about us. There was a crowd of lordly fifth formers in front of us, and some first-form shrimps just behind. We appeared to be safe.

'What did you want to say?' I asked, cautiously quiet all the same.

'It's about *what Beanie saw*,' said Daisy, and I could tell that she was being careful too, in a Daisyish way. 'Something she said, about what *they* looked like – it's been stuck in my head all morning.'

'*Ordinary-ish*,' I said, grinning a little as I remembered.

'Not that!' said Daisy. 'That was simply dreadful and can be ignored. The other thing. She said they looked like grown-ups. Like *parents*.'

'But she only meant—' I began.

'No, Hazel! People often say more than they mean, and they do it quite unconsciously. What if that was our' – she lowered her voice even further – '*our first real clue*? Because . . . what day is it?'

'Friday,' I said.

'Not just *Friday*! What's this *particular* day? Think logically.'

'*The Friday of the Anniversary*,' I said, understanding. 'And . . . and that means all the parents are arriving. You think . . . you think they might have *really* been parents?'

'I think there's at least a strong possibility,' said Daisy, nodding. 'Parents wandering about in the woods before the Anniversary begins properly. And if I'm right – well! There's something *quite* obvious that we need to do *before* we go up to the scene at lunch. Do you see, Hazel?'

'We need to find out which parents are supposed to be coming to the Anniversary!' I said. I took my biscuits from the pile and followed Daisy across the lawn towards the pond. 'But how?'

'Oh, it should be easy enough. There must be a list. A third former could help— Bother, ignore that. But we can find it, and we will. Now, let's tell the others of our plan!'

I looked at her. Daisy's face was lit up with eagerness. She had a purpose. Here was my Daisy Wells, at last. I bit back all my questions and simply smiled at her.

'What's up?' asked Kitty, as we arrived at the pond. 'Have you been plotting without us?'

'Are we going to the woods already?' asked Beanie, her face peaky with worry. 'I don't know if—'

'We're not going to the woods until lunch time, as I told you,' said Daisy. 'And you mustn't worry so much about being caught. Remember that everyone will be more distracted than usual because of the Anniversary, as well as my cunning plan. But yes, we *have* been talking privately, because Hazel and I are still by far the most senior detectives in this society.'

'It's really not fair,' grumbled Lavinia. 'We're supposed to be working together! Hey, Beanie, can I have your biscuits? I'm *starving*, and you're just nibbling them.'

Beanie passed her biscuits to Lavinia with a sigh, and Lavinia bit into them.

'So?' asked Kitty. 'What's the *cunning plan*? What genius idea have you had?'

'I am going to ignore your arch tone of voice,' said Daisy, 'and merely say that it has occurred to us that the people Beanie saw on the ridge may *actually* be *parents*, down in Deepdean for the Anniversary! And *if* that is true, then there is something we must do as soon as possible, before we visit the woods. We *must* get a copy of the RSVP list for the weekend. If Beanie really did see a murder, and it involved the parents of a Deepdean girl, then there will be one guest on that list who does not arrive tonight – for the most horrid reason!'

2

'But we can't just steal the list!' said Kitty.

'Of course we can,' said Daisy, rolling her eyes.

'No, we *can't*,' said Kitty, more forcefully. 'There's only *one* list. Haven't you been paying attention? Miss Lappet is in charge of it, and she's been fussing about it for weeks – I heard her talking to Miss Barnard about how the table settings keep on having to change as parents RSVP. It never leaves her side.'

'Well then!' said Daisy, though I could tell from her quick frown that she was momentarily thrown by the fact that Kitty knew more than she did. 'Well then, if it's up to date, all the more reason why we need to see it! If a father telephoned this morning to say that his wife won't be attending at the last minute, we need to know.'

'But how are we supposed to get hold of it?' asked Lavinia. 'Miss Lappet is hiding in Barny's office, like she does every bunbreak – and bunbreak is almost over.'

I thought – and then the most Daisyish plan came into my head, quick as a wink.

'We just need to keep to timetable,' I said. 'Isn't that right, Daisy?'

Daisy looked at me, her eyes very slightly narrowed.

'Because,' I went on, 'we've got History after bunbreak. With Miss Lappet!'

'AH YES!' said Daisy, relieved. 'Watson is quite right. All we need to do is cause a diversion just before History starts, take the list from Miss Lappet, and Hazel will copy it down during the lesson. Easy.'

'*Easy*,' repeated Kitty, raising her eyebrows at me.

'Easy,' I agreed – although I was not convinced it would be.

'Well, hurry up, Detectives!' cried Daisy. 'Let's go!'

We stood together outside Miss Barnard's door in Big Girls' wing. I felt uncomfortable, prickly with sweat on my palms and my temples. I took deep breaths, and told myself it would all be all right.

Daisy knocked.

There were flustered, rustling noises behind the door, and then it was pulled a little way open and Miss Lappet's head popped out to glare at us.

'What do you want, girls?' she snapped. 'I'm rather busy!'

'Oh, Miss Lappet!' said Daisy, eyes wide. 'I'm *so* sorry to bother you, but I'm terribly worried about my History exam. I haven't been able to get question three out of my head all week – I'm sure I bottled it and I don't know what to do!'

'Indeed, Wells, your exam was quite dispiriting,' said Miss Lappet. 'Question six was your Achilles heel – whatever were you thinking?'

I saw a flash of real panic in Daisy's eyes – and then she snapped back into being Deepdean Daisy.

'Oh, Miss Lappet, it's so hard – everything simply slides out of my brain! I do try, I really do. Only, not being here for so long . . .'

Miss Lappet tutted. 'Wells, really,' she said. 'You must apply yourself!'

'But – but – I *do* try,' gasped Daisy, and she dissolved into pretty tears. It was a childish trick, but it worked.

Miss Lappet came out of the study, a large pile of papers in her arms. We all stared at them – I saw Daisy look too – and then we pretended not to. At the top of the sheaf was a much-scribbled-on page titled *RSVPs*. My heart jumped. *The list!*

Daisy began a stumbling apology for herself, and Miss Lappet muttered and tutted and tried quite desperately to pull herself away, but every time she stepped backwards, Daisy's wails rose again, and she was forced to stop her retreat.

The bell went. 'Oh, for—' said Miss Lappet. 'Come along, girls, it's time for History. Wells, now do stop this nonsense and act your age.'

We proceeded down Library corridor together, our eyes on the list – but just as we passed the Library, Amina stepped out of the doorway.

'Hello, Miss Lappet!' she said, bobbing her head respectfully – for, as I had noticed, although Amina was full of wild stories and naughtiness, she was always polite to mistresses. 'May I help you? May I carry your things?'

'Dear girl, of course!' said Miss Lappet.

'Wait!' gasped Daisy. 'I mean – Miss Lappet, we were already here! Let *me*!'

'But I have already had an offer, Wells. Here, El Maghrabi' – and we had to watch in horror as Amina took the papers from her, clasping the precious list to her heart, and walked beside Miss Lappet all the way to History.

We all glanced at each other in desperation. There was nothing polite or grown up that we could do.

Luckily, though, Lavinia is still not polite in the slightest. Just as we were approaching the History room, she shouldered forward and knocked Amina as hard as she could. Amina gasped, and all the papers she was carrying fluttered to the floor. We all pounced, and in the chaos of collecting the scattered essays I caught hold of the RSVP list and stuffed it, heart pounding, into my book bag.

'Fourth formers!' cried Miss Lappet. '*Really!*'

'Amina tripped me,' said Lavinia, folding her arms.

I expected Amina to deny it, but she did not. She pressed her lips together, her eyes glittering – and then she seized Clementine's elbow and went rushing away with her into History, looking back at us and whispering something into Clementine's ear that made her giggle. I felt an uncomfortable twinge.

'Ugh!' said Daisy, rolling her eyes. 'Quick thinking, Detective Temple. That was work worthy of *me*. Hazel, copy that list quick, before Lappet misses it!'

And that was how I spent Miss Lappet's History lesson – in writing down names, not of kings and queens, but of lords and ladies, viscounts and viscountesses, knights and princes.

Amina glanced over at me once or twice, her expression curious, but for Daisy's sake I stared at her as blankly as I could manage, and she sighed and bent her head back down to her work.

Past cases have taught me never to guess when it comes to evidence, so I did not merely write down the couples (thirty-eight of them), but the men on their own (twenty), and the women on their own (six, one of whom was Lavinia's mother). I also wrote down the Council members (ten of them), and the brothers and fiancés of the Big Girls who were coming to Saturday night's gala dinner. It was a horridly large suspect list and I felt quite exhausted by all the names my cramped hand had scribbled down.

'Miss Lappet?' said Daisy, five minutes before the bell. 'I can hear something outside. It sounds like . . . Goodness, it sounds like Miss Barnard calling your name!'

Miss Lappet exclaimed, jumped up and dashed out of the room, and I stood and walked to the front of the class, with Kitty as cover. We both put the essays we had been working on down on Miss Lappet's desk, and I put down the list with mine.

As I did so I could not stop thinking about something I had copied down, a note Miss Lappet had made this morning.

Mr Hilary North ~~and Mrs Julia North (née McKay '22~~; *Betsy North, 2nd form) Message, 3rd July: Mrs North is indisposed. Mr North will arrive on his own.*

3

'Now, for the woods!' cried Daisy as we stepped into the shade of the trees opposite House after lessons were over for the morning.

'I can't believe you're making us miss lunch,' I said.

I had told the others what I had discovered – that Betsy North's father might be our first real suspect.

'If there's *actually* a dead body, you'll be glad you didn't eat anything beforehand,' said Daisy, beaming. 'And aren't I clever to create a diversion? Of course, no one can resist a box of chocolates from a well-wisher. I simply telephoned the Deepdean sweetshop and told them that Jennifer Stone's boyfriend wanted to send her a box of chocolates. Matron's telling Jennifer off, and all the Big Girls are eating the chocolates or getting ready for the Anniversary, so no one's noticed that we're not in the Dining Room! Now, on with our treasure hunt.'

'Treasure? It's a dead body, you ghoul,' said Kitty, picking her way carefully through the leaves.

'I hope it isn't,' whispered Beanie. 'I know what I saw, but I don't . . . I don't want it to be real. I don't like murder.'

I patted her reassuringly – but her words started up my nagging worry all over again. What if Beanie had been wrong? What if there was no mystery? What would that do to Daisy?

We clambered up through the woods, brambles catching at our regulation socks, twigs scratching our bare legs, stumbling over on hidden roots and rabbit holes. Sun and birdsong dappled down through the branches above us, and insects whined around our heads. As we disturbed it, the earth smelled heavy and slightly rotten.

Kitty gave a shriek. 'I just stood on something that crunched!' she squealed. 'Look at it, look, there are *bones*.'

My heart jumped automatically with excitement and horror before I even had time to remember that anyone murdered a few hours ago would not be a skeleton yet. I turned to Kitty and saw that she was pointing at something very small and clumped-together on the ground. Lavinia bent over it and gave it an appraising stare.

'Owl pellet,' she said briefly. 'They eat mice and things and then spit their skin and bones back up. It's normal.'

Beanie and Kitty wailed in unison and clung to each other, and I steadied myself against Daisy's arm. There is far too much countryside in England, full of hundreds of tiny horrors.

'It's all right, Hazel,' said Daisy soothingly. 'Look, did you know that those mushrooms there will kill you? Plants are glorious: there are all sorts of dreadful ways to die in the natural world.'

'DAISY!' I said.

'Oh, all right, come on, Watson,' said Daisy, rolling her eyes. 'We've got to keep climbing.'

We did climb, up and up for what seemed like miles. Daisy and Lavinia were annoyingly cheerful about it, but Kitty was making faces about the dirt on her clothes and Beanie was looking more and more peaky. I had to keep holding onto trees for support, so that my palms went the odd orange colour of the lichen that is everywhere in Oakeshott Woods.

At last we came out at the top of the ridge that Beanie had described. It was hot up here, the sun striking down between the green leaves of the trees. The wood around us was rustling with a thousand living things. We turned to look behind us, and saw House below, through the trees, our familiar dorm-room windows studded into its side. I could make out the curtains blowing in the breeze, someone's school tie hanging out to dry. Beanie *could* have seen people up here from where she had been standing, but not the details of their faces.

Below House were the sports pitches, and then the school itself. I turned my head the other way and saw the roads and gardens of Deepdean town.

'I wish we were at lunch,' I said, folding my arms and trying not to pant.

'No you don't – remember it's *Friday* lunch,' said Daisy. 'It's only fish pie. All right, Beanie, is this where you saw them?'

Beanie looked about and then nodded. 'I remember that tree was above them,' she said. 'It's got a funny dead bit there.'

'Excellent. This is the place – and look, we've already proved something. There is a line of sight between *here* and *there*, so Beanie *could* certainly have seen what she says she saw. Now we must hunt for clues. Can we prove the second part of her story?'

Lavinia immediately crouched down and began to shuffle her hands through the dirt.

'Hold hard!' said Daisy. 'We must be scientific. *Look* about the area. What do you see, apart from the marks of our arrival?'

'A footprint!' said Kitty immediately, gasping. 'There, look. And another one! Two people's.'

'Indeed, Detective Freebody,' said Daisy. 'They are only faint impressions, but they are there. What else?'

'These ones are facing towards school, away from Deepdean town,' I said. 'Look where they're pointing. And then I think . . .'

'I think I can see a struggle,' said Daisy, nodding. 'Look at the way this print is dug in at the toes. Anything else?'

'There's a man's footprint over there that's facing back into town,' I said quietly. 'Several of them. And—'

Suddenly I found it hard to breathe.

'And they're going back alone,' I finished.

At last, I believed.

4

'But where's the body?' breathed Kitty. 'Oh, Lord, what if it's still HERE!'

Beanie shrieked and clutched at her, but Daisy rolled her eyes.

'It's quite clearly not here any more, is it, Detective Freebody?' she said. 'Otherwise we would be standing on it. But look – look at that print facing back towards town. What do you notice about it?'

'It's deeper,' I said, feeling a shiver go right through me.

'Yes!' cried Daisy. 'Much deeper. Don't the rest of you see? Now, what does that suggest? That when he began to walk back the way he came, he was carrying something heavy. Something like . . . *a body*.'

Kitty shrieked this time.

'But wouldn't we have seen it when we looked out of the window?' asked Lavinia sceptically.

'No,' said Beanie. 'No, look. These bushes, they block the view a bit – I could only see the people from the waist up, I remember that now. When she fell, he must have knelt down over her, so they were both out of sight when we all looked!'

'And he only got up again after the bell went and we had to go to lessons!' said Daisy. 'It makes sense, it all makes sense.'

She looked at me, and I could almost feel her vibrating with excitement – or perhaps it was just that every bone in my own body was finally humming with detective fever.

'Now, before we go following that step and looking for the body, we must make a closer examination of this scene. Everyone stand here, backs together, facing outwards.'

We did. I saw Kitty squeezing Beanie's hand encouragingly, and Beanie smiling wanly back at her.

'Now, begin to walk outwards, very slowly, in a straight line,' ordered Daisy. 'Look about you as you go, and as soon as you see anything that may be a clue, shout. Do not touch anything unless I tell you to – this may be crucial evidence!'

'Are you sure we should touch it at all?' asked Kitty. 'Won't the police want to see it?'

'The police are not here,' said Daisy grandly. 'But . . . you make a good point. No touching ANYTHING without using your handkerchiefs, and you have to put it back afterwards.'

She nodded to us all, and we began.

I found myself next to two of the footprints facing towards House, indentations in the grass and soft soil. One was a large man's shoe, and one, slightly smaller, was a woman's, with a pointed toe and slight heel. The woman was clearly not short or petite – this print was larger than my own foot, and she had pressed down the earth more than the slender Beanie would have done.

I sketched them quickly in my casebook and made a note of their sizes. The prints looked quite fresh, the grass inside them still pressed down. No one had been up here since then apart from us, I was sure.

Then I called all this information out to Daisy, who made a pleased noise.

'I found something!' called Lavinia. 'It's a matchbox. Ooh, it's *foreign*!'

'What sort of foreign?' asked Daisy sharply.

'French, I think,' said Lavinia. 'It's got the Arc de Trump on it.'

Kitty giggled. 'You never do listen in French lessons, do you?' she asked.

'Shut up, Kitty. At least I know what the Arc de whatever *is*!' said Lavinia. 'It's in Paris, so there.'

'All right, Lavinia, make a note of where you found it, wrap it carefully in your handkerchief and carry on,' said Daisy.

We kept on walking. It was hotter than ever, and my hair was coming out of its plait and hanging around my face. I wiped my forehead with my handkerchief and breathed in deeply.

'Ooh!' squeaked Beanie. 'I've found something! Come and see, come and see – I think this is important!'

'WALK BACK IN YOUR OWN FOOTSTEPS!' shouted Daisy. 'But all right, Beanie, we're coming.'

We met back up in the middle of the ridge. Lavinia held out the matchbox in her grubby handkerchief for us to see. It was indeed printed with a little image of the Arc de Triomphe and the words CAFÉ BAR, and was only about half full. Then Beanie held out what she had found, and we all gasped.

I was expecting a note, but this was more than that. A rectangle of rich creamy paper with a gold edge and gold lettering.

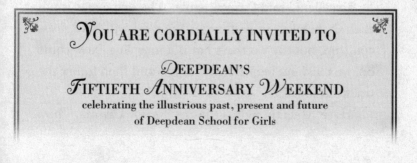

YOU ARE CORDIALLY INVITED TO

DEEPDEAN'S
FIFTIETH ANNIVERSARY WEEKEND
celebrating the illustrious past, present and future
of Deepdean School for Girls

We all looked at each other. Daisy had been right, I thought, in a fresh rush of excitement.

'They *are* parents!' said Kitty excitedly.

'Parents or Council members,' I said, remembering the list. 'Guests at the Anniversary, though, Daisy – you were right!'

'Of course I was!' cried Daisy, but I could sense her relief. 'Proof at last! And now our next move is clear. We have the crime scene, and we have the guest list. We know who ought to be coming as a couple. So all we need to do is match the grown-ups who *do* arrive at the concert tonight with the ones who *ought* to – and work out who's missing. Beanie, can you think of *any* other distinguishing features of the man you saw? Anything that might help us this evening?'

Beanie's forehead wrinkled. 'The man was in . . . oh, just a beige mac and a soft dark hat,' she said. 'You know, ordinary! The woman, though, she was wearing a lovely hat. It was such bright green that I could see it properly. Oh yes, I remember!'

'Excellent,' said Daisy warmly. 'The beige mac is not entirely helpful, since tonight the men will have dress coats on, but the woman's hat is a nice clue. Now come on, we must put back this invitation and then follow the tracks to town!'

'Have you thought, though,' said Lavinia, 'how

horrible this is, really? After all, if we're right, someone's mother is dead, and she doesn't know it yet.'

We all fell silent, and all we could hear was birdsong.

5

After that, the mood changed. I was suddenly certain that we would come upon a hastily covered corpse at any moment, and certain that I could not bear it if we did.

We stepped nervously down the hill towards Deepdean town, tracking the man's heavy progress through the undergrowth in snapped twigs and fallen leaves.

'There!' cried Daisy suddenly, pointing ahead, where something was shining bright green with a slash of red against the softer green of a cluster of brambles. 'It must be the woman's hat Beanie saw!'

'Oh *no*,' I whispered. This was proof of the most horrid kind. Kitty and Beanie clung together, and even Lavinia looked rather pale.

'Heavens!' said Daisy. '*You're* all no help.' And she went marching up to the hat and poked at it with a stick.

My vision blurred.

'She's not here!' called Daisy, with a note of regret in her voice. 'It's all right, you idiots, it's just the hat. It must have fallen off her head. Oh, do look, it's divine! Hmm, let's see . . . ordinary size, some long, dark hairs caught in its band – and a milliner's mark, MARCELLE ROZE, PARIS. *Paris!*'

I crouched down beside her. 'Another clue leading back to Paris,' I said quietly. 'The victim was there – and perhaps the murderer too, if they were married.'

'Wouldn't it be lovely if it were Clementine's family?' asked Daisy.

'Daisy!' I said. 'It'd be awful. Poor Clementine! And, thank goodness, it doesn't fit the list. I remember only her father RSVP'd. It's just as you said – this evening we need to look for a woman who RSVP'd that she would attend, but who never appears. What shall we do now?'

'Keep on looking, of course!' said Daisy. 'And take one of those hairs. There are lots, and the police won't need all of them.'

'So you *do* want us to go to the police?'

'Humph!' said Daisy. 'Absolutely not.'

'But . . . look at the evidence' I said. 'A crime's been committed here, Daisy. And we're running out of time to find the body before we have to turn round and go back to House. Don't we need to tell someone?'

'No!' said Daisy. 'We'll find it!'

But although we continued to track the prints back towards Deepdean town, we found nothing else. No clothes, no handbag, and certainly no body.

'Bother it!' said Daisy at last, after Beanie had fallen down into what Lavinia told us was a badger sett and burst into overexcited tears. We were almost out of the woods by then, and it was clear that we had missed something.

Lavinia kicked a tree stump.

'Beanie, do stop crying,' said Daisy. 'And, Lavinia, stop trying to hurt that tree. Now, we must not be daunted. We must go back to House, tidy up as quickly as possible before the bell goes, and behave in an entirely normal fashion until we have a chance to come back and look more carefully.'

'When?' asked Kitty critically. 'I'm not coming back at night, and neither is Beanie. The parents are all descending later today for the concert and then there are things all weekend – we can't just *miss* the Anniversary, and if we tried we'd be stopped!'

'I would *absolutely* miss the Anniversary,' said Lavinia.

'I don't think we need to miss anything,' I said, struck by an idea. 'I know what we have to do.'

Daisy argued with me all the way back down to House, but I was certain her complaints were mostly for show. We managed to creep up the main stairs and back to our dorm without attracting the attention of Matron or the prefects, and we cleaned ourselves as best we could in our basin of water.

Our legs were still rather scratched, and our socks were absolutely ruined, but most of the mud brushed off our pinafores, and our shoes were all right as long as you didn't look directly at them.

I took a deep breath, and then Daisy and I went back downstairs and knocked at Matron's office door.

'What do you want, Wells, Wong?' she asked.

'Hazel needs to make a *very* urgent telephone call,' said Daisy.

'You girls rely on the telephone entirely too much,' said Matron. 'It's not healthy. Why can't you write a letter?'

'It's an *important* family matter concerning this weekend,' Daisy said, and behind her I looked as tragic as I could.

Matron sighed and narrowed her eyes and said, 'Oh, go on, then. But *only* to the first pips.'

'Yes, Matron!' we gasped. I dialled the operator as quickly as I could and whispered the number I wanted. Daisy crowded next to me to listen in.

There was an agonizing pause, and then Inspector Priestley's voice said, 'Hello?'

'It's Hazel Wong!' I gabbled in a whisper. 'I can't talk for long, but Daisy and I need your help – we think there's been a murder in Oakeshott Woods but we can't find the body.'

'WHAT?' said Inspector Priestley.

'It happened this morning. Beanie saw it, and we went to look at the crime scene and found *clues*. We think the victim and the murderer are both *parents* coming to the Anniversary, but we can't keep investigating in the woods because of all the Anniversary events this weekend,' I said – and then the pips went and I slammed down the telephone, breathing as though I had just won a race.

I did not know if it would work. *But*, I thought, *it has to.*

6

We came out of the office just as the school bell went. Kitty, Beanie and Lavinia were waiting for us by House's front door.

'Hurry up!' called Kitty, waving her hand. We rushed over to them, Daisy knocking into the first-form shrimp Emily Dow, who squeaked and sat down on the floor with a bump, her mouth open. There were dark circles under her eyes, and I thought she looked rather thin.

'Oh, poor Emily!' cried Beanie, rushing over to help her up, but before she could get there Emily jumped to her feet and ran away.

'Never mind her,' said Daisy as we stepped outside into the summer air. 'Now, hurry down to school! Once you're past Old Wing entrance, meet by the Founder's statue so we can have a Detective Society meeting before French. Mamzelle won't mind if we're late.'

The sun was on our hats and the sound of other girls' laughter and footsteps was all around us. It was hard not to feel excited, buoyed up by being on a case. And it was the most brilliant fun to dodge through the Deepdean corridors on our way to a secret Detective Society meeting once again.

We all gathered around the Founder's statue, and I took out my casebook.

'Present: Daisy Wells, Hazel Wong, Kitty Freebody, Rebecca Martineau and Lavinia Temple,' I whispered. 'The case is—'

'The Case of the Disappearing Body!' said Daisy. 'No, wait, the Mysterious Murder in Oakeshott Woods! So, we may not have a body, but we have enough evidence to prove that the crime really did take place. A man – most likely the father of a Deepdean girl – strangled a woman in Oakeshott Woods this morning, and then he carried her body away, back to Deepdean town. We found a hat and a matchbox, both from Paris, proving that the victim – and possibly the killer as well – has been there.'

'And recently!' said Kitty. 'That hat is this season, I'm sure of it.'

'Very good, Detective Freebody. And the fact that it was abandoned in the woods – why, a woman would *have* to be dead to leave a hat from a Paris *atelier* behind! Now, at Vice-President Wong's suggestion, we have contacted the police in the person of Inspector Priestley. But we cannot rely entirely on his help. So our next steps must be to use the list. The first event of the Anniversary weekend is tonight, of course – the concert. Our theory – made stronger by the discovery of that invitation in the woods – is that our killer is a man coming to the Anniversary who ought to arrive as part of a couple, but instead will arrive alone. Now, how many couples on the list, Hazel?'

'Thirty-eight sets of parents,' I said. 'And of the ten Council members, there are two married couples. Forty couples in total!'

'Forty men! Well, that divides nicely,' said Daisy, pleased. 'Five of us, eight potential suspects each.'

'What do you mean, eight each?' asked Lavinia suspiciously. 'You don't want us to tail *eight* people at once?'

'Of course not!' said Daisy. 'This evening I want each of us to *take note* of eight men each – watch them as they come in, and then cross them off our suspect list as soon as we see that they're here innocently with their wives. Hazel, you're in charge of writing out smaller lists for each of us this afternoon. Put down the grown-ups' names, and then the names of their daughters, so we know who they are. Once we have our lists, we must learn them thoroughly so as to be ready for this evening. I want each of us to arrive at the concert ready to sniff out even a *hint* of suspicious activity – suspicious activity being, in this case, any missing female guests.'

'And remember Paris,' I said. 'If you do find any men who fit, do everything you can to find out whether they or their wives have recently been to Paris. And whether they smoke!'

'Yes, exactly!' said Daisy. 'Now, I want reports from you all at the end of the night – and I want *proper* investigation, detectives. No shoddy work!'

Kitty rolled her eyes. 'You never trust us,' she said.

'With good reason!' snapped Daisy. 'No one is as good at observation as I am, not even Hazel, and I have been training her for two years.'

'*Training* me!' I exclaimed. 'I've been a detective for exactly as long as you have.'

'Hush, Watson,' said Daisy. 'You have improved marvellously in that time. And, Beanie – remember that you are a crucial part of this mission. As well as all that, you must be looking about you all the time for the man you saw. I know you say you didn't get a good look at him, but posture and gestures are everything.'

'Yes, Daisy,' said Beanie, frowning and chewing her plait. 'I'll do my best.'

'Excellent,' said Daisy. 'Really, this mystery man doesn't stand a chance!'

7

For me, that afternoon was made of lists. I copied out what seemed like endless names, until I really felt I knew every person who would be stepping through Old Wing door that evening. And it was a good thing I did . . . but I only discovered that later.

I had given Kitty, Beanie and Lavinia their own parents to watch – it seemed only fair – and I gave Daisy Amina's people, for I knew she would be watching them jealously anyway, whatever her list said. Beanie had the couples from the first-form parents, Lavinia had the second formers', Kitty had the third formers'. Daisy had the rest of the fourth form and the fifth form, and I had the Council members and Big Girls' parents. I also – privately – memorized the names of the single men and women, which included Clementine's father. Of course, it seemed likely that Beanie was right, and she had seen a married couple – but what if she had not?

What if the pair she had seen were both on the RSVP list, but not as a couple? Or what if the victim was a woman who was never supposed to arrive at Deepdean, although the man was? Or the other way round – the woman was a guest on the RSVP list, but the man was not? We had only found one invitation in the woods, after all, and we had no way of knowing whether it had belonged to the man or the woman. I have detected enough cases not to know that we should never make assumptions. But I did not say so to Daisy, not when her eyes were so bright and there was a skip in her step at last, not when she was in control of a case, and of the Detective Society, and happy.

The afternoon passed in a blur and I was not the only one distracted. The school was fizzing with excitement about that evening's concert. It was rumoured that some really rather famous Old Girls would be performing – most excitingly Artemis Turnbull, the opera singer. Half-melodies came faltering and floating out of the music practice rooms, and the corridors echoed with singing. Sophie Croke-Finchley was missing from lessons, of course, to prepare for her piano solo, and Beanie was also missing, for she was a member of the choir. ('Who wants to sing in the *choir*!' said Daisy to me. 'No one notices you!')

In English, Miss Dodgson was so distracted that she set us Big Girl work by mistake, a composition on someone called A. E. Housman, who none of us had ever heard of. We stared at Miss Dodgson's title ('*Terence, this is stupid stuff.' Explain why we should care about poetry*) blankly.

'Is that a poem?' Daisy hissed, unimpressed. 'If it is, I don't see the point.'

We all sat paralysed, none of us willing to point out that we had never even read the poem. Luckily, just then Miss Dodgson caught sight of Miss Lappet outside the classroom and leaped up to speak to her about adjustments to the walking play, leaving us free to talk.

'My papa's coming tonight,' said Clementine smugly. 'So's Sophie's parents and Amina's. What about *your* people, Daisy?'

Lavinia kicked her chair.

'Busy,' said Daisy unconcernedly. 'But my uncle's coming to Leaving Prayers.'

I was quite sure that was a lie. I tried not to make a face at her.

'It doesn't matter, though, does it?' asked Amina, turning round in her chair to stare at us. 'Whether or not they're here, I mean. My parents are always telling me to be good and not wicked, even though they're hardly perfect themselves. But if they weren't here, I'd miss them. It's bad either way. *You* know.'

And she smiled at Daisy.

Daisy glared back at her. 'I don't know *anything*,' she snapped. 'I don't know what you mean.'

'Oh . . .' said Amina, blinking, 'See here, I was only trying to be nice!'

There was a frozen pause, during which the whole form looked from Daisy to Amina and back again.

'Anyway,' said Lavinia at last, 'Sophie's going to bungle her solo, I know she is.'

'Hey!' said Clementine, and the tension was broken. We knew how to behave when there was nothing more than dorm pride at stake, and, as we all began to rag each other as usual, I felt quite relieved.

After dinner, we trooped down to school in a tidy crocodile, a little too warm in our formal blazers and hats under the early evening sun. English summer days stretch on for ever, the sky still a clean blue until hours after lights out, the sun striking onto our faces before the wake-up bell sounds. It makes me feel a little dizzy, as though I never really sleep, and I felt rather dizzy now – and not only from the lonely knowledge that my parents, and Daisy's, would not be there that evening. After all, we were on a case. Had the Inspector really listened to my telephone call? Had he really believed me, and would he come and help us?

Each of the Detective Society members were clutching lists in their hands. *It ought to be simple*, I thought: *one victim, one suspect, one crime*; but my thoughts were in a tangle that only became more knotted the more I worried at them. Say we discovered that one of the fathers was unexpectedly without his wife. How could we be sure that we knew the reason for it? How could we *prove* what he had done? We had a hat, a few smudged footprints, an invitation and a matchbox – and our word; the word of five silly, scared schoolgirls . . .

. . . And then we were stepping through Old Wing entrance, and my thoughts were cut short, because we found ourselves in an atmosphere that at first felt quite unlike the Deepdean I know.

Old Wing entrance hall is large and square, with wooden floors and wood-panelled walls. Usually the effect is rather like stepping into an echoing, school-smelling box. But this evening it was very different. A long piece of plush red carpet had been unrolled across the floor, and candles glowed on long, thin candelabras. And the whole space was absolutely swarming with grown-ups.

Fathers and mothers in beautiful clothes circled about, clustering together in chattering groups. They looked so imposing and sensible, just like people at my father's parties back in Hong Kong. I tried to remind myself of what Daisy and I have learned – that simply appearing old and important does not mean you really are – but it was rather difficult in the circumstances.

Miss Lappet, her ship-like figure encased in a beetle-shiny purple dress, was standing with her feet together, nodding and smiling with all her teeth at the grown-ups as they went by, and next to her was our cool, elegant headmistress, Miss Barnard, her hair newly waved, and wearing a soft grey silk gown, saying a gentle word to each set of parents as they arrived.

Just behind her was another tall, thin woman in a long-sleeved black dress, her striking, sharp-featured face looking oddly familiar – and then she and Miss Barnard both made the same little motion with their lips and I understood what I was seeing.

'That's Miss Barnard's sister!' whispered Kitty to me. 'Her name is Mrs Rivers!'

I realized I knew Mrs Rivers – her name was on my list of single women, one of the Council members. I had imagined her as old – a white-haired lady who looked rather like our friend Alexander's grandmother – but in real life her hair was dark and her face a more interesting version of Miss Barnard's. She was very beautiful for a grown-up, and a wedding ring with a large ruby glinted on her finger.

'She's on the school Council,' Kitty was still whispering. 'Her husband was the head, but he died last year and she's taken over. She's meant to be awfully fierce. She was the one who made sure Barny was hired.'

I stared at Mrs Rivers with interest. I wondered whether this was why Miss Barnard was always so calm and serene – because her sister was determined enough for both of them.

Daisy motioned to Kitty, Beanie and Lavinia, and we all crowded around her.

'All right, Detectives!' she whispered. 'The game's afoot. Use your lists – and in the event you do find a likely suspect, investigate him thoroughly. Be charming, be rude, be confused – I don't mind, as long as you make sure that he doesn't get away without explaining *why* he's alone. Ready?'

We all nodded.

'Then let's go!' cried Daisy.

And our mission began.

8

Despite my recent practice at the Rue, I am still nervous when faced with this sort of bold detective work. For a while, everyone seemed to mix up into a tall, chattering, well-dressed blur, and then I began to pick out faces from the crowd.

Daisy moved towards a round, calm woman who looked just like Rose and Jose, and a man with glasses who looked exactly like Sophie Croke-Finchley. Next to them were a man and a woman who stood out starkly from the rest of the pink-and-white tweedy mothers and fathers.

They both had light-brown skin, and clothes that I could tell were expensive. The woman was wearing a pretty little cloche attached to a wispy chiffon scarf that was tied under her chin, and matching gloves, and the man was in a high felt hat. They were talking together as they stared at the crowd, and the man was smoking an elegant cigarette. They looked rather proud and unapproachable, but then the man bent and whispered something into the woman's ear, and her face creased up in a huge smile. Of course, it wasn't hard to guess whose parents they were, but that grin left me in no doubt. These were Mr and Mrs El Maghrabi, Amina's parents. I should not have been watching them, but I was too fascinated to look away.

'Mama! Baba!' cried Amina, rushing up to them with her arms out, her smile just as wide as her mother's.

I saw one mother whisper something to another, pursing her lips disapprovingly, and felt myself bristle, for I knew what they were saying. *Not quite nice, not quite English* – all the things they might say about *my* parents. And for the first time I wondered whether it was in fact a good thing that my father was not here. I saw that Amina knew what the whispering people were saying, and I saw that she had decided not to care, and I wondered, suddenly, if her dramatic stories were calculated to make herself defiantly stand out, just like our friend George's clothes do.

My eye was suddenly drawn away from the El Maghrabis to a slender, fair-haired man in a beautifully tailored suit. He looked like someone I knew, I thought, or perhaps that was just because he was so handsome. He moved like something coiled and ready to spring, and I saw mothers flutter as he passed them and fathers gaze at him open-mouthed. I thought for a moment that he was on his own, but then an equally tall and handsome dark-haired woman in a beautiful long-sleeved dress, a bright silk scarf knotted jauntily about her neck, parted the lookers and gigglers. He took her hand, pulled her to him and kissed her on the cheek in front of everyone. I blushed.

'That's Mr and Mrs Thompson-Bates!' said Daisy, suddenly beside me. 'Lallie Thompson-Bates's people. Lavinia's playing her in the exhibition match tomorrow, you know. The father's an awfully good tennis player. He goes to Wimbledon every year and he nearly beat Bunny Austin last time.'

'Oh! I've seen him in Lavinia's tennis magazines,' I said, realizing.

'Quite so,' said Daisy. 'Now, stop gaping at Kitty's ruled-out suspects and try to find some of your own, if you please.'

'What about you?' I asked her. 'Why are you talking to me instead of investigating?'

'I am giving you some much-needed guidance,' said Daisy. 'Also, Sophie's mother just walked in so her father's ruled out. Ooh, look, there's Pippa Daventry's father! Remember that rumour about him having a secret wife in Australia during our case last year? Perhaps he's murdered her! Oh no, bother, there's his wife in that awful pink outfit. Well, that's one to cross off your list.'

Then I caught sight of someone rather more promising. This man was tall and red-haired, and he made me think of a sleek wicked fox. He was smoking a cigarette, and quite alone – that is, until the Big Girl Jennifer Stone went running up to him squealing, 'Daddy!'

'That's Mr Stone!' said Daisy. 'Is he one of your suspects, Hazel? I happen to know through Uncle Felix that although he pretends to be a banker, he is secretly a smuggler – remember I told you about him during our first case?'

'He's not on my list of couples,' I said, showing her. 'He was only ever supposed to arrive on his own.'

'Bother!' said Daisy. 'Ooh, hold on, there's Astrid Frith with a man— Excuse me!'

She wriggled away through the crowd, and I was left watching Jennifer Stone and her father. What if the murderer *was* a single man, as I had thought?

'. . . Little Jenny Wren!' Mr Stone was saying. 'How are you?'

'Like you care!' Jennifer grumbled. 'You didn't come last exeat, and you told me you would.'

'Now, look, I couldn't help that. I was travelling – you know how it is. Paris one day, Rome the next. But I'm here now, aren't I?'

Jennifer scowled, but I felt electrified. *Paris!* And recently too! I could not ignore that – I would be a bad detective if I did. I took out my *other* list and circled Mr Stone's name.

Daisy came darting back up and seized my arm. 'One for you! Alice Murgatroyd's father's alone, and he shouldn't be!' she said. 'Mrs Murgatroyd was on the RSVP list. I heard him telling Alice that her mother is "off learning mysticism in India", which is exactly the sort of thing you *would* say if you'd just killed her in the woods.'

Alice was a Big Girl who was rather hard and cool (she smuggled cigarettes into House every term and was quite rude to younger girls), but all the same, I thought, she did not deserve to lose her mother. No one did. I circled Mr Murgatroyd's name on my list.

Then we all heard Beanie shriek.

We turned round, hearts pounding, and saw her running into the arms of a large bald man in a very loud checked suit. He did not look as though he belonged at Deepdean any more than Mr and Mrs El Maghrabi did – he was burly and (I knew that this was what the other parents were thinking as they stared at him) rather common-looking, but it was clear that Beanie did not care in the slightest.

'Daddy!' she shrieked, kissing him on both cheeks.

'My little Becky!' he said affectionately, ruffling her hair. 'Not so little any more – look at you!'

Then Beanie stepped backwards and looked about, and her expression changed. I watched it fall, from excited joy to frightened confusion.

'Daddy,' she said, 'where's Mummy?'

9

I reached out to seize Daisy's hand, and found that she was already reaching for mine. We clung to each other in horror as Mr Martineau said, 'Oh, Becky, I'm so sorry to disappoint you. Mummy isn't feeling very well again. We were all packed to come, and then she had a funny turn and . . . well, she's had to go back into hospital for a few days. But she wanted me to tell you that she loves you, and she wishes she could be here.'

'But she promised,' said Beanie emptily, her lip trembling. 'She promised she'd be here, she *promised*, and so did you.'

'Now, you know Mummy's not been well. You know that.'

'BUT YOU PROMISED ME!' Beanie shouted at him, shaking her hands out of his grasp, and she went running away towards the Old Wing cloakroom.

The rest of the Detective Society went pounding after her. We were missing the opportunity to watch our suspects further – but, despite what Daisy says, some things are more important than the case at hand.

We found Beanie hiding behind a clump of coats and sobbing.

'I'm not crying,' she said loudly. 'Only babies cry and we're almost fifth formers now.'

'BEANIE!' said Kitty, and she went diving behind the coats and dragged out Beanie, who looked very mournful.

'I just thought Mummy would be here,' she said. 'She was supposed to be here.'

Daisy and I looked at each other. Mrs Martineau was supposed to be getting better – that was what we had been told, although exactly what illness she had was mysterious to us. But if she was getting better, why was she not here?

And it was impossible to ignore that we had been looking out for a husband without his wife, and here one was. The fact that he was the father of one of the Detective Society's members was a horrid shock, but not enough to rule him out.

'Here,' said Lavinia roughly, and I could see she had had the same thought. 'If you want to know more suspects, Mr North's alone, just like the list said he'd be.

Very suspicious. And I just saw my father come in without stupid Patricia. *He* might be the murderer. Wouldn't that be a turn-up for the books?'

Both Daisy and I flinched, and tried not to look at each other. 'Don't be an ass, Lavinia. You don't want parents who are murderers,' said Daisy quickly. 'That's not a nice thing to say. But if he's here alone, then he's certainly a suspect.'

'I know what you're thinking,' said Beanie, 'but it *wasn't* Mummy and Daddy I saw. I'd have recognized them anywhere, and it wasn't them. I'm not upset because I think they're mixed up in this case. It's not that at all! It's just – Mummy was supposed to be BETTER!'

There was a knock at the cloakroom door.

'Fourth formers!' called Miss Lappet. 'Come out of there! You are needed to escort the parents to the Hall. Temple, your father and mother and – well – are here, and Martineau's poor father looks utterly at sea. You mustn't be rude!'

Beanie looked frozen.

'We mustn't be rude!' said Kitty in a very good imitation of Miss Lappet's voice once she had left. 'Come on, Beans. I'm sure your mum is quite all right. Come on, let's go and talk to your dad and you can make certain. You'll only be frightened until you know.'

Beanie sniffed miserably. Kitty handed her a handkerchief and squeezed her arm.

'Buck up,' she said.

'Yes, do focus, Detective Martineau,' said Daisy. 'There is a mystery to solve and we must all be rigorous. I have identified Mr Murgatroyd as a suspect. What about the rest of you?'

'Mr North,' said Lavinia. '*And* my father.'

'I think we ought to add Mr Stone to the list,' I said. 'I know he was supposed to be here alone – Mrs Stone died a few years ago – but I heard him tell Jennifer that he'd been to Paris recently! That might be important.' I had been preparing to suggest Clementine's father as well, but I had not seen him at all.

Daisy stared at me, and then she shrugged and said, 'All right. So far, so good. Four suspects, *and* we've ruled out plenty of parents too. We must keep watching. Come on! Once more into the breach, dear Detectives.'

Out we went into the entrance hall again. Beanie's father was standing where we had left him, looking very lost indeed. Next to him was a large, black-bearded man who looked very fierce. He folded his arms and scowled, ignoring Mr Martineau – and I knew who he must be.

'Lavinia!' gasped Kitty at exactly that moment. 'Your father looks exactly like you!'

'He does not!' snarled Lavinia, folding her arms and scowling too, and we all burst out laughing. Even Beanie smiled wanly. Suddenly I felt more cheerful.

'Father, you're late,' shouted Lavinia at her father. 'Where are . . . YOU know?'

'Lavinia, you're *making* me late!' roared Mr Temple. 'Patricia's gone inside, and so has your mother. If we don't hurry, there'll be war. Come on, idiot girl!'

Off they went towards Library corridor, arguing furiously. Kitty sidled up to Mr Martineau, Beanie in tow, and bore them both away very carefully.

Old Wing entrance was quite deserted at this point, and Daisy and I really were about to be late.

But then someone slipped through the doorway and stood staring around, as though he was lost. I got a sort of half-look at him at first, and then I spun round in shock.

I ought to have expected it, but somehow I had not.

It was Inspector Priestley.

10

'What are you doing here?' asked Daisy, looking just as surprised and delighted as I felt.

'You summoned me,' said Inspector Priestley. 'I drove down in my car this afternoon. Would you have preferred I flew?'

We were still gaping at him, so he added, 'I had some leave to take from my station. There hasn't been much time for holidaying this year. Before I motored down, I also had a word with the Deepdean police. I let them know I'd had a tip-off that there may have been illegal activity in Oakeshott Woods this morning.

'Really?' I gasped. '*Why?*'

'Because, against all probability, when you've told me that something terrible has happened, it always has. You have been right again and again, and I would be no sort of policeman at all if I did not believe in your detective powers by now.'

I felt like a hot-air balloon rising into the sky.

'Yes, but how are you going to explain why you're at our concert?' asked Daisy, and I came back down to earth with a bump.

'After you told me it was the Anniversary, I took the precaution of telephoning your headmistress's office,' said the Inspector. 'I told the woman I spoke to that I would be representing Miss Wells in place of her uncle. I also telephoned *him*, before you ask, mentioning that I would be in the area, and he gave his consent to my taking his place at the festivities, as a . . . sort of family friend, let's say. I thought it prudent to stay near you while this is cleared up. Agreed?'

'Agreed,' I said thankfully.

'Excellent,' said the Inspector. 'Now, quick, tell me all about the case.'

We rushed into the Hall for the concert just as it was about to begin, having briefed the Inspector as fast as we could about what Beanie had seen, and what we had found in the woods – and I could not have felt more obvious. Heads turned and tuts rippled away from us like pebbles into water. I saw Lavinia sitting between Mr Temple and blonde-haired Patricia on one side, and a woman with Lavinia's heavy eyebrows and dark eyes on the other. So Lavinia was wrong – Mr Temple could be ruled out. I saw that Clementine was sitting alone too – her father was still not there. We therefore had only three concrete suspects so far: Mr Murgatroyd, Mr North and Mr Stone.

I dipped my head, noticing that the Inspector's mac was crumpled and frayed at the cuffs and his hat was out of fashion – and, of course, he was a policeman, something frightening and not at all nice. Even Daisy's gold hair and polished, carefully bored expression could not save us from being looked at.

Miss Barnard moved forward onto the stage. We ducked down into the first three seats we could find as she began to speak.

'This is a great occasion,' she said in her calm, quiet voice that nevertheless carried through the Hall. 'Deepdean School for Girls is fifty years old. Fifty! When the Founder opened Deepdean's doors in 1886, she was told that such a school was not necessary, that no one needed or wanted to educate their daughters. But now, in 1936, we have more than proved those people wrong. We live in a brave new world where women may vote. They may sit in a court of law and the Houses of Parliament. Why, one day I believe we shall even see a female Prime Minister. What a wonderful example she shall be for her sex! This weekend we celebrate our current girls, as well as welcoming home many past pupils, women who have gone out into the world and done commendable things. Many of them now have daughters or granddaughters here, and some – like myself – have returned to inspire more young minds through the wonder of teaching. Tonight we begin our Anniversary celebrations by showing you the brightest of our musicians, girls whose talents will cheer and delight. Please listen carefully and applaud them as they deserve. They are a credit to our school, and I am proud to introduce them to you all.'

'Dull!' Daisy muttered in my ear. 'Deadly dull! Oh, what a bother this weekend will be – so many tiresome events to get through when all we want to do is go out and hunt for the body.'

'Don't be gruesome, Madam Super,' whispered Inspector Priestley from her other side.

Daisy narrowed her eyes at me, and I had to fight not to laugh.

The concert began. The choir sang (Beanie looking sick with misery), a third former played the flute, Sophie Croke-Finchley played the piano (her father cheered in the wrong place and had to be subdued by his wife), and then, as four staid fifth formers were playing a string quartet, a sharp, high-pitched noise rang out from all over the Hall.

An alarm clock was trilling to my left, and another behind me. It took me – and everyone else, from the startled glances I saw – a moment to realize what we were hearing, and in that time three more went off, one up in the balcony, one just below the stage and one two rows in front of where we were sitting.

'TURN OFF THAT NOISE!' bellowed Miss Lappet.

Everyone looked about them, to see who was looking guilty. 'I'll bet it's Binny and her rat friends!' hissed Kitty, but I was staring at the row in front of me, where Amina was sitting with her parents. Her shoulders were shaking with mirth – and when she looked over at Clementine I knew who was behind the prank. Next to her, Mr El Maghrabi was elbowing his daughter and Mrs El Maghrabi turned on Amina crossly, her smile gone.

Miss Lappet, and Mamzelle, and Miss Dodgson, had to scuttle about, turning clocks off and becoming more and more flustered, while we all tried not to giggle – and then, at last, the final clocks stopped with a shrill thump, and there was no sound in the Hall. It was as though we had imagined the interruption. But, of course, we had not. Miss Barnard's lips were pinched together, Miss Lappet was beetroot-red, and Rev MacLean was coughing into his dirty old handkerchief in a way that I suspected was really a snigger.

Miss Barnard came striding back on stage, clearing her throat.

'Many apologies for that interruption, ladies and gentlemen,' she said. 'If the girls behind it would come and see me at the end of the concert, I have a few words to say to them. And many apologies to the string quartet. An excellent performance – it was a pity that it was cut short. Now, before we begin the next section, I wanted to bring on a very special guest. She was a music scholar during her time at Deepdean, and now, of course, she is one of Europe's shining lights – as well as being the mother of our current third-form pupil, Ella. May I welcome . . . Mrs Artemis Turnbull!'

Applause clattered around the Hall, but when it died away, Miss Barnard was still alone on the stage.

'Mrs Turnbull!' she called. 'Mrs Turnbull? Has *anyone* seen Mrs Turnbull?'

PART THREE

CURIOUSER
AND
CURIOUSER

1

'Artemis Turnbull is missing!' said Daisy to the rest of us as we walked back up to House together after the concert had ended – or, rather, after it had been brought to a hasty conclusion. Mrs Turnbull's unexpected absence had finally ruined the celebratory mood. Mr Turnbull was stony-faced, refusing to answer Ella Turnbull's tearful questions or speak to the mothers and fathers who were all crowded around him, looking for answers.

Miss Barnard, though, seemed more concerned about the prank. As we filed out, I saw her in a huddle with Mrs Rivers and the El Maghrabis – Amina, arm in arm with Clementine, must have owned up to it. Mr and Mrs El Maghrabi both looked furious, Mrs Rivers' face was stony, and Miss Barnard was as cross as I had ever seen her.

'I only wanted to have a bit of fun,' I heard Amina say, as we passed her. 'It wasn't serious! Everyone does this sort of thing in England. See here, I'll apologize!'

'This is not how we behave at Deepdean,' snapped Mrs Rivers. 'Really, I expected better from you!'

Is Amina really in trouble? I wondered. I saw from a slight quirk in Daisy's lips that she had the same idea, and it pleased her – but I remembered a long-ago Games lesson and a mistress saying something similar to me, and I could not feel glad about it.

Daisy and I paused at Old Wing entrance to say goodbye to the Inspector.

'You saw!' Daisy hissed at him urgently. 'Mrs Turnbull is missing! And remember, we told you that Mrs Murgatroyd and Mrs North are too. We have identified four suspects: Mr Turnbull, Mr Murgatroyd, Mr North and Mr Stone. Get those clodhopping policemen to search the woods for the body immediately!'

'I am surprised you trust me to organize them, Madam Super,' said the Inspector, his mouth twitching upwards.

'I don't,' said Daisy. 'But I trust everyone else less. Anyway, *we* can't do it. We have to be back at House for our bedtime soon. Ugh, what a hideous word! Really, when I remember our lives in London . . . we are far too grown up for *bedtime*!'

'You really will make them look?' I asked. 'You promise?'

My heart was pounding. I was not sure Daisy was sounding entirely credible.

'I promise,' said the Inspector, and he caught my eye and smiled at me. I felt suddenly calmer. *Something* had happened in the woods, and he would find out what it was. 'And I promise to let you know the results of the expedition tomorrow morning, during your . . . what is the word . . .?'

'Our exeat morning,' said Daisy. 'Tomorrow you may accompany us into town from the hours of ten until two, but we have to be back in time for the beginning of the exhibition matches.'

'My grammar school did not prepare me for any of this,' said the Inspector, with a slightly haunted look in his eyes. 'I will see you tomorrow at ten a.m. precisely, Madam Super, Miss Wong. And now, if you'll excuse me, I'm off to the police station to organize a search for a body.'

We joined Kitty, Lavinia and Beanie, who had hung back to wait for us. I could feel Daisy fizzing next to me, hating the idea that with every step we took towards House we moved away from the official investigation.

Swallows were swooping parabolas above our heads in the last of the day, and a bat skittered around the trees like a scratch at the edge of my vision. 'Why *didn't* we know Mrs Turnbull was missing?' Daisy burst out. 'Kitty! She was one of yours!'

Kitty shrugged her shoulders. 'Mr Turnbull kept telling people she was on her way!' she said defensively. 'He was red in the face about it. I was watching to see whether it was true, but then Beanie's dad arrived, and . . . I was distracted. I forgot to tell you. Anyway, he might have been telling the truth!'

'Detective Freebody, you can't *believe* people!' said Daisy. 'How many times . . . Well, never mind that now. Inspector Priestley is organizing the police to hunt for the body while the light lasts this evening. If all goes to plan, we may know by tomorrow morning who the woman in the woods is, and, by extension, the man who strangled her. The case may be over!'

Kitty, Beanie and Lavinia looked cheerful – but I detected a catch in Daisy's voice. If the case was over, we would go back to being ordinary. If the case was over, Daisy would lose her special purpose – she would become nothing more than the girl who could not even get onto a school team without help.

And I truly did not know what I hoped for from the search.

SUSPECT LIST

1. *Mr Turnbull.* His wife Artemis (an opera singer with an international reputation) was supposed to perform at the concert on Friday night, but she did <u>not</u> attend!

2. *Mr Stone*. According to Uncle Felix, he is a smuggler! He has also recently been to Paris.

3. *Mr Murgatroyd*. His wife is allegedly in India, but is this true?

4. *Mr North*. We know he telephoned on Friday morning to tell Miss Lappet that his wife would not be attending the Anniversary weekend — <u>very suspicious!</u>

2

That evening, Oakeshott Woods were shot through with torchlight and shouting, and Daisy and I crouched by the window after lights out, in the last of the day, and watched. Although we could not be part of the hunt, it turned out that we could spy on it – just a little – from our dorm window.

I felt as though I had lit the touchpaper of one of Miss Runcible's fireworks and seen the whole sky explode above me. And, once again, I felt strangely torn about this search. Would our eighth murder mystery be over before it had even properly begun? And what would that do to Daisy?

I turned to look at her and saw her leaning against the dorm window, her chin on her arm and her gaze fixed on the faraway ridge. She barely blinked. The curtains billowed around her, and her nightie billowed a little too, so she looked like part of the fabric of the dorm.

I was worried that she would decide to slip down the drainpipe and do something stupid, so I forced myself to stay up with her. But I must have slept at some point, for my worries chased me into my dreams. In them, Daisy took wings and flew like an avenging angel to scoop up the culprit – who sometimes looked like Mr Murgatroyd, sometimes like Mr Turnbull, sometimes like Mr North and sometimes like Mr Stone – and carry him off to prison.

I woke up with a snap on Saturday morning, before the wake-up bell, when everything was quiet and clean. I flung myself upright – I had slipped down into an uncomfortable heap on the floor – and found Daisy exactly where I had last seen her, beside the window. Her eyes were open, still gazing out on the woods, but she jumped when I got up and put my hand on her shoulder.

'Who goes there!' she hissed. 'Oh, Watson, it's you.'

'Did they find the body?' I asked, my voice a little blurry.

'They've stopped hunting,' said Daisy. 'Hours ago, so they must have. It's over, Hazel.'

She sounded wan, and I knew it was not just from lack of sleep. I stood next to her and we leaned together, ear to ear.

'I wonder who she was?' I asked.

'We'll find out soon enough,' said Daisy. 'But – oh, how annoying that we weren't there! Now the police have taken over, I know the Inspector will just hand the rest of the case to them. He might be a fairly competent policeman, but he's still a policeman, and they are all clodhoppers in their souls.'

'He *might* let us keep on helping,' I said, trying to cheer her up, even though I did not think that was likely. 'He listened to us, didn't he? And – and there are lots of places we can go that the police can't. Haven't we seen that, in all our cases? We're different from them, and that's good!'

'Humph,' said Daisy.

'Oh, stop feeling sorry for yourself!' I said. 'We did something important, Daisy, we really did. The body is someone's mother, remember? She needed to be found. We did the right thing, you know.'

But I felt rather deflated too.

It is funny now to remember that feeling I had when I thought the case was over – before . . .

Well.

Because when we clattered down to breakfast, after we had washed and dressed and done our hair, I found a note in my pigeonhole.

'It's from the Inspector!' I said, unfolding it. 'And – oh, *Daisy*!'

I held it out to her, so she could read it.

No joy from the woods. No body.
Do we need to think again? I will be with
you at ten this morning.

I felt sick. All my secret worries bubbled up again. Beanie had been wrong. Daisy had believed what she wanted to. We *were* silly schoolgirls, after all.

Daisy was gaping, her face blank with confusion. My heart ached for her.

'The murderer's moved it!' she said. 'He must have! He – how – oh, *bother.*'

But then I saw the glow come back into her face.

'Hazel, the mystery is not over yet! We must not stop being detectives! We must keep working – we can't let a little thing like this stop us!'

'Of course, Daisy,' I said, biting my tongue.

At least for a little longer, I thought, *Daisy has this case, and can be happy.*

But in the end, it was Daisy who was right.

3

'There has to be a body,' Daisy kept on muttering at breakfast. We were all huddled at one end of the fourth-form table, having a whispered and urgent meeting. 'Somewhere! There has to be!' She rattled her spoon furiously around the bottom of the jam jar until I was half afraid she would crack it.

'It could be hidden somewhere in Deepdean town,' said Lavinia. 'Or – ooh, it could be in the Pavilion! I'll look this afternoon when I'm changing for my match.'

The Anniversary, of course, was beginning in earnest today, with the exhibition matches in the afternoon and then the gala dinner that evening.

'It's *not* in the Pavilion,' Daisy snapped. 'That makes *no* sense. We know the murderer went back towards Deepdean town, not towards the school and the sports pitches. We tracked his movements! No, if the body is anywhere, it's in town.'

'Well, we've got time to look for it, haven't we?' I said. I had decided to humour her, and there was a part of me that still hoped that it was true. 'We've got four hours to get into Deepdean town and look about for clues.'

'*Some* of us have,' said Lavinia. 'An adult has to sign us out, and *my* father probably won't even remember my match this afternoon, let alone take me out this morning.'

'And I told Daddy I didn't want to see him,' Beanie said wanly. 'So I'm stuck here too.'

'Oh, Beans!' cried Kitty. 'Well, it's a jolly good thing that Mum and Dad will be here to take Binny and me out in half an hour. The rest of you can tag along – they won't mind us slipping away once we get into town.'

'Binny will,' Lavinia pointed out. 'She'll sniff out that something's odd.'

'I can't help that!' said Kitty. 'I tried to bump her off plenty of times when she was a baby, but it never worked. It's not *my* fault she's so dreadful.'

'You must just do your best to shake her off. Once you've got away, come and meet us.'

'How are *you* getting out?' asked Kitty. '*Your* parents aren't here!'

Daisy flushed. 'The Inspector is coming to get us,' she said. 'We will be discussing the case in the Willow Tea Rooms, and then we will be searching the town for anything suspicious.'

'What are you lot talking about?' asked Amina, leaning over from the other side of the table.

'Escaping from my little sister,' said Kitty quickly.

'Oh,' said Amina, 'I thought you might be trying to hide from your parents. Mine are taking me and Clementine for a Talk about the alarm clocks this morning. They're going to go on and on about me being a good little girl so I don't get expelled, I can tell.'

'So what if you are expelled?' asked Daisy. 'And why are you talking to us? You're not in our dorm.'

Amina gazed at Daisy and grinned. 'I shan't be really. My father will make sure of it. I asked to come here – England is *the* thing at the moment, you know. I shall just explain again that pranks are part of being an English schoolgirl and promise to be perfect from now on – all the mistresses love me, so it won't be too difficult. And I don't understand your obsession with *dorms* here!'

'Did you really ask to come here?' I said. I was wondering if I was right about what I had guessed the night before: that Amina's dramatics were just a front to hide that she felt rather out of place at Deepdean.

'Of course. My parents agreed to it. And the prank was worth it, wasn't it? It was the most exciting thing that's happened for weeks – after all, what's the point of life if it isn't exciting?' asked Amina, genuinely surprised.

'Oh!' said Daisy. '*Exactly!* Hazel, haven't I told you . . . I mean, that's ridiculous. I've finished my toast, so let's get ready to go into town. Amina, go and talk to your *friend* Clementine and stop bothering our dorm.'

She dragged me away out of the Dining Room, her chin held high, and Amina stared after us, a rather deflated expression on her face.

Mr and Mrs Freebody appeared on the front steps of House just before ten in a cloud of jollity, seeming perfectly delighted to be told that they were suddenly looking after four girls rather than two.

'My goodness, darling, what a lot of children we have now,' said Mrs Freebody with a giggle, as we signed ourselves out for the morning under Matron's icy glare. 'I'm sure I don't remember giving birth to *all* of them.'

'Nor do I,' said Mr Freebody, winking. 'But if they say they're ours, they must be.'

Kitty rolled her eyes and huffed, and Mr Freebody elbowed her cheerfully. Mrs Freebody had both arms around Binny, who was turning red as she struggled to get free.

'You are the worst parents in the world,' she complained.

Mrs Freebody said, 'I know, my darling,' and beamed fondly down at her. Mr Freebody took his wife's hand.

'UGH,' said Kitty. 'Dad, Mum, come *on*, people are staring! Why are you so AWFUL?'

I hurriedly looked down at my feet. It always surprises me when parents get on. I feel suspicious of it and in awe of it, all at once.

'Where would you like to go, darlings?' asked Mrs Freebody. 'We could go round the shops, or have tea. There's something we'd like to—'

'Actually, we want to look at the shops on our own,' said Kitty.

'Oh!' said Mrs Freebody. 'But we wanted to . . . well, you are fifteen now. I suppose you are too old to enjoy spending time with your boring parents, aren't you?'

'Quite right!' laughed Mr Freebody, with an effort. 'Here, you'll be needing some spending money.'

'*I* want to go to the pictures,' announced Binny quickly, narrowing her eyes at us. 'There's a matinee of *Flash Gordon*.'

'Well, your mother and I will just spend our morning together, then,' said Mr Freebody. 'Won't we have fun! You'll be sorry you missed it.' He squeezed Mrs Freebody's shoulders and she smiled – but there was suddenly something tense behind their expressions, and I wondered that neither Kitty nor Binny could see it.

But just then I saw Inspector Priestley striding up to House's door in his mac, a stern look on his face, and I knew I had to put my questions about the Freebodys aside.

4

We walked through Deepdean town, the Inspector rather awkward and formal beside us. He was not used to behaving like an uncle rather than a policeman – and it was odd for us as well. It felt as though bits of our lives had been stitched together wrong, patched up so their patterns were all confused.

The morning sun was warm on my face, and the whole town smelled of flowers and petrol and freshly baked buns. I thought how strange it was to be in Deepdean town so early on a Saturday. Usually, fourth formers are only allowed out from three to six in the afternoon, and only to a list of appropriate locations. The Willow Tea Rooms was not one of them – although we had covertly visited it once before, under rather unpleasant circumstances.

I linked my arm through Daisy's and tried not to let my nerves show. Was the Inspector about to destroy all Daisy's hopeful visions about the case?

The Inspector refused to say anything until we arrived at the pretty front of the Willow Tea Rooms. Daisy shoved open the door, its bell tinkling sweetly, and a waitress in a frilly apron showed us to a table in the corner of the room.

We ordered a pot of tea, and some scones with cream and jam, and three rounds of sandwiches, for an early lunch – we did not want to eat at House if we could help it. Then the Inspector sat back, sighed and said, 'As you know, we have encountered something of a problem.'

'We!' said Daisy. 'The *police*, you mean. They can't find—' The waitress went bustling by and she lowered her voice. '*They can't find a body* in a small stretch of woodland, even though we gave them *plenty* of hints.'

'The hints are not what concerns me,' said Inspector Priestley. 'We found the clues you mentioned: the hat, and the matchbox, and the invitation. *Something* happened on that ridge. But we looked for as long as we could and not a trace of a body did we find. Which means that, without any evidence that a murder has taken place beyond Miss Martineau's testimony – without the body itself – the Deepdean police are not inclined to listen to me. Remember that I am no longer one of their number. I'm a London policeman now, and they don't enjoy that fact over-much.'

I felt like a seesaw. 'But . . . you still think there *was* a crime?' I asked.

'Of course there was, Hazel!' cried Daisy.

'I do,' said the Inspector, and our eyes met again. 'But . . . only in the most unscientific way possible. From what I saw, and what you told me, I am certain that something dreadful happened yesterday, but I can't prove it any more than you can.'

'So, what you're saying is . . .'

'I have used up my credibility,' said the Inspector. 'It is, unfortunately, all gone. Unless we discover more evidence that a crime has been committed – again, a *body* would be extremely useful – I cannot act in an official capacity. Now, would you like me to suggest next steps?'

'No,' said Daisy, nose in the air. 'We don't need—'

I pinched her, hard, under the table. I knew what was going on in her mind. Detection was still something we did alone, and everyone else we invited into the Detective Society was only there for my sake. Daisy did not really believe in the detective talents of anyone else in the world – and that, although Daisy is one of the most brilliant detectives I know, is one of her greatest weaknesses. I have learned that the more people there are to rely on, the easier a case may be. The Detective Society now has branches on two different continents, and that makes me feel reassured. I know that my family is safe in Hong Kong, because our friends are there to protect them.

'I mean to say,' Daisy went on, glaring at me, 'that we don't need you to take the lead. We can all work it out *together.*'

Our tea arrived, and I took a bite of scone. There was something about hearing that the Inspector still believed in Beanie's murder. It made me trust myself again, and it made me want to carry on pushing forward with the case. 'We can still watch our suspects,' I said, rather stickily. 'And find out where their wives *really* are.'

'Indeed,' said the Inspector. 'And – well, if there is a body, it must be hidden somewhere. As I said, you have been right too many times for me not to listen to you now, despite the results of the search last night. May I suggest that while you work on the suspects, I scout the town for the more grisly side of the investigation?'

Daisy and I looked at each other.

'You may,' said Daisy. 'Not a bad plan, in fact. For a policeman.'

The Inspector smiled. 'Now, eat up,' he said. 'I'm well aware that detecting is hungry work.'

I looked at him across the table. It seemed so strange that we should be working *with* the Inspector on this case – but it was proof that things really had changed at Deepdean.

5

We stepped back out of the Willow Tea Rooms, its bell jangling behind us. Inspector Priestley nodded sharply to us and slid away, shoulders hunched and looking like nothing more than a bored man out for a walk.

I took a deep breath. It was time to detect.

While we were in London, we'd had several very useful weeks of lessons from Daisy's Aunt Lucy about things that are never taught at Deepdean. We know how to throw off pursuers, how to disguise ourselves, and how to follow a suspect so that they never notice we are there. We were in need of all those skills now.

We moved through the crowds, and as we did so we caught sight of Kitty, Beanie and Lavinia, with Binny trailing them like a dark cloud. We circled round them, keeping to side streets and ducking into shops from time to time – and at last we turned a sharp corner and ran straight into them. Before Binny saw, Daisy seized

Kitty and Lavinia's wrists, I took Beanie's, and we dragged them sideways behind an ornamental flower arrangement.

After a moment, I popped my head round the side of the arrangement and saw Binny shoving her way through the throng of shoppers, looking about furiously. We had evaded her – for now, at least.

'All right!' Daisy hissed at the other three. 'We've been speaking to the Inspector, and we've agreed that he's going to search the town for possible dead bodies while *we* watch our suspects. We'll split them up, so we don't all move about together. Hazel and I will watch Mr Turnbull and Mr Stone. Lavinia, watch Mr Murgatroyd, and Beanie, you follow Mr North. Kitty, try to stick with Lavinia or Beanie – but if Binny comes back, you must distract her.'

'That's hardly fair!' complained Kitty.

'She's *your* sister,' said Lavinia.

'Yes, but – oh, all right,' said Kitty.

'Remember, we want to find out *everything* about them,' I said. 'Where they've been recently, obviously, and anything about where their wives are supposed to be now. We ought to watch Ella, Alice and Betsy too, and get any information out of them that we can – they might know something about where their mothers are.'

'Which means listening *and taking notes*,' said Daisy.

'Not me!' said Beanie. 'Please, Daisy, you know writing things down confuses me.'

'You don't have to take notes,' I told her. 'Daisy didn't mean it.'

Daisy made a face at me. 'Hardly!' she said. 'And we all ought to hurry, before we miss anything more. We only have a few hours until we have to be back at House!'

6

Daisy and I set off again – and, almost immediately, we were in luck.

We walked down a narrow side street, red-brick houses on each side of us, and then popped out again on the main Parade to find Mr Turnbull and Ella standing just ahead of us, talking to Miss Barnard and Mrs Rivers. I had to remind myself, again, that Miss Barnard and Mrs Rivers were sisters.

Daisy froze and then fell to her knees. 'Golly, I seem to have dropped my hairpin!' she sang out, and I crouched down beside her, trying to look as though I was hunting for a dropped hairpin, but all the while listening with all my might.

'Glad we ran into you!' Miss Barnard was saying. 'Such a pity about last night. I really was counting on having Artemis at the concert. Have you heard from her?'

'I do apologize,' said Mr Turnbull, shifting from foot to foot, one hand on Ella's shoulder. Ella, a blonde third former, wriggled uncomfortably, looking as though she would rather be anywhere else. 'Artemis was to motor down later and meet me at the concert – she said she had some things to finish up in town – but she never appeared. When I returned to the Majestic last night, there was a telegram waiting. Apparently, Artemis's, er, *friend*, an extremely eminent composer, requested at the last minute that she remain in London to sing at *his* concert after another performer dropped out at the last moment. But she has assured me that she will be at the dinner tonight, and I hope she will make her apologies to you then.'

'Mama never comes to things like this,' said Ella, rather bleakly. 'She's too busy travelling all over the world being famous.'

Both Mrs Rivers and Miss Barnard made clucking, sorrowful noises and Mr Turnbull gave a snort that he tried to turn into a cough.

'Artemis was always ambitious!' said Mrs Rivers, shaking her head. 'I remember that about her. I had to squash her a little, for her own good, but I couldn't help being impressed. I knew she'd make something of herself.'

'Oh yes,' said Miss Barnard. 'An unforgettable child. She was in the third form when I was in the fifth, and when Jean was a Big Girl, you know.'

Ella twitched, and I could understand why – it was so odd, thinking of mistresses and parents being at school at all, let alone *together*.

'I always thought we should hear great things of her, and we have,' Miss Barnard went on. 'She is a wonderful singer, and Deepdean is proud that she has found such acclaim. That is what this weekend is about, of course, so we cannot be *too* upset when our alumnae are successful.'

'True, true,' said Mrs Rivers.

'In fact, we really ought to be glad of it!' Miss Barnard went on, warming to her subject. 'I hope that Deepdean prepares girls for *all* the challenges and opportunities they may face in life, no matter how unlikely they may seem. Why, I had no idea when I was here that I would become the headmistress, and Jean could never have guessed that she would be called upon to step in as the head of the school Council *and* of a large company when poor Mr Rivers passed away—'

Mrs Rivers looked suddenly distraught. Miss Barnard caught sight of her sister's face and stopped speaking. There was an awkward pause.

Mr Turnbull coughed and said, 'Well, if you'll excuse me, Ella and I must go – we shall be late for lunch.'

He strode away, Ella bobbing along behind him, and Miss Barnard turned to us. We had been seen.

'Wells, Wong, are you quite all right?' she asked, gently concerned.

'Oh, Miss Barnard!' cried Daisy, straightening up. 'We were looking for my hairpin – many apologies.'

'Make sure you don't ruin your uniforms doing it, if you please,' said Miss Barnard. 'I am relying on all you girls to be nicely presented at all times this weekend.'

'Sorry, Miss Barnard; yes, Miss Barnard,' we muttered, and rushed away in as ladylike a way as we could.

'That girl,' I heard Mrs Rivers say behind us, 'looks familiar. Wells – related to the Fallingford affair, I presume? How is she . . .?'

'For heaven's sake!' cried Daisy, once we were out of earshot. 'Why won't people stop talking about . . . well, never mind that. What did we learn?'

'Mrs Turnbull is definitely missing,' I said.

'Indeed! She was allegedly at a concert in London last night – not hard to prove – so why is Mr Turnbull so twitchy? Oh, I'd like to see that telegram, to see whether it's real, or only made up by Mr Turnbull! D'you think we ought to go into the Majestic? It's that hotel further up the Parade. It's awfully grand.'

'Perhaps,' I said cautiously.

'Well, never mind that at the moment. All right, so we know that Artemis Turnbull is still unaccounted for. Anything else?'

'We know she used to go to Deepdean,' I said, 'along with Miss Barnard and Mrs Rivers!'

'Ugh! Yes. But that can hardly be useful, Hazel. After all, Old Deepdeanites are two a penny this weekend. Every other mama used to be a girl here. The more interesting thing is finding anyone who *didn't* go here.

'Anyway, Hazel, Mr Turnbull is a most intriguing suspect. He seems rather cross with his wife, doesn't he? Oh, I wish we could be flies on the wall at the gala dinner tonight to see if Mrs Turnbull really does make an entrance and, if not, how Mr Turnbull behaves! If only we were Big Girls, so we could be there! It's so unfair that we're excluded . . .'

'What are you planning?' I asked suspiciously.

'Nothing!' said Daisy, and turned away.

7

'People are such bothers!' Daisy hissed as we walked through Deepdean Park, in between the flower beds and the small children playing with their nannies. We were on the hunt for Mr Stone and Jennifer, but they were proving elusive. The first-form shrimp Emily Dow trailed past us with her parents, powerfully built Mr Dow holding forth on his own school memories while Emily and her round, mousy mother cringed behind him.

'Why won't our suspects arrange themselves neatly in a single area so we can observe them easily!' complained Daisy.

'They will tonight,' I pointed out.

'Yes,' said Daisy, her eyes going misty for a moment. 'About that, Hazel. I think—'

I caught her arm and squeezed it.

'What?' asked Daisy. 'Is it Mr Stone? *Oh!*'

It was not Mr Stone – but it was something else quite concerning.

Mr and Mrs Freebody were sitting on a bench at the edge of the park. She was weeping, her handkerchief pressed to her eyes. He was trying to comfort her, but as we watched she pulled away from him angrily.

'What shall we do?' I gasped. It felt sacrilegious to watch them, but of course Daisy was not worried about that.

'Circle round and listen in!' she said at once. 'They don't appear to have seen us yet. We must get behind them, creep up and find out what they are saying.'

'But we can't!' I said. 'What if we find out something dreadful?'

'Then Kitty ought to know,' said Daisy callously. 'I'd want to, if they were *my* parents.'

I bit back my reply.

We circled through the park, trying to move casually enough not to be noticeable, and as soon as we were out of Mr and Mrs Freebody's line of sight we dashed towards their bench. There was a useful tree a few paces away from it, and we leaned against it, our faces turned away, and tried to look as though we were not listening in.

Mr and Mrs Freebody were still talking. They were using hushed voices, but we could catch a few words – and what we heard gave me a distinctly grubby feeling.

'I don't know what to do!' Mrs Freebody was saying, between sniffles. 'I was hoping we could tell them today, but just look at them both – they already don't want to be near us!'

'Now, you're being over-emotional,' said Mr Freebody.

'*Don't* call me over-emotional!' snapped Mrs Freebody, and she began to sob harder. 'Oh dear, they'll be so cross – especially Binny. What if they grow up with abandonment issues?'

'We've already sent them to boarding school, darling. I hardly think this will be much worse.'

'But what if it is? What if they resent us? Oh, I can't bear it! We should never have—'

Mr Freebody pulled her into an embrace, and I decided that I did not want to listen to any more. 'Come ON, Daisy!' I said. 'We shouldn't be here!'

'But this is important, Hazel! It may be the key—'

'It isn't the key to anything! They're just . . .' I could not work out what on earth Mr and Mrs Freebody *were* talking about, so I let the sentence drop. 'Come on, we've got to look for Mr Stone!'

'Well,' said Daisy, sighing, 'there is one thing I do know. Marriage causes *far* too many emotions. This is why I shall never marry. You should be careful, Hazel.'

'I'm not going to marry Alexander!' I said. 'He doesn't think of me that way.'

'*Did* I say anything about Alexander?' asked Daisy, poking me cheekily. 'No! Then why would you say—'

'Stop it, Daisy!' I said, elbowing her, and Daisy smirked and went quiet.

8

We finally caught up with Mr Stone by the entrance to the Majestic, in the middle of a quiet but fierce argument with Jennifer – one that made our ears perk up. We ducked behind the nearest pillar and listened.

'Daddy, what did I say after the last time!' Jennifer was hissing. 'You're far too old! It's shameful! And Mummy's only been dead for three years! Why can't you just be a widower like *ordinary* fathers?'

'I'm hardly . . . Jenny, really . . . now, see here, I have every right to marry again – and what about you, by the way? I heard about the chocolates from your *admirer*. We'll discuss *that* later.'

'DADDY!' shrieked Jennifer.

I remembered Daisy's diversion from the day before, and flinched. But what was this about Mr Stone getting married? Ought there to have been a woman here with him this weekend after all?

I was desperate to hear what he would say next, but then Mr Stone, his cigarette halfway to his mouth, paused so suddenly that I thought we had been compromised. But it was another pair of girls who had startled them – Beanie and Lavinia. They trotted up to the front of the Majestic, and Mr Stone and Jennifer walked away towards Deepdean Park, still muttering at each other angrily.

Daisy hissed through her teeth. 'Amateurs!' she muttered. 'Schoolgirls!'

'*We're* schoolgirls,' I pointed out, though I was disappointed as well.

'We are so much more, these days!' said Daisy. 'Don't you feel we've moved on, Hazel?'

I did not say anything.

'Oh, there you are!' said Beanie. 'We've got lots to tell you!'

Daisy glared at them. 'Can't you see we were watching some suspects? You've scared them off. Look!'

'Well, they're gone now,' said Lavinia, shrugging. 'D'you want to hear what we've found? Kitty's holding off Binny, by the way. She's trapped her in the sweet shop.'

'Oh, go on, then,' said Daisy ungraciously, 'now you're here.'

'We got stuck behind the Thompson-Bateses on the Parade at first,' said Beanie. 'So we didn't *exactly* hear anything important about the case, but we did hear something important about Lavinia's match this afternoon. Mr Thompson-Bates was being horrible to Lallie about . . . about . . . what was it, Lavinia?'

'Her form not being up to snuff,' said Lavinia. 'Her lob's weak, which is marvellous to know. Mrs Thompson-Bates just stayed quiet and looked bored. She must be tired of hearing about it – she's been touring with him this spring. I've seen snaps of them both in all my magazines. They always get into the Who's Who pages because Mrs T-B's family's something important.'

'Irrelevant!' said Daisy. 'Mr Thompson-Bates is not a suspect, as you well know. Hurry up.'

'But anyway, then we went into the Lyons, pretending to look for Dad, and we saw Alice Murgatroyd talking to Mr Murgatroyd. Apparently her mother telephoned House this morning to say that she's going to stay in India and climb a mountain. Alice said she talked to her, and Mrs Murgatroyd said she was sorry to be missing the Anniversary. So she's not dead, if Alice spoke to her, so we can rule her out of being the body, and Mr M of being the murderer!'

'Excellent,' said Daisy. '*We* had a good run of it too. We heard Mr Turnbull talking to Barny and Mrs Rivers, and Mrs Turnbull is still *definitely* missing. And just before you barged in, Hazel and I overheard Mr Stone and Jennifer, and Mr Stone was saying some very interesting things about getting married again. What if he has a secret fiancée, and she was the woman in the woods?'

'Except why would he tell Jennifer about her *today*?' I asked. 'If he killed her yesterday, I mean.'

'Watson makes a point,' said Daisy, frowning rather. 'Oh dear, there's Kitty, and Binny. Quiet, please – we can't let the third formers know what we've been up to!'

I thought two things. First, that for all Daisy was certain she was more grown up, being at Deepdean was pulling her back into all the silly little games that schoolgirls played.

And second, that we had lost our chance to talk to Beanie and Lavinia about what Daisy and I had overheard in the park. Something was up with Mr and Mrs Freebody – but what was it? Ought we to tell Kitty?

9

The morning had been warm and fresh, but that afternoon, as we all gathered on the sports fields for the exhibition matches, clouds clustered overhead. My skin felt sticky and my head ached – it was suddenly unbearably hot. Fathers were loosening their ties uncomfortably, some of them even leaving their jackets slung across little garden chairs – fearfully bad form – and mothers were fanning themselves with their programmes. The tea tent was doing a roaring trade in cool drinks.

I managed to get behind Mr Turnbull at the tea stand after I heard him chivalrously offering to fetch Mrs Thompson-Bates a glass of squash. 'Any word from Artemis?' she asked, glamorous in a pair of dark glasses and another jaunty scarf. 'She was two years below me, and she had quite a pash on me. I was Tennis Scholar, of course, so it's understandable.'

'She should be here this evening,' said Mr Turnbull, twitching, at which point Mr Thompson-Bates appeared and put his arm around his wife.

'No time for drinks, Cordy – Lallie needs us before her match,' he said, squeezing her shoulder. They both turned away from Mr Turnbull rather pointedly, and he was left alone clutching his glasses of squash.

I felt a nudge behind me and turned to see Daisy, eyes shining with excitement. 'I've been going through the jackets!' she whispered to me. 'Lucky for us some of the fathers have forgotten how to behave politely. *Anyway*, I looked in Mr Turnbull's wallet and he's got *francs* in his. Which means that he must have been in France very recently indeed! He is becoming more suspicious by the minute.'

'What about Mr Stone and Mr North?' I whispered back, not bothering to point out to Daisy that looking through people's wallets was very nearly stealing. I knew she would only sniff and tell me not to be dull.

'Mr Stone's got his wallet on him, bother him,' said Daisy, 'which proves he has a suspicious mind.'

We both looked over to see Mr Stone striding through the crowd, handsome and rakish with his red hair gleaming under the dull clouds. Jennifer ignored him – clearly still smarting from their argument earlier – and Mrs Rivers, dressed in a high-necked dark-green frock, tutted and narrowed her eyes at them both. Mr Stone winked at her, and she flushed and took a large gulp of her lemonade.

'Mr North's wallet only had pounds and shillings in it, though,' Daisy went on. 'A pity. Of course, that doesn't mean he *hasn't* been to France recently as well, but we have no way of confirming— Oh goodness, look who it is! By the tree!'

I turned to look where she was pointing, and saw the Inspector lurking under the old oak tree at the edge of the hockey pitch. He looked overwarm in his mac, and he had his large hands wrapped uncomfortably around one of the very small cups the maids at the tea stand were giving out.

'Good grief!' said Daisy to him, as we sidled over to say hello. 'That dreadful coat makes you look entirely out of place!'

'Thank you for your comments, Madam Super,' said the Inspector, wrinkling up his forehead at her. 'Most helpful, as usual.'

'I'm only saying!' said Daisy. 'If you behave wrong, it makes people nervous. You know some of the girls have recognized you – it isn't *so* long since you were here for the Bonfire Night murder, after all. They'll begin to talk, and then we'll be scuppered. Look at Mrs Rivers, glaring at you as well as at Mr Stone!'

Inspector Priestley sighed. 'And how should I be behaving?' he asked.

'Look happy to be here, for goodness' sake!' cried Daisy. 'And talk to the parents. We found francs in Mr Turnbull's wallet, which is deeply suspicious, but none in Mr North's. Mr Stone has his wallet with him, so we can't check that. We need to find out whether or not he's been in Paris lately.'

'Did you manage to find anything in town?' I asked, as Inspector Priestley unbuttoned his coat, revealing a cheap dark-blue suit beneath it.

'Not yet,' said the Inspector. 'But I'll keep looking after the gala dinner tonight too. Now, Madam Super, who ought I to be speaking to?'

'Perhaps it's best that he's wearing his coat!' said Daisy, as the Inspector ambled away once we had pointed out our suspects. 'That suit is off the rack! Oh dear, I suppose an inspector's salary isn't up to much. Now, Hazel, I keep on thinking about the dinner. It *eats* at me that we're not allowed to be there, which is rather ironic. I wonder . . . I do wonder . . . if we could somehow manage to be on the spot . . .'

10

Lavinia's exhibition match against Lallie Thompson-Bates was at three, and all four of us (and the Inspector) lined up to cheer her on.

Daisy nudged me. 'Look!' she whispered, nodding to our right. There was Mr North, with Betsy beside him. They were standing on the edge of the crowd, talking together animatedly.

I nodded to Daisy, and we both began to sidle towards the Norths, all the while keeping one eye on the game. Even I could tell that Lavinia was playing good tennis, and she was soon two games up. Lallie was small and slight, not strong enough to chase after every ball, and I saw her becoming more and more frustrated. She was no match for Lavinia.

It did not help that her parents were also in the crowd, and it was quite obvious to everyone that Mr Thompson-Bates was not happy. After every shot his daughter missed, he would bellow, 'COME ON, LALLIE! HIT IT!' Then he would turn to Mrs Thompson-Bates and mutter angrily in her ear, while she quirked an eyebrow and sighed.

'She's *useless*!' Mr Thompson-Bates shouted, as Lavinia went another game up. 'Just look at her!'

On court, Lallie faltered.

'Darling, really – remember your second round against Sato in '33,' murmured Mrs Thompson-Bates. 'Temper will get you nowhere.'

Mr Thompson-Bates breathed through his nose and squeezed her hand, momentarily soothed. Mrs Thompson-Bates smiled tightly behind her sunglasses.

We had now arrived at a spot just behind the Norths – and, of course, they seemed to have stopped talking. Betsy was now staring straight ahead at the game, her arms folded, while Mr North, a tall, dark-haired man with a thin face and bright blue eyes, shifted from foot to foot and looked bored.

Back on court, Lavinia thrust her arm into the air and slammed the ball over the net.

'GO IT, LAVINIA!' our dorm all shouted – and our words were echoed by a deep voice in the crowd behind us.

I turned to see Mr Temple, his beard combed and a yellow cravat around his neck, his arm about a bottle-blonde woman in a very clingy afternoon dress and pearls.

'HOORAY, LAVINIA!' she shrilled, and out on the court Lavinia flinched and flushed, and made a very cross face. The ball came at her and she slapped it away with her racket, so it flew over Lallie's shoulder, bounced on the line and buried itself in the long grass. Lavinia's mother, on the other side of the crowd, applauded pointedly, and Mr Temple glared at her.

'Point to Temple,' said Miss Talent, umpiring.

'Nice for *her* to have *her* mother here,' Betsy North grumbled pointedly.

Mr North sighed. 'Not this again, Betsy,' he said. 'You can't be cross. Mummy's just—'

'Home with smelly *Roger*!' said Betsy, curling her lip. 'It's always *his* fault when she isn't somewhere. Like this weekend! Whooping cough! I bet he doesn't *really* have it. I didn't hear him coughing on the telephone with Mummy this morning.'

I felt Daisy's elbow in my side, and I gave her a quick nod to let her know I'd heard.

'HIT IT, LAVINIA!' Mr Temple whooped.

'Would you mind NOT shouting?' Mr Thompson-Bates asked crossly, turning towards him.

'MIND?' growled Mr Temple. 'What business is it of YOURS, James?'

'My DAUGHTER is trying to WIN the MATCH, Michael,' said Mr Thompson-Bates.

'James, darling, temper . . .' said Mrs Thompson-Bates.

'Cordy, *dear*, can't you *see* I'm *talking* to Mr Temple?' said Mr Thompson-Bates, his lips white.

Lavinia and Lallie both looked over at the commotion.

'Oh, hello, Lavinia darling!' cried the blonde woman next to Mr Temple, waving her hand excitedly. 'It's Patricia and Daddy! We're here! You're doing EVER so well!'

Lavinia narrowed her eyes, threw the ball into the air and slammed her racket into it as though she was crushing the skulls of her enemies. It burned through the air over Lallie's head.

'Game, set and match!' called the umpire.

Lallie burst into tears. Mrs Thompson-Bates gasped. Lavinia smashed her racket on the ground. Mr Temple laughed nastily and said, 'Just like the time I beat you at the match at Weston, remember, James?'

Mr Thompson-Bates swung about and punched Mr Temple square in the face.

All in all, it was quite the most exciting exhibition match I had ever seen.

11

'So we know Mrs North's alive!' said Daisy, when the two of us were back in our dorm after the match. 'Stuck at home looking after Betsy's little brother. An absolute washout on Mr North – did you hear Betsy mention that she talked to her mother on the telephone this morning? So she's very much accounted for! I think, therefore, that we are down to *two* suspects: Mr Stone and Mr Turnbull. And that, Hazel, is why even though Deepdean has not seen fit to invite us, we *must* get down to school this evening and spy on the gala dinner. We have absolutely NO choice in the matter!'

'I think we *do* have a choice,' I said, although I could not help smiling.

'Hush, Hazel,' said Daisy, her eyes sparkling. 'Now, the dinner will take place only in the main body of the Hall. The upper balconies will be quite empty, you know. Imagine if someone was to hide up there and watch events!'

'I think it ought to be two people,' I said, 'just in case.' Despite myself, I was beginning to enjoy this case thoroughly.

'Yes, Watson!' cried Daisy. 'Excellent, most excellent. Now all we have to do is wait for this evening, so we can escape!'

At seven p.m. we all clustered together in the hallway to watch the Big Girls and prefects go down to the gala dinner. They were all dressed like grown-ups, in bright silks and soft chiffons, their hair up.

All the Big Girls were allowed to invite a guest (fiancés were acceptable, brothers far better, and boyfriends were not allowed), and Kitty was thrilled because Emmeline Moss was bringing her brother, who was a dish.

'He's so handsome!' she sighed. 'Oh, if I didn't have Hugo . . . Daisy, why are you wriggling?'

Daisy, of course, was fizzing to be on the spot, at the dinner, in the room with our suspects. The last Big Girls had barely stepped through the front door before she whirled round to us and cried, 'Come on, let's go up to the dorm!'

I saw Amina's head turn to look at us. 'What's the hurry?' she asked. 'Are you planning something? Is it a prank?'

'No!' snapped Daisy. 'We are *much* too grown up for pranks, unlike *you*.'

136

'You're just jealous,' said Clementine, coming to put her arms about Amina's shoulders, 'because our prank last night was brilliant.'

'I don't care,' said Daisy loftily. 'Come on, Dorm. We have important things to discuss!'

When we arrived back at the dorm Daisy pushed the door shut and leaned against it.

'Detective Society! As I told the idiots downstairs, we have important things to say. Hazel and I have been discussing the matter, and we have decided that now we are down to two suspects, we *must* get down to school to watch the gala dinner. We need to see how Mr Stone and Mr Turnbull behave – and whether Mrs Turnbull appears, as she has apparently promised she will!'

Kitty, Beanie and Lavinia all began to complain, of course.

'Silence!' hissed Daisy. 'We can't *all* go, that would be foolish. We stand a much greater chance of being caught if we're all together – and, more importantly, we need several people to remain up here as cover.'

'But—' Kitty began.

'NO arguments, Detective Freebody! I am still the President of the Detective Society – my word is law!'

'It does make sense,' I said to the others. 'Really. We can't all go, and we have to make sure we're not caught.'

'Ugh!' said Lavinia. 'Can't one of us three go, at least?'

'I suppose *one* more person could,' I said, 'couldn't they, Daisy?'

'No!' said Daisy. 'Well . . . oh bother – but not you, Lavinia; you don't creep well at all. And not Kitty, either. Beanie, you can come. No arguments!'

Beanie beamed, looking happier than she had all day, and I was glad Daisy had chosen her.

'Now that's decided, we have to get out of House,' said Daisy, pacing about the dorm like a caged tiger. 'That's easy enough – or at least it ought to be. Everyone, help me get the sheets off the beds. Quickly!'

As Daisy tugged at one of the knotted sheets – a knot that Aunt Lucy had taught us a few months before – I pushed the dorm window open wide and stared out into the evening. It was still light – by my wristwatch it was ten past seven – and I could see each tree of Oakeshott Woods. We would have to creep very carefully indeed so as not to be caught. My eyes were drawn to the empty ridge where Beanie had seen . . . whatever it was she had seen, and I shivered despite the warmth of the evening.

'We shall now tie one end of the sheets around my bed,' Daisy ordered. 'Kitty, sit on it, and Lavinia will hold the rope. Is everyone ready?'

'Why am I sitting on the bed?' Kitty protested.

'Because you have no upper body strength, Detective Freebody. Mind you, neither has Hazel – and I have told her a thousand times that she needs to work on her fitness if she wants to be a good detective. Now, on the count of three, we shall begin. Ready? One – two – THREE!'

12

Creeping down to school and all the way into the Hall that evening – *this* evening: I have nearly caught up now – gave me a distinctly prickly, terrified feeling. Old Wing entrance was open when we arrived, and it was easy for us to slip in, but the still-lit lamps and the carpets indented with the marks of high heels and men's dress shoes made me jumpy. Of course, Daisy and I have been at school after hours illegally before, but never when we knew so many other people were there. It did not help that Beanie trembled with nerves every time we heard even the slightest sound.

Up the little spiral staircase that led onto the balcony we went at last – and there we were, staring down at the Hall, which was filled with chattering grown-ups and Big Girls, and glowing with candles.

'Ooh!' gasped Beanie, poking her head over the edge of the balcony. 'They've got the nice napkins out!'

'*Down!*' whispered Daisy, batting at her. 'We mustn't be obvious!'

We crouched down, our noses against the wooden fretwork of the balcony, and peeked through to watch what we could.

It did not take me long to catch sight of the first of our suspects. Mr Stone's red hair shone in the candlelight as he took his place at the fourth table from the stage. Daisy nudged me quite painfully, and I saw that Mr Turnbull was on the same table. As well as Mr Stone and Mr Turnbull, Amina's parents, Mr and Mrs El Maghrabi, were there, and Lallie's parents, Mr and Mrs Thompson-Bates, along with the first former Emily Dow's parents, who we had seen walking through Deepdean Park that morning.

'At least Lavinia's father's not on the same table as Mr Thompson-Bates!' said Daisy to me, grinning. 'But where's the Inspector, though? He said he'd be here. Well, it's a good thing we decided to see for ourselves!'

'He's over there,' I whispered, after some craning about and looking. 'See – on that table on the Gym side.'

'Oh well, that's no good!' said Daisy. 'He's with Mr Martineau and the unimportant parents, almost as far away from the stage as the Big Girls! He'll never be able to watch our suspects! Really, as I said – it's lucky that we're here!'

'Thank you for bringing me,' whispered Beanie, eyes glittering. I noticed that she was pointedly looking away from where her father was sitting next to an empty space, and my heart hurt for her all over again.

There was a moment's lull in the chattering. I tensed, in case someone had caught sight of us – but the pause had been caused by ten solemn, well-dressed people, eight men and two women, processing into the Hall.

'The Council!' whispered Daisy in my ear.

Mrs Rivers, wearing a strict royal-blue high-necked dress and looking both fierce and fiercely glamorous, moved forward and took a seat at the head of Mr Stone and Mr Turnbull's table. The others sat too, one Council member at the head of each table, and now I could see that there was one empty place on Table Four, between Mr Thompson-Bates's blond head and Mr Dow's broad shoulders.

'*Mrs Turnbull isn't there!*' I whispered.

'Yes indeed!' said Daisy. 'She's still missing, Hazel! She's not here! Oh, he lied to everyone this morning. I knew it! I knew he was suspicious!'

I tried not to let Daisy's excitement colour my thinking. We did not *know*, yet, that Mrs Turnbull was our missing woman. We could not be sure – but, all the same, I now thought that she must be.

Mrs Rivers was at Table Four's head, with Mr Turnbull opposite her at the other end. On Mrs Rivers' left-hand side was Mr El Maghrabi, then nervous-looking Mrs Dow, foxy Mr Stone and smiling Mrs El Maghrabi. On the other side of Mrs Rivers was Mr Thompson-Bates, then a space for Mrs Turnbull, then Mr Dow, his thick neck wrapped in a Weston Old Boys' tie, and finally dark, beautiful Mrs Thompson-Bates next to Mr Turnbull.

I watched as Mrs Rivers leaned forward across the table and said something to Mr Turnbull at the other end. She gestured to the empty place where his wife should have been, which made him slump in his seat and blush angrily. Mr Stone replied with something that looked as though it was supposed to be a joke, but Mrs Rivers sat up very straight, tossed her head and turned quite deliberately away from him to speak to Mr Thompson-Bates. Mr Stone scowled, his handsome face twisting, and leaned across Mrs El Maghrabi to mutter to Mr Turnbull.

I was desperate to know what they were saying, and I could tell that Daisy was too. She watched the table, open-mouthed. A curl of gold hair had escaped from her schoolgirl plait and was tickling her nose, but she did not notice it in the slightest.

I made a careful sketch of Table Four and its occupants (I have tucked it into the beginning of this account, if you want to see it for yourself) and tried to follow what was happening, as the Deepdean maids began to circulate with the wine.

'They're doing it wrong!' whispered Daisy. 'Oh, Chapman and Hetty would have a fit! Look at Nancy and Beryl's form – dreadful.'

'Mmm . . .' I said vaguely, for I still do not understand the niceties of waiting at British dinner tables. All my eyes could see was a gentle black-and-white dance, as figures darted backwards and forwards and glasses glinted amber in the candlelight.

The first course was brought out – an aspic, on plates emblazoned with Deepdean's crest. I saw Mrs Dow turn to Nancy, serving the plates, and shake her head, motioning her aspic away tearfully.

Mr Dow leaned forward across the table and said something that made Mr Stone and Mr Thompson-Bates laugh, and Mrs Dow looked stricken.

'Poor Mrs Dow!' Beanie whispered. 'She looks so unhappy to be here! And everyone's being so horrid to her . . . oh, look! Mrs Rivers is going to tell them to stop!'

But although Mrs Rivers was speaking, every face at Table Four turned towards her, what she was saying was clearly not designed to soothe Mrs Dow. Mr Stone laughed again, and Mrs Dow put her hands up to her face. Then she simply stood up and went rushing out of the Hall. She brushed past Mrs Rivers quite violently and almost knocked into Beryl, serving the wine. Beryl hovered, looking awkward, and then at last decided to move on, leaving Mrs Dow's glass empty.

'I don't think Mrs Rivers is a very nice person!' said Beanie. 'Or Mr Dow!'

Nancy, meanwhile, was having more bad luck with her plates. Mrs El Maghrabi waved her aspic away as well, as did her husband.

'Vegetarian, do you think?' asked Daisy – but, for once, I knew an answer she did not.

'They're Muslims!' I said. 'It must be a pork aspic – you're not allowed to eat pork if you're Muslim.'

I looked back at Table Four. Mrs Rivers was now talking to Mr El Maghrabi – and it seemed that all was not well there, either. Mr El Maghrabi's face was grim, and he snapped something at her. Mrs Rivers' head jerked back, and she replied, waving her hands furiously. Whatever they were discussing must be quite unpleasant.

Further down the table, Mr Stone was staring fixedly at Mrs Rivers, as though there was something burned onto her forehead that only he could see. At last he got up and went over to her, bending down to whisper in her ear. Mrs Rivers turned on him with an angry expression, pointing back at his seat.

'She's telling him to go away,' said Daisy. 'Oh, what on earth is happening?'

'They all hate each other!' said Beanie. 'Is this – is this what you thought you'd see?'

I was fascinated.

Mrs Turnbull and Mrs Dow's empty seats, Mr and Mrs El Maghrabi's empty plates, and Mrs Rivers' banishment of Mr Stone seemed to have frozen Table Four into silence. No one spoke except to ask for the salt and pepper.

At last the first course was cleared. I looked at my watch, and saw that it was after eight. The main course was served rather hesitantly by Nancy – roast pork on plates, accompanied by platters of roast potatoes and vegetables. Again, Mr and Mrs El Maghrabi waved their plates away, Mr El Maghrabi now quite angrily.

Mr Turnbull began to speak to Mrs El Maghrabi, while Mr Dow tried to get the attention of Mrs Thompson-Bates, sitting next to him – but she was playing distractedly with her clutch bag in her lap and hardly noticed him. I thought Mrs Rivers and Mr Thompson-Bates had moved onto the safe topic of tennis (or so it seemed, from Mr Thompson-Bates's wild and enthusiastic arm gestures), while Mr El Maghrabi was trying his best to get the attention of Mr Stone, who was still staring at Mrs Rivers.

And then – and then – Mrs Rivers coughed. She held her napkin daintily in front of her mouth to hide it, but she coughed again, and again: big, racking chokes that had Mr El Maghrabi and Mr Thompson-Bates turning to her in concern. At last Mrs Rivers doubled over, her hands on her stomach, and gasped out something that I was quite sure was 'Help!'

The table wobbled as she knocked into it – and we all looked on, aghast.

'What's happening?' gasped Beanie.

'It can't be!' Daisy breathed. 'Hazel, it can't be – surely it can't?'

I could barely believe my eyes. But as Mrs Rivers continued to choke and gasp, bent over in agony, I was quite certain I knew what I was seeing. I had seen it before, once, at Daisy's house, Fallingford. It is a horrid memory, one I try not to think of very much – but here it was again, brought to life.

Mrs Rivers looked for all the world like someone who had been poisoned with arsenic.

Mr El Maghrabi leaped up and bent over Mrs Rivers, and Mr Thompson-Bates got up too, pushing him aside. Mr Stone shoved his chair back and ran to her, his foxy face grey and horrified.

Mrs Thompson-Bates fell back in a faint and Mr Turnbull caught her, looking stricken. Mrs Rivers, meanwhile, was gasping and foaming at the mouth.

'Get a doctor!' screamed Mrs El Maghrabi, seeming to have the greatest presence of mind of anyone. 'Quick! Help! A doctor, please!'

The Inspector pushed his way through the crowd, and so did Miss Barnard. She knelt beside her sister, dabbing at her forehead and whispering desperately in her ear. Nancy dropped the tray she was carrying with a great clatter and dashed out of the Hall, to return five minutes later with a panting Mrs Minn, our school nurse. Mrs Minn bent over Mrs Rivers, who was by now fitting horribly.

'Oh no! Oh no! Oh no!' Beanie was whispering in my ear, tears in her eyes.

I felt dizzy with shock. How could this be?

'She's been poisoned!' cried Mrs Minn. 'We must get her to San. Someone help me lift her. Hurry!'

Mrs Rivers was carried out of the Hall, Miss Barnard running after her in a panic, leaving all the other guests in horrified confusion.

I looked at my watch again – it was 8:42 p.m.

And that was the moment that death truly came to Deepdean, and the reason why I am writing all this up.

1

I hardly remember Daisy's and my escape from the Hall balcony, just a blur of dark and then light, a rush of running up Oakeshott Hill, hearing rustling in the trees, feet stumbling on the grass by House, and Lavinia and Kitty's white faces at the window as we climbed up into the dorm again to collapse on the floor, gasping.

'Where's Beanie?' cried Kitty. 'What happened?'

I sat up, and Daisy leaped upright and stood in the middle of the dorm room, trembling with excitement like a dog who has smelled a fox.

'Someone's been *poisoned*!' she cried. 'We saw it, we were there! Someone's poisoned Mrs Rivers! Beanie's staying to watch the other people in the Hall – otherwise we have no way of knowing if they show symptoms of poisoning as well.'

'*Mrs Rivers* was poisoned?' said Kitty blankly. 'And why would you leave *Beanie*—'

'I know, I know, but we didn't have *time*,' said Daisy, pacing in circles. '*Someone* had to watch. Now, the Big Girls will be—'

The front door to House slammed open, and the hallway was suddenly filled with shrieking noise. We could hear it all the way up the stairs and along the corridors and through the closed door to our dorm.

'Kitty, you go running downstairs looking frightened and make the Big Girls tell you what's happened. And watch *them* for any signs of poisoning! Go! We need as much information as possible. We'll wait here.'

I couldn't think why she did not volunteer to go herself. She looked as though she was ready to run a mile.

'Hazel, Lavinia, get out the things for a midnight feast. We shall be needing it – this is going to be a very long night, and we need to begin with a Detective Society meeting *at once*.'

'What are you going to do?' asked Kitty.

'*I* am going to plan our next steps,' said Daisy. 'I must admit that not even I was prepared for this. The case has absolutely turned on its head. The only thing we do know is this: Mrs Rivers has just been poisoned *in our own school* – and the poisoner shall *not* be allowed to get away with it!'

'First things first,' said Daisy, when Kitty had returned, bubbling with second-hand gossip from the Big Girls about the horrid incident they had witnessed, and we were all seated in a circle on the floor. 'Cut me a slice of cake, if you please, Kitty . . . Excellent. Now, I shall call this extraordinary meeting of the Detective Society to order. Present, Daisy Wells, Hazel Wong, Kitty Freebody and Lavinia Temple. Absent on Society business: Rebecca Martineau. To discuss: the poisoning of Mrs Rivers, and the continuing mystery of the murder in Oakeshott Woods. Hazel, will you give me the new facts of the case?'

I took a deep breath and said: 'Victim: Mrs Rivers. Time and place of crime: Deepdean School Hall, during the gala dinner on Saturday night. The victim was carried away at 8:42 p.m. We don't know if she's dead yet – or if anyone else will be affected – but Daisy and I have seen this before. It's arsenic poisoning . . . it has to be.'

'Indeed, it looks like it. And, really – good grief! I must admit that I was not expecting someone entirely unconnected to the investigation thus far to be *poisoned.*'

'At least you're admitting you don't know everything, for once,' said Lavinia.

'Oh, do stop it!' said Daisy. 'I could hardly say anything else. This has thrown the whole case on its head. Why on earth was Mrs Rivers poisoned this evening? Does it have anything to do with what Beanie saw in the woods? Is this the *same* mystery, or quite another one?'

'It has to be another one, doesn't it?' said Kitty.

'But the suspects we were watching were both on Mrs Rivers' table!' I said. 'Mr Turnbull and Mr Stone. That's too much of a coincidence. I know we need to wait to see if anyone else in the Hall has been poisoned before we jump to conclusions, but . . . it's not likely, is it? I mean – it's not the simplest explanation.'

'This is very true,' said Daisy. 'Life is extraordinarily odd, but the fact is that *usually*, when several crimes occur together, they do so because one single person or group of people is behind them. So, Detectives, give me some suggestions that would fit all our facts.'

'What if Mrs Rivers saw the same thing Beanie did?' suggested Lavinia. 'She might have been walking in the woods, and seen the strangling – or the murderer . . . seen him dragging the body! And the murderer might have found out. So *she* might have died because she knew too much.'

'Mr Stone *was* staring at her oddly all the way through dinner,' I said. 'And Mr Turnbull looked terribly upset at something she said to him – I think it was about Mrs Turnbull not being there. What if she said that because she wanted to needle him, because she knows that he killed Mrs Turnbull yesterday?'

'Good,' said Daisy. 'Excellent, and very true. This could be the answer. Except that . . . when we heard Mrs Rivers talking to Mr Turnbull in Deepdean town this morning, she didn't sound as though she was suspicious about Mrs Turnbull yet, did she? Bother! It doesn't quite fit.'

'Wait,' I said suddenly. I had suddenly got a creeping feeling all up and down my back. So *many* things did not quite fit, not unless . . . 'I've had a thought. I think you're right, Daisy, that this must be connected to what Beanie saw, but . . . what if what Beanie saw *wasn't* actually what she thought she did?'

Everyone stared at me.

'Explain,' said Daisy.

'Well,' I said. 'Beanie saw a man strangle a woman on the ridge. We went up it and looked, and we proved that the man and woman were there, that they struggled, and that the man carried the woman away. But – what if she wasn't *dead* when she was carried down the hill again? What if she was only unconscious? The green hat we found had dark hairs on it, didn't it? Mrs Rivers is dark-haired. Well . . . what if the woman Beanie saw was *Mrs Rivers*? And what if the murder she thought she saw yesterday didn't really happen – until this evening?'

2

'Good heavens,' said Daisy.

I felt trembly with all the thoughts dashing through my brain. This – at last – made sense. 'Mrs Rivers has been wearing high-necked dresses,' I said, remembering. 'It might have been to hide the bruising!'

'That is . . . Why, that is an entirely elegant solution, Watson! It requires us to alter some of our thinking, but it fits perfectly. If you are right, we are still looking for a man who is attending the Deepdean Anniversary, but his victim is no longer a mystery to us. That means . . . that means that even if Mrs Rivers *does* die of poisoning this evening, there has only been *one* murder thus far, not two!'

I was still working through everything. It all fitted – all of it – except . . .

'But if it *was* Mrs Rivers Beanie saw being strangled, why didn't she come forward to say what happened?' I asked. 'Why didn't she tell the police?'

'That's not hard to work out,' said Daisy. 'I assume the man threatened her. After all, he almost killed her.'

'Yes, but why wouldn't she just go to Miss Barnard's office, or speak to the Inspector at the exhibition matches?' I asked. 'She'd feel safe at Deepdean, since she used to go here when she was a girl.'

'Hazel, you are being difficult,' said Daisy, with narrowed eyes. 'There are lots of ways to threaten someone. You can do it with just a look or a word at the right moment. And he might know a secret of hers – something that would be ruinous to her if it came out.'

'We know Mrs Rivers' husband is dead!' said Kitty. 'Barny said so yesterday, didn't she? Ooh, what if Mrs R murdered him!'

'How very sensational of you, Kitty,' said Daisy. 'But, yes, that is the sort of thing I mean. Now, if Mrs Rivers believed she was in danger, she could have been taking care not to go about on her own. If so, it would explain why she was always seen with Miss Barnard. But in a crowded room, at one of the Anniversary events, she would have felt safe enough to let her guard down. Of course, we now know that she was not safe at all!

'I think it makes sense to suggest that Hazel is correct in her assumptions, and that the woman strangled in the woods and the woman poisoned at dinner tonight are one and the same. We only have one victim! So, what do we know about Mrs Rivers? And why would someone try so hard to bump her off?'

'She's on the school Council, of course,' said Kitty at once. 'She's Barny's sister – er, the headmistress's sister – and she used to go to Deepdean too. And she used to have a husband, but he died.'

I remembered something else Miss Barnard had said in Deepdean town that morning. 'When her husband died, she took charge of his company,' I added.

'What *is* the Council, by the way?' asked Lavinia. 'You keep on talking about it, but I've no idea what it is. What do the Council members do?'

'They are a fearfully important group!' said Daisy. 'They decide things like where our fee money goes, who works at Deepdean, and who is allowed to attend it. And when girls do truly awful things, it's the Council who decides that they can't be at Deepdean any more.'

'That's stupid,' said Lavinia.

'That's *life*!' said Daisy. 'It happens everywhere. So that's Mrs Rivers – or, at least, the beginning of understanding her. An old Deepdeanite, a powerful member of the school Council, a widow, the sister of the headmistress. But we certainly must discover more about her, at our earliest opportunity. Write that down, Hazel.

'Now, the next question is *who*? Who could have murdered her this evening?'

'Anyone in the Hall, of course,' said Kitty. 'Or anyone in the kitchen!'

'No!' I said. 'That's not true. Daisy and Beanie and I were watching the whole dinner, from the moment they all sat down. The way the food and drink was served – the wine was all from bottles and decanters, the first course and main courses were handed out at random on plates, and the rest of the main course was served on platters by Beryl and Nancy. The poison couldn't have been in anything sent out from the kitchen – there was no way of knowing who would get what.'

'Hazel is quite right,' said Daisy. 'I recall distinctly that, during the first two courses, the only people who approached Table Four were Nancy and Beryl, the maids on dinner duty – and members of Table Four itself. Mr Stone and Mrs Dow were the only two people who got up from their places and went past Mrs Rivers. Apart from them, no one came near her. So the only people who might have been able to pass her something, or put something into her food or drink . . .'

'Were the people on Table Four with her!' I said. 'Mr Stone, Mr Turnbull, Mr and Mrs Thompson-Bates, Mr and Mrs El Maghrabi, and Mr and Mrs Dow.'

'Yes, but we can narrow things down even further,' said Daisy, eyes extremely blue. 'Beanie saw a *man* on the hill, strangling the woman we now believe was Mrs Rivers. Therefore we must be looking for a *male* murderer.

Our suspect list is *five* – Mr Stone, Mr Turnbull, Mr Thompson-Bates, Mr Dow and Mr El Maghrabi. Now, does anyone have thoughts as to why one of *them* might want to murder Mrs Rivers?'

'If she's in charge of who's allowed to be at Deepdean, what if she was threatening to expel one of their daughters?' I said.

'Oh, *very* good, Watson!' said Daisy. 'And I know just the person. Amina's prank yesterday made Mrs Rivers furious. We saw Mr El Maghrabi in a heated discussion with Mrs Rivers over dinner – perhaps they were arguing about whether she should be allowed to continue at Deepdean. What else?'

'What if she wouldn't give a girl a scholarship, or make them a prefect?' I suggested.

'Why would parents care, though?' asked Lavinia. 'Mine wouldn't.'

'Ugh, you're lucky!' said Kitty. 'Mine are already awfully worried that I won't be a prefect. Parents get all het up about the stupidest things where their children are concerned.'

'That is an excellent observation, Detective Freebody,' said Daisy, and I knew that she, like me, was thinking about what we had overheard between Kitty's parents in the park. 'Let's see, isn't Lallie Thompson-Bates in line for a tennis scholarship, and Ella Turnbull for a music scholarship? And Jennifer Stone's a Big Girl – she might be a prefect next year.'

We all pondered these ideas.

'I'm sure Mrs R had a dark past!' said Lavinia with relish. 'I bet she's a cheat or a thief – or a murderer herself, like Kitty said!'

'Or what if she's a smuggler, along with Mr Stone!' cried Kitty. 'Perhaps that's why he was staring at her.'

'Detective Freebody, I shall bar you from this meeting unless you are more sensible,' said Daisy. 'Come on, Detectives, think harder!'

'We *are* thinking!' said Kitty. 'It's you who're rejecting perfectly good suggestions!'

'What about method?' I said, as loudly as was safe, for it was quite clear that we had got as far as we could with motive. 'Are we quite sure what she died of?'

'I don't think there's much doubt,' said Daisy. 'Arsenic! We know those symptoms, Hazel. And if so, it's fearsomely easy to get hold of, as we know well. Rat poison, fly papers ... it's everywhere! But you are correct, we must discover exactly where the murderer got it from, and when and how he administered it. Arsenic takes at least half an hour to work, so I would suggest that Mrs Rivers must have taken it during the first course – either in her food or in her drink. I think we must stage a re-creation of the scene to work out how our poisoner could have given Mrs Rivers the dose. And as the case has changed so much, we need an entirely new suspect list! But first, I believe that it is time to discover a little more about the people on Table Four – and relieve Beanie, of course. Hazel, it is time for another night-time excursion.'

Suspect List

1. **Mr Turnbull.** His wife Artemis (an opera singer with an international reputation) was supposed to perform at the concert on Friday night, but she did *not* attend! MOTIVE: Possibly worried about Ella's music scholarship? We must discover more. NB Where is <u>Mrs</u> Turnbull? Mr J was a suspect <u>before</u> the poisoning!

2. **Mr Stone.** According to Uncle Felix, he is a smuggler! He has also recently been to Paris. MOTIVE: None yet – but he was observed staring angrily at Mrs Rivers on more than one occasion and at dinner he got up and spoke to her. We have observed him smoking. He was a suspect before the poisoning!

3. **Mr Thompson-Bates.** MOTIVE: Possibly worried about Lallie's tennis scholarship (he seemed upset at her exhibition match), but we must discover more.

4. *Mr Dow.* MOTIVE: Unclear – but Mrs Dow seemed very unhappy at the dinner.

5. *Mr El Maghrabi.* MOTIVE: Possible that he wants to stop Amina from being expelled?

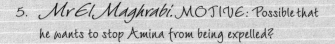

PLAN OF ACTION

1. Find out whether Mrs Rivers is truly dead.

2. Find out more about Mrs Rivers! Why would someone want to murder her?

3. Discover more about our five suspects.

4. Discover how the murderer got hold of the arsenic.

5. Stage a reconstruction, to work out how the poison was given to Mrs Rivers.

6. Speak to Inspector Priestley to confirm that the poison was arsenic – and that no one else was affected.

3

We climbed down the rope of sheets again. I was beginning to worry that it would rip under our weight and my hands were aching from clinging to it.

'*Psst!*' came a little voice as we reached the bottom of the rope – and Beanie stepped out of the shadows. She was trembling, but her shoulders were set and her hands were clenched. I am always more impressed with Beanie's bravery than almost anyone else's, for I know how much it costs her.

'I watched for ages,' she whispered. 'The Inspector made everyone on Mrs Rivers' table stay in the Hall so he could see if they become ill. I think he thinks what you do – that someone else on Table Four must be responsible for what happened to her.'

'And?' asked Daisy eagerly.

'Nothing,' said Beanie, shaking her head. 'No one's ill at all. But they're all looking at each other as though they can't believe it. Mrs Dow came back – or rather the Inspector made her come back. She and Mrs Thompson-Bates can't stop shaking, and Mr Stone looks as though he wants to cry.'

'*And?*' I asked.

'And Mrs Minn came in looking very upset, just before ten. She whispered in the Inspector's ear and then he looked very serious. He said something to them all and then Mr Stone *did* cry.'

'Crying!' said Daisy. 'That's interesting – very interesting. Mr Stone keeps on having dramatic emotions around Mrs Rivers! Make a note of it, Hazel.'

'Mr Thompson-Bates was almost sick too, but not with poisoning, just horror. I think – I'm sure – Mrs Rivers is *dead*!'

'So it *is* a murder,' breathed Daisy. 'What's the Inspector doing now, Beanie?'

'Questioning them, I think,' said Beanie. 'He looked all official.'

'Good, good,' said Daisy. 'Go on back up to the dorm, Detective Martineau. Hazel and I will go and investigate our suspects' rooms while we have time.'

'You've done excellently well,' I said to Beanie. 'Thank you.'

Beanie beamed. And I knew that, although she was frightened, this evening had been important to her. After what she had discovered about her mother yesterday, she needed a distraction as much as Daisy did. They were both hiding from something in their lives that they could not bear to face yet.

It was quarter past ten and finally turning dark as we began to make our way towards Deepdean town at last – not the way to school, but the way that winds down through Oakeshott Woods, a way hemmed with trees that rustled coolly around us as though they had secrets. Every lift and flinch of a branch in the wind made me start, and Daisy had to put a soothing hand on my shoulder.

'It's all right, Hazel,' she whispered. 'We've survived much worse, haven't we?'

We had – but, all the same, I was afraid. There was so much unknown in this case. Mrs Rivers' poisoning had tripped us up, a sly foot stuck out from a row of desks when your eyes are on the mistress calling you up to the front of the form room for punishment, and now I felt I could not trust that anything was safe and as it seemed. At last I was sure that this was at least an attempted murder – but that certainty was dreadful.

We came out of the woods, into the curving twilit streets of Deepdean. It was almost half past ten by my wristwatch, and the lights in most houses were burning low, doors closed, curtains drawn. A few dogs barked as we walked by, but we met no one until we turned out onto the Parade. Its lamps were lit, a few cars gliding smoothly along the road, and there, next to Deepdean Park, we saw the Majestic Hotel, as bright as a ship on the ocean.

'Where to?' I asked Daisy.

'Round the back,' she said at once. 'Come on, let's go!'

The back of the Majestic was darker, dingier – but there was a light above a little black door that stood half open, and this was what Daisy motioned me through.

We crept inside, my heart thumping in my chest in case we were stopped and questioned, but although I could hear the clatter and steam of a kitchen somewhere ahead of us, and a rumble of voices beyond that, we saw no one.

'This way,' said Daisy, pulling me through yet another door and into a room that, for a moment, I thought was full of clouds. Heaps of whiteness, a soft, clean smell and a rolling warmth – but then I blinked and saw that we were still firmly on the ground. The clouds were only linen: towels and tablecloths and handkerchiefs all piled up together. It was like House's airing cupboard, but enormous.

'Oh!' I said, startled. 'Daisy, what are you doing?'

'Getting our disguises,' said Daisy, busily sorting through the piles. 'Here, look!' She held up something frilly, looking absolutely triumphant. 'Chambermaids' aprons and caps. Put them on, hurry up! We won't have long before the Inspector has finished questioning our suspects, and then they'll come back to the hotel. We have to use every minute of that time!'

'But, Daisy . . .' I began, looking down at the black tunic and trousers I was wearing, the set I had brought back from Hong Kong. It was not exactly a maid's outfit, even with the addition of a white apron, or at least not the outfit of a maid in England, but I realized that, as usual, Daisy was quite correct. We would look all right, just about – and it was a very clever idea.

4

Which was how I came to be padding through the corridors of the Majestic Hotel, holding a pile of towels, on my way to Mrs Rivers' room.

Daisy had found a list of rooms and guests on the service corridor's wall, heavily marked up with notes, master keys hanging next to it. 'Time is of the essence,' she had snapped, her eyes blazing blue. 'Hazel, you go to Mrs Rivers' room first and find out all you can from it before the police arrive – for arrive they will. Once you've done that, go to Mr Stone's and Mr Turnbull's. I shall take Dow, Thompson-Bates and El Maghrabi. Remember, if you're stopped, say you're new and you're going around turning down the sheets in all the rooms. Understood?'

'Understood!' I said. 'Daisy, I know all this as well as you do.'

'Of course you do,' said Daisy. 'That is why I am allowing you to search the room of our murder victim alone. It really is quite an honour, Hazel. You should be pleased.'

I sighed. Only Daisy could make something so nice seem somehow rude.

But here I was outside Mrs Rivers' room, and it was time to detect. I took a deep breath and thought of Hetty, and Bridget, and Ping. I had to pretend to be them – and our time at the Rue Theatre had taught me that I *could* pretend to be someone else.

I knocked on the door and, as confidently as I could manage, unlocked the room and stepped inside.

The lamp was on, and the bed was made, but there were papers scattered across the desk.

I looked at the desk first. It had several photographs on it – and they must be important, I thought, if Mrs Rivers had brought them with her to the hotel.

There was one in pride of place, of Mrs Rivers standing next to an old, white-bearded man, her wedding ring glinting on her finger. Mrs Rivers looked happier than I had seen her this weekend. This, I thought, must be her husband – and if it was, I was not sure he looked much like a murder victim, or she a murderer. He was beaming at her, and she at him.

Next to that photograph was another, much older – a school photograph labelled '1919' of a group of serious girls in uniform, the mistresses next to them in old-fashioned clothing, their hair rolled. From the blurry building behind them, I saw that this was Deepdean, and when I squinted closely at faces, Miss Barnard and Mrs Rivers both jumped out, slender and pretty, standing with the older girls. I looked at the lower forms, and there was a plump, sad little girl that could have been Mrs Dow; a solid fair-haired third former who had a look of Ella Turnbull about her; and a beautiful fifth former who, clutching a tennis racket like a pet, must be Mrs Thompson-Bates. The only face I could not find was Mrs El Maghrabi's, although there were two tall girls with darker skin, their arms folded, looking as uncomfortable as I had felt when I first arrived at Deepdean.

I moved on to the papers. There was a letter, half written: *Dear Sir,* it began, *I am aware that I am not my husband, but I certainly am his replacement at the Rivers Corporation and will therefore act in accordance with his wishes. Given that I will certainly not reconsider your removal* . . . Apart from the letter, there were several pages of accounts, neatly annotated; a note from a Lord Hill about the next meeting of the Deepdean Council (20th July); and a telephone message from Miss Barnard to invite Mrs Rivers to lunch on Monday. *Poor Miss Barnard!* I thought suddenly. Monday lunch would never happen.

That bit of paper had been torn off the pad next to the telephone. I looked at the pad itself, and saw the indentations of words on the blank page – deep scores and scratches that did not correspond to the words of Miss Barnard's message. Something else had been written, something not on the desk.

I took the wastepaper bin and tipped it up. Little bits of paper came scattering out, settling on the carpet like leaves. Whatever the message had been, Mrs Rivers had taken care to tear it up. So I turned back to the pad on the desk. I picked up the pencil next to it and carefully shaded over the paper. Words began to appear, white against the grey – and what they said made me catch my breath. They looked like attempts at a note, begun again and again and crossed out every time.

Tom – I won't
Tom, you must stop this
Tom, really, this is
Tom – I only want to be left in peace
Tom, I can't love you

Tom? My breath caught. I pulled my copy of Miss Lappet's list, now rather dog-eared, out of my pocket and scanned through it. There!

Mr Thomas Stone (Jennifer Stone, Big Girl)

Tom was *Mr Stone*!

And Mrs Rivers was warning Mr Stone off, for some reason – something to do with love. She still wore her wedding ring, even though we knew she was a widow, and the photograph of Mr Rivers remained on her desk. I suddenly remembered what Mr Stone had been saying to Jennifer, about getting married again. Mrs Rivers must have been the person he meant! But if she was, it was clear that she was not as interested in remarrying as he.

What if Mrs Rivers *had* rejected Mr Stone, and he had been angry at the rejection – so had decided to take matters into his own hands?

5

I hurried through the corridors of the Majestic once again – and as I did so I passed another chambermaid. The guests I had seen so far had ignored me entirely, but the maid caught my eye and stared at me in frank confusion. I gave her a little smile, but she did not smile back. Instead she frowned and turned away.

My heart was pounding as I reached Mr Turnbull's door, knocked and let myself in.

And there, sitting at the desk, was a heavy-set, blonde woman. She was on the telephone and, as I came in, she raised her eyebrows at me crossly and waved her left hand, sparkling with a diamond and a fat gold band, towards the bed.

I startled in surprise – but then, of course, I remembered that it was not odd at all for a chambermaid to tidy a room while someone was in it. I took a deep breath, summoned every shred of housekeeping knowledge I had, and tiptoed forward to turn down the bed. The woman went back to her conversation.

'No!' she said. 'Yes . . . No . . . I've just got in. Three-hour drive! Quite exhausted. Honestly . . . No, I don't know where he is. He ought to be back from the dinner by now . . . Yes! After all that – so rude of him. And it's not as though I've been on tour for a month. We only had breakfast together at Claridge's yesterday morning, before he set off . . . Yes! Men . . . I know he's cross about the concert, but, really, what was I supposed to do? When Figaroni asks, you can't say no . . . Oh yes! It was wonderful! A thousand each night, at least . . . What . . .? No, go on . . .!'

She was still talking as I tiptoed out of the room. I tried to keep my face calm and straight, but my hands were shaking and I felt wild with nerves. And I knew I had heard, and seen, something very important.

I had found Mrs Turnbull.

She was not dead at all, and she did not have dark hair. With that, the last possibility that she could have been the woman Beanie had seen in the woods on Friday vanished. And Mrs Turnbull had just given Mr Turnbull an alibi. If he had been having breakfast with his wife on Friday morning at Claridge's Hotel in London (even I knew that London was where Claridge's was), then he could not have been strangling anyone in Oakeshott Woods at the same time. The drive from London, as Mrs Turnbull had said, was several hours at the best of times. The timings simply did not work – and we had narrowed down our suspect list for the strangling in the woods to four.

But as I walked towards Mr Stone's room, I was stopped by the chambermaid I had seen earlier. She came hurrying towards me, a man in a smart suit rushing along in her wake, and when she caught sight of me she pointed furiously.

'There!' she said. 'Her! She doesn't work here! What is she doing here?'

I backed away in horror. 'I'm – I'm new!' I said. 'I'm just here to—'

'She sounds posh!' cried the chambermaid. 'I *told* you she doesn't belong.'

'You're quite right,' said the man. 'Now, you, explain yourself at once. I'm the hotel manager and I certainly didn't hire you!'

'She's a thief! I'm sure she is!'

'I'm – I'm not!' I stammered. 'I'm really not, I . . .'

And then I gave up and simply ran. I tore down the rattling back stairs, the chambermaid and her manager calling out behind me. I scrambled along the service corridor, tearing off my white apron and cap, and burst out of the little black back door into the summer night.

I crouched in the bushes, panting as shallowly as I could and watching as the chambermaid and the manager stood at the door talking to each other angrily about telephoning the police.

'She won't be hard to find,' said the chambermaid, 'her being foreign and all.'

At last they stepped back inside the hotel.

The bushes rustled next to me, and then Daisy's voice said, 'Wotcher, Watson. You've been compromised, I see.'

I gasped a little. There had simply been too many surprises, too close together. 'They didn't catch me!' I said at last, rather weakly. 'Anyway, what are you doing out here?'

'I am here because I completed my mission quickly!' said Daisy. 'No one saw me, but they *did* see you, and that is not good at all. Well, we shall have to hope that they don't bother the police about it. What did you find?'

I told her about Mrs Turnbull, and about Mrs Rivers. Even in the darkness, I could see Daisy's eyes going wide.

'I didn't manage to get to Mr Stone's room, though,' I finished.

'Well!' said Daisy. 'Under the circumstances, I think

you can be forgiven. Good heavens! So, we have ruled out one suspect – and we have a very interesting new motive for Mr Stone! Now, about the others . . . I went to Mr and Mrs El Maghrabi's room first, and that was interesting. There was a whole stack of old newspaper clippings about Mr El Maghrabi's company – and the Rivers Corporation was mentioned in some of them! There was a trade deal that went wrong, and Mr El Maghrabi clearly blames Mr Rivers personally. His name's circled and some quite rude things are written about him in the margins. Most of the notes are in Arabic, of course, but enough of them are in English for me to be able to tell.'

I remembered the business letter Mrs Rivers had been writing, and told Daisy about it. 'It sounds like Mrs Rivers was doing what she thought her husband wanted,' I said. 'So what if the vendetta against Mr Rivers became one against *Mrs* Rivers?'

'Oh, very interesting!' said Daisy, nodding. 'Good, Watson. Then there's Mr Thompson-Bates. Betting stubs and cigarette packets in all his jackets. He's a smoker, and a gambler! I went through the wardrobe and it's clear they've both been to Paris recently. Mrs Thompson-Bates has plenty of clothes from this season with Parisian labels on them – as well as some *gorgeous* pieces of jewellery. They look like family heirlooms –

she really does come from money! There are some spaces in her jewellery box, though . . . I wonder whether Mr T-B pawned the pieces to pay off his debts? He must have got the money from somewhere creative, because I found the book he records his tournament progress in, and he's been on a losing streak. He hasn't got beyond the third round since January, which is not good at all, Hazel.

'And finally, Mr Dow. He's like a grown-up schoolboy! He's got the 1919 Weston school pin on his desk, and a school photograph from 1915, with Mr Temple, and Mr Thompson-Bates, and Mr Stone in the photo too. And remember, Mr Dow was wearing a Weston Old Boys' tie at dinner! They were all at school together.'

'Isn't that odd?' I asked.

'Not really,' said Daisy, shrugging. 'Weston is one of the only schools that matters, just like Deepdean.'

Something else had occurred to me. '1915 . . .' I said thoughtfully. 'That's almost the same time as Mrs Rivers was at Deepdean. Do you think they all knew each other?'

'Oh, very good, Watson!' said Daisy. 'Now, that's clever. What if they did? *Most* interesting! All right, I think we have made very successful inroads into the case. Now it is time to hurry back to House, before anyone misses us!'

Suspect List

1. ~~Mr Turnbull. His wife Artemis (an opera singer with an international reputation) was supposed to perform at the concert on Friday night, but she did not attend! MOTIVE: Possibly worried about Etta's music scholarship? We must discover more. NB Where is Mrs Turnbull? He was a suspect before the poisoning!~~ RULED OUT from the strangling! Mrs Turnbull is safe and sound — and she has given her husband an alibi for the altercation Beanie saw in Oakeshott Woods on Friday morning!

2. Mr Stone. According to Uncle Felix, he is a smuggler! He has also recently been to Paris. MOTIVE: None yet — but he was observed staring angrily at Mrs Rivers on more than one occasion. We have observed him smoking and at dinner he got up and spoke to her. He was a suspect before the poisoning! He seems to have been in love with Mrs Rivers, but she was trying to rebuff him. Did he take revenge?

3. Mr Thompson-Bates. MOTIVE: Possibly worried about Lallie's tennis scholarship (he seemed upset at her exhibition match), but we must discover more. He has a gambling addiction, he smokes and he also has been on a losing streak in his tennis games. Has he been pawning his wife's

jewellery? But how does this fit in with the murder?
NOTES: He has been to Paris recently!

4. *Mr Dow.* MOTIVE: Unclear – but
Mrs Dow seemed very unhappy at the dinner. He
was at Weston at the same time as Mrs Rivers was
at Deepdean – did they know each other?

5. *Mr El Maghrabi.* MOTIVE: Possible that
he wants to stop Amina from being expelled? He seems
to be obsessed with Mrs Rivers' dead husband and
his business deals – does he have a vendetta against
the Riverses? Did he murder her to get revenge?

PLAN OF ACTION

1. ~~Find out whether Mrs Rivers is truly dead.~~

2. ~~Find out more about Mrs Rivers! Why would
someone want to murder her?~~

3. ~~Discover more about our five suspects.~~

4. Discover how the murderer got hold of the arsenic.

5. Stage a reconstruction, to work out how the poison was
given to Mrs Rivers.

6. Speak to Inspector Priestley to confirm that the poison
was arsenic – and that no one else was affected.

6

Sunday morning dawned bright and clear.

I know because I saw it.

I woke up in the soft, pencil-hued hush that comes before the sun to find Daisy prodding me. She was crouched next to my face, her hand over my mouth, her eyes fever-bright and the colour high in her cheeks.

'Hazel,' she said, 'something is Up.'

'Have you been to sleep?' I asked, once my heart had stopped beating so wildly. 'And I *know* something's up. There's been a murder.'

'I don't need sleep – none of the greatest detectives have time for it. Anyway, someone has to keep watch on the situation, since *you* fell asleep.'

'I was awake half the night writing up the case!' I said indignantly. 'What's happened?'

'The doorbell keeps ringing,' said Daisy. 'I took it upon myself to listen in from a safe hiding place – I had to be cunning because awful Amina woke up too and was sniffing about – and it's not good at all. Mrs Rivers is *definitely* dead, and parents have been arriving asking to take girls away because of it. Matron wouldn't let them at first, but then Rose and Jose's mother Mrs Pritchett raised an enormous stink and Matron gave in. They've gone from our year, and Astrid Frith from the Big Girls, and Alma Collingwood from the third form. And then Miss Barnard came by. She's been crying, you can tell – I didn't think she was capable of being so rattled. She's usually utterly serene.'

'Her sister *died*, Daisy!' I pointed out. 'Imagine if it was Bertie . . . imagine what *you*'d do!'

'Don't even *think* it, Hazel. I should kill anyone who even *tried* to hurt Bertie. But this is quite different. Anyway, Barny was terribly upset, but she told Matron that she wanted the Anniversary to carry on. Chapel this morning is going to become a service of remembrance on the lawn, because the Hall is the scene of the crime – the police absolutely think this was a murder; it's not like Fallingford – but the garden party and the play will go on quite as normal. Still, it's going to be odd if half the girls and their parents have left by then.'

'But what if our suspects leave too!' I cried.

'They won't,' said Daisy confidently. 'The Inspector won't let them. They're suspects, after all! But that is not important, Hazel. The point is that if we don't hurry up and solve the case, it won't just be this weekend that's ruined. Deepdean is in trouble. If girls don't come back next term – if there aren't enough pupils – the school might *close*.'

'It wouldn't!' I said. 'Last time—'

'Last time Barny pretended there hadn't been a murder until the case was over,' said Daisy. 'She can't lie like that again this time, and she obviously doesn't want to either. And remember the time before that, with Miss Bell? Deepdean barely survived it. I don't know if it can again, Hazel. And if it doesn't . . .'

We stared at each other, and I felt sick to my soul. If Deepdean closed, we might be sent to different schools. I might even be called back to Hong Kong. I had been feeling as though we might be growing out of Deepdean, but I was not ready to say goodbye to it yet, and I knew Daisy needed Deepdean even more than I did. Without it, she lost the heart of who she was.

'We *have* to solve this case,' Daisy said fiercely. 'And we have less than two days to do it. As soon as Leaving Prayers is over on Monday, *we'll* have to leave, and we'll lose our chance to observe our suspects.'

'I know!' I said. 'It's all right, Daisy. We'll solve the case – I know it.'

'I knew I could depend on you, Watson,' she said.

Then she stretched out beside me and fell asleep.

It was no good me trying to do the same, now that my own brain was crawling with worries, so I propped myself up very carefully against the cold metal of my bedstead and carried on writing up the case.

Warming air blew in through the open window (in the summer term, at least, Matron's obsession with fresh air is almost nice) and the rest of the dorm slept. Lavinia growled, Kitty breathed softly, and from Beanie's bed came a small regular hiccupping noise. At last I slipped out of bed, crawling over Daisy (who did not respond) and crept over to Beanie's side. She usually sleeps with her head wrapped in her sheets, but today they had slipped away from her face, and I saw that it was damp with tears.

'Beanie!' I whispered, and shook her shoulder.

'Mummy!' said Beanie quite clearly, and then rolled over away from me.

I went back to bed, more upset than ever. Mrs Rivers' murder was solvable, it had to be.

But Beanie's mother was a problem I did not know how to fix.

7

The wake-up bell went off with a bright clatter, and we all leaped out of bed, Daisy calling out orders for that day's investigations to everyone as we dressed. She did not mention what she had said to me – that Deepdean might close down. It felt too terrible to say out loud, in daylight, but we kept glancing at each other nervously.

'What are you two hiding?' asked Lavinia at last.

'Nothing!' I said, feeling myself blush.

'Liar,' said Kitty, rolling her eyes. 'All right, let's go!'

But Beanie glanced at me, her brow furrowed, and I could tell that she was not fooled. The concern on her face carried on all the way down the stairs to breakfast.

We stepped into a Dining Room in chaos. Girls were gathering and whispering together – in the toast queue, next to the porridge vat, and at each form's table.

'Gone!' I heard. 'Yes, overnight – her mother wouldn't let her stay. It's because of the MURDER!'

In a way it was lucky for us, for, in the drama, all the usual breakfast rules were relaxed. Second-form shrimps daringly passed the butter to fifth formers, and third formers were boldly speaking to Big Girls. There was an atmosphere of high excitement – but when we sat down at the fourth-form table, Amina looked anxious and withdrawn. Clementine and Sophie sat protectively on either side of her, and of course Rose and Jose Pritchett were not there.

'They've been taken home,' Amina told me, noticing me looking. 'Rose and Jose. Because of what happened.'

'What do you mean?' said Daisy innocently.

Amina made a face. 'You know perfectly well!' she said. 'Everyone's fearfully upset about the murder. Rose and Jose have gone, and their mother . . . she said something awful about *my* parents being suspects. Which isn't true! All right, they were on the table of the murder victim, but they've got no reason to kill her. They didn't even know her!'

'That's not true! I heard that your father *did* know Mrs Rivers,' said Daisy. 'And he hated her.'

'So?' flashed Amina. 'Baba hates most people. See here, he didn't do it. Neither of them did!'

'You can't stop people wondering about it, though,' said Daisy.

'Can't I?' asked Amina. 'Well! I'll show you – and everyone! Clementine, come *here*!'

She went into a furious huddle with Clementine, and as Daisy leaned in to try to overhear what they were saying, she glanced over at me in a way that I knew meant *Get on with it, Hazel Wong*. I looked about at the rest of the room to see what use I could be.

Lavinia had found a new tennis magazine and was sitting reading it, ignoring everyone. I nearly nudged her to pay attention – but then I saw that she had her back very pointedly to the third-form table, where Lallie Thompson-Bates and Ella Turnbull were in the centre of a supportive ring of girls, wailing and dabbing their faces with handkerchiefs. I was reassured – Lavinia was on the case after all. Beanie had gone over to where Emily Dow was sitting on her own at the first-form shrimps' table. She was murmuring something to Emily, who had her head lowered and her shoulders slumped. Which only left . . . the Big Girls' table. I turned towards it, and saw Jennifer Stone in the middle of another huddle.

'How do *I* know if he did it?' I heard her say. 'I hardly speak to him, honestly. He's always travelling about – you've seen the postcards. And he never tells me anything. He's getting *married*, apparently, and he only bothered to tell me yesterday! If he wants me to simply believe that he didn't do it, he's out of luck.'

The other Big Girls looked delighted and scandalized all at once, but before I could hear any more, the gong went for the end of breakfast.

8

As we walked down to Sunday chapel, the Detective Society were rather subdued. We were all thinking over what we had seen and heard.

'Oh, it's all awful!' said Beanie at last. 'Rose and Jose having to leave, I mean, and Emily Dow so sad.'

'Why is Emily Dow sad?' I asked. 'What did she say to you?'

'Well, I saw she'd been looking very thin and pale recently,' said Beanie – only Beanie would have noticed this about one of the shrimps, I thought, feeling a rush of affection for her. 'So I asked if she was all right. The other girls in her dorm don't like her. They're horrid to her and they don't let her walk down to school with them. She's been miserable all year! I feel horrid that I never realized before.'

'But you're a fourth former!' said Daisy. 'Why would you notice shrimps?'

'Because I used to be just like Emily,' said Beanie. 'In first form I wanted to leave Deepdean as well. Everything was awful, until Kitty and Clementine fell out in spring term and Kitty began to walk with me.'

'Pity I wasn't there yet,' said Lavinia, nudging her. 'We could have run away together. Look, doesn't anyone want to know what I found out from the third form, and that magazine I was reading?'

'Did you find out anything? I thought you were just being rude!' said Kitty.

'Don't be stupid. I was listening in to them talking. Mrs Thompson-Bates has begun travelling with her husband this year on his tours – that's why Lallie is a boarder now. The magazine had a story about them too, about how in love they still are. *Grim*. But it had photos of Mr and Mrs Thompson-Bates together at the French Open last month. Now, the French Open is held at Roland Garros, and that's in *Paris*!'

'Well!' said Daisy. 'That is . . . that is really quite useful work, Detective Temple. It corresponds with what we saw in the T-Bs' room last night: they both have new-season clothes from Paris. Now, what else?'

'Jennifer was telling everyone about Mr Stone's mysterious fiancée,' I said. 'And . . . well, she doesn't like it, or him. I think she's suspicious of her father.'

'By contrast, Amina most certainly is *not*,' said Daisy, nodding. 'She seemed quite furious at my suggestion – not a bit logical! Now, this is all useful. But this morning I want us to proceed with another important part of our plan – staging a re-creation of the crime!'

'How are we supposed to do that?' asked Kitty. 'It's chapel!'

'About that . . .' said Daisy. 'I have had a quite brilliant idea. Would you like to hear it?'

'Oh yes!' breathed Beanie.

'Well,' said Daisy, 'just wait until we're past Old Wing entrance, and I shall tell you.'

At Old Wing entrance we were met by Miss Lappet, her bosom heaving expressively and a tragic expression on her face.

'Girls!' she said to us. 'Due to – to an unfortunate event last night, there has been a change of plan. Chapel will now take place on the lawn, not in the Hall, because – well, you will be informed in due course. Now, run along to the lawn, and please don't fuss. Everything is all right.'

That was, of course, the best way to convince us that nothing was all right. It always amazes me how much grown-ups think they can get past us, as though they believe we are only given brains when we turn twenty.

We were determined to play her game, though, so we all curtseyed and scuttled by – but as soon as we were through familiar wood-panelled Old Wing, its candles extinguished and its rolled-out carpet beginning to look scuffed from so many feet, and into the chequerboard of Library corridor, Daisy wheeled about and faced the four of us.

'Detectives!' she hissed. 'Miss Lappet's silly stammering has proved to us that the mistresses are trying to hide the truth of the situation from us girls. We must ignore her and get into the Hall to take a closer look at Table Four.'

'We can't!' said Kitty.

'Of course we can!' said Daisy, folding her arms. 'All we need is to use a little elementary subterfuge and—'

'Oh. We're not *all* getting out of chapel, are we?' said Beanie sadly.

'Detective Martineau has understood it,' said Daisy. 'We are not all getting out of chapel. Only Hazel and I are. Now, NO ARGUING, Detectives Freebody and Temple! We have only a few minutes to put my brilliant plan into practice. Hazel, take off your hat and give it to Kitty.'

I took off my regulation straw boater and held it out to Kitty, who snatched it rather crossly. Daisy handed hers to Beanie, as though she was conferring an honour.

'Now, Beanie and Kitty, you must *be us* as well as yourselves at chapel. Get in the fourth-form row, place your extra hat on your hand and hold it out next to you, as though you were standing beside another girl. The mistresses will count the number of girls in each row, but they'll do it from the hats they see. Five hats means five of us, even if two of us are really in the Hall!'

'It's a stupid plan,' said Lavinia. 'What if Clementine or Amina snitches on us?'

'If they do, hit them. Anyway, do you have a better plan?' asked Daisy.

'No,' said Lavinia. 'You'll be caught, that's all.'

'Detective Temple, I am never caught,' said Daisy. 'Hazel sometimes is, because she is not as good at sneaking as I am. But she is still better than any of you, which is why she is coming with me, while you go to chapel. Now, when I give the signal, you go left out of Library corridor, onto the lawn. Move quickly, so as to distract any eyes, and we'll hide and then go right into the Hall. Are you ready?'

Lavinia, Beanie and Kitty nodded, rather reluctantly, and Daisy took my hand. 'On three,' she said. 'One, two, *three*!'

The others took off at a run down the corridor, and Mamzelle, standing guard at the door into the garden, shouted out, 'Gurrrls! *Lentement, s'il vous PLAÎT!*' As we had hoped, she did not notice Daisy and me, lurking against the wall. The two of us were free to creep away, past the Library, towards the Hall.

We were in luck. The door into the Hall from Library corridor was open and, when we peered inside, the great shadowy space was empty. There was the stage, with its heavy curtains tied back and its vast frieze of painted women hovering high above it. There were the carved wooden balconies, stained-glass windows casting coloured patterns across them.

And there on the polished wood floor of the Hall, where the rows of seats for Prayers are usually set out, were ten rectangular tables, each covered with a white cloth. Their chairs were pushed back, napkins scattered across the floor like empty ghosts, and cutlery disarranged, as though the guests had only just left. I thought of our friend George, and his obsession with the story of the *Mary Celeste*, and shuddered.

'Quick!' hissed Daisy. 'We don't have much time! Those clodhopping policemen must be around somewhere, and they'll be back before we know it. Hazel, let's discover what we can from the unlucky Table Four.'

'Was that a Hong Kong joke?' I asked, for to my Chinese family the number four is as unlucky as thirteen is to Daisy.

'Indeed it was,' said Daisy. 'I do listen to you from time to time, Hazel. Now, here we are! Table Four! Let us see what we can see.'

9

We were back at the crime scene, the table where Mrs Rivers had been taken ill only a few hours before. I stared around at it, remembering what I had seen last night, and shuddered.

The number 4 was carefully inked onto a bit of gold-edged card in the centre of the tablecloth, and snuffed candles and pretty summer blooms from the Deepdean flower beds were arranged in vases along it. A salt cellar was overturned next to Mr Turnbull's place, and its matching pepper pot sat forlornly by Mrs El Maghrabi's. A gravy boat, whose contents were hardening unpleasantly, sat beside Mr Stone's plate. There was Mrs Turnbull's untouched setting, and the empty places of Mr and Mrs El Maghrabi and Mrs Dow. Mr and Mrs Thompson-Bates, Mr Turnbull, Mr Stone and Mr Dow's plates had congealing bits of meat and vegetable on them. Only Mrs Rivers' plate and glasses were entirely missing.

'Taken away to be tested,' said Daisy, nodding. 'Even the worst clodhopping policemen have some standards. But, oh dear, Hazel, I see the first problem! If the poison was administered during the first course – the aspic – that plate and wine glass would have been cleared away and washed before Mrs Rivers was even taken ill. Oh, what a waste of evidence! Now, let's see. Aside from that first course, is there anything here that *only* Mrs Rivers ate or drank?'

I shook my head. I was again remembering Mrs Rivers' final moments, and I hated the images that were spinning around my head – of her twitching and gasping for air, and of an unknown hand that had reached out and spilled poison into her glass or onto her plate.

'I don't understand how it could have happened,' I said. 'How did we miss it? We were watching all the time!'

'Well, we must just try to work that out,' said Daisy, 'by sitting down and attempting to recreate the circumstances of the crime.'

'But what if the police do come back?' I asked uncomfortably.

'So what if they do?' cried Daisy. 'We must move quickly, that's all. And we needn't worry about disturbing things. They will already have thoroughly photographed the crime scene, so we can move objects about without compromising the investigation. But put on your gloves, anyway, just to be on the safe side.'

I was privately amused at that. Daisy may still be outwardly rude about the police, but she has learned to care about not disturbing police work.

I pulled on my light summer gloves and got out this casebook, with my notes about the place settings. Daisy moved about the table, squinting at the silverware and sniffing the glasses and muttering distractedly to herself.

I stared at Mrs Rivers' empty seat. It looked so . . . so ordinary, so tidy. If I had not seen what had happened with my own eyes, I should never have believed it. Slowly I began to circle the table. I ran my hand across Mr Thompson-Bates's chair first, then stepped round Mrs Rivers' chair from right to left, as he had done to help her when she had been taken ill. Mr El Maghrabi was next – and I remembered the argument he'd had with Mrs Rivers – and then Mr Stone's. Mr Stone's place was nearer the other end of the table from Mrs Rivers, separated from her place by a flower arrangement, two candles and the gravy boat, but I remembered how he had got up and gone to stand beside her for a moment. His opportunity was clear.

Then I moved on again, all the way to the other end of the table. Here was Mr Turnbull's chair, directly opposite Mrs Rivers'.

Four empty chairs on either side separated them.

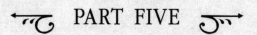

PART FIVE

The Life
of the Party

1

I froze. Daisy ducked.

There in the door of the Hall was Miss Lappet, her bosom heaving with emotion.

'I cannot BELIEVE THIS!' she bellowed. 'Fourth formers MISSING CHAPEL! DESPORTING themselves at the SCENE OF – OF *A TRAGEDY.*'

So the rest of the school must have been told about Mrs Rivers, I thought. I was trembling, and I felt like water all over, but there was a small part of me that was quite still and calculating.

'Excuse me,' said a quiet, deep voice behind Miss Lappet. 'I'm afraid this is *entirely* my fault.'

Miss Lappet wheeled about – to see the Inspector standing there, his forehead wrinkled up in apology, hands in the pockets of his mac.

'I asked them to meet me here,' he went on politely. 'Or rather, I asked them to meet me *outside* the Hall. I have been rather . . . dragged into this case, I'm afraid, and I am aware that I may have to miss the rest of the day's festivities. I was hoping to make it up to them by—'

'By allowing them to poke about at the *scene of a crime*?' cried Miss Lappet.

'By offering to take them out for an early lunch before the garden party this afternoon,' said the Inspector.

'That is quite out of the question,' said Miss Lappet, narrowing her eyes at him. 'The girls have acted shockingly, and, even if it was possible for me to allow them out on a *Sunday*, I would not do it. However . . . well, if it was *your* idea . . . I understand that our rules may be confusing to someone like you. Girls, if you go back to House immediately, we shall say no more of this. Do you understand?'

'Yes, Miss Lappet,' we murmured, heads bowed. I could feel my heart pounding.

'Good girls,' said Miss Lappet. 'Come along now – no running, though! Inspector, please follow us to Old Wing entrance.'

'Oh, there's NO need to take us out of Deepdean, Miss Lappet!' trilled Daisy.

'I can hardly trust you, Wells,' said Miss Lappet. 'Come along – I'll walk with you.'

And, just like that, Miss Lappet escorted us out of the Hall.

Daisy took my hand and squeezed it, and I knew she was boiling over with indignation. Once again, it felt as though we were losing our grip on Deepdean.

2

'Lappet's still watching,' said Daisy grimly to me and the Inspector, as we began to climb the hill to House. 'Standing there watching us, as though we're up to no good! I'd forgotten how diabolical it is to be a schoolgirl!'

I agreed. We had been watched in Hong Kong, quite intensely, and in London we had been stuck in the enclosed world of the Rue for most of the time – but there is a special quality to the way we are monitored at Deepdean, as though we are hovering on the edge of wickedness at all times, and only a careful grown-up eye can stop us falling prey to it.

'But we *are* up to no good, I suppose,' I said.

'Everyone *else* is up to no good!' snapped Daisy. 'But *we* are detectives, and detectives attempt to *stop* bad things happening! We are quite different from the rest of humanity, Hazel, and I wish you would remember that.'

'An interesting point of view, Madam Super,' said the Inspector.

The road to House curves a little as it winds upwards, like Kitty's hair when she puts it in curlers. There are rows of tall white houses on each side of it, and rows of smart dark cars parked up and down it.

'Daisy . . . Hazel . . .' said Inspector Priestley, 'walk more slowly, if you please. I believe we have until we reach the top of this hill to talk.'

'What do you want to speak about?' asked Daisy.

'The case, of course,' said the Inspector. 'Don't you want to know what happened to Mrs Rivers?'

That caught Daisy's attention at once.

'Poison! Arsenic, we think.'

'Well, they're still testing that,' said the Inspector. 'But between you and me, it looks as though the coroner will agree with your assessment. Good work, Madam Super. That's the *what*. The *how* is more puzzling.

'I saw your associate Miss Martineau hovering on the balcony above the Hall last night, while I was interviewing suspects, so I would guess you already know something about last night's events. What you may not be aware of is that none of the other guests on Table Four, or any other table in the Hall, have shown any ill effects. This does seem to have been a random mistake. No, this was quite specifically targeted at Mrs Rivers.

'As well as that, I want to tell you I was being truthful with your mistress earlier. I am now a part of this case, for both good and bad. Good, because, after Mrs Rivers' death, the local police at last believe that something is going on at Deepdean School. Bad, because, now they have the bit between their teeth, they have no interest in being delicate. They would like to shut the entire school down while they investigate – I have only just persuaded them that this would be unwise.'

'*Shut it down?*' Daisy and I both cried in horror.

'Indeed. And that is – well – only one problem that we face. They also believe that one of the maids is behind the poisoning. Now, I'm certain that they are not. I spent many minutes speaking to Beryl and Nancy, the girls who served Table Four last night, and I am convinced that they have no idea what happened. They harbour Mrs Rivers no ill will, nor were they paid by anyone else. They had nothing to do with this crime, I am certain of it.'

'Of course they didn't!' said Daisy. 'Hazel and I proved that in our reconstruction just now – they couldn't have done it, and nor could anyone pretending to be them. It has to be someone else at Table Four!'

'You and I agree. But until we can prove who the culprit really is, Nancy and Beryl will suffer. They are currently being held at Deepdean police station, and although I am doing my best to have them released as soon as possible, I doubt I will succeed.'

I was horrified. Yet again, a crime at Deepdean had been pinned on innocent people.

'We're working as fast as we can! We already know that Mr Turnbull can be ruled out,' said Daisy. 'He wasn't at Deepdean on Friday morning and there's no way he could have passed poison to Mrs Rivers without poisoning someone else. So we're down to four suspects: Mr Stone, Mr Dow, Mr Thompson-Bates and Mr El Maghrabi.'

We quickly told him what we had learned about each of our suspects.

'But – what about the women on the table?' asked the Inspector, frowning.

'We've realized something else as well,' I explained. 'We think that what Beanie saw – it must be connected to Mrs Rivers' murder. What if the strangling in the woods wasn't a murder, but only an attempted one? What if the killer tried again last night, and succeeded at last?'

'You think *Mrs Rivers* was the woman your friend saw?' asked the Inspector, his forehead wrinkled with interest. 'That would make sense – and it would explain why we found no body on Friday evening. So your theory is that we're looking for a man – the man seen in the woods, who is also one of the men on Table Four last night? Well! That does put us in an interesting position.'

I heard him say *us*, and felt very grown up.

'Why *interesting*?' asked Daisy.

'Because I don't see how to convince the Deepdean police of your theory at this stage. They won't like the idea that this murder was committed by a wealthy parent – and nor do they acknowledge what Miss Martineau saw on Friday morning. To them, this is a simple case of a maid poisoning a guest.'

'But *you* believe us?' I asked. I wanted to make sure – because I had hardly believed myself at first, but I did now, most fiercely.

'I am certainly inclined to. You have been right more times than can be explained away by luck.'

'*Luck!*' cried Daisy. 'We are not lucky, we are excellent detectives. How dare you—'

'*I am* not *doing you down!*' said the Inspector, as crossly as I have ever heard him say anything. 'Will you stop behaving as though I were about to take the case away from you!'

We both jumped a little.

'You are doing excellently. You are at least three steps ahead of the police – what you have learned is far beyond what they know. And therefore it would be remiss of me not to congratulate you on what you have discovered so far, and ask you to carry on. I will continue to help the Deepdean police with their official investigation – but, quite frankly, I doubt I can be as efficient as the two of you. I will do my best to help you – I will try to impress upon your suspects that they *are* still suspects in my eyes, and thus they must stay at Deepdean until the end of the weekend – but the rest is up to you.'

'*You want us to solve the case for you,*' whispered Daisy with shining eyes. 'You see, Hazel? We *shall* be the world's foremost consulting detectives by the time we are twenty!'

I saw that the Inspector was smiling and I knew that he did not mind.

Daisy's whole face had gone pink. '*We accept,*' she whispered giddily.

'So do I,' I said. 'But – when will we see you next?'

'When *shall* we three meet again? Well, I hope to be at tonight's play, but I will almost certainly miss the garden party due to police business. I assume you know what you are doing next?'

It was so strange to hear him speaking as though we were equals – or, rather, as though we were the experts. But where Deepdean was concerned, perhaps we were. Daisy and I knew all its nooks and crannies, all its traditions and oddities. We ought to be listened to – and the miracle was that at last we were.

3

We arrived up at House to find Kitty, Beanie and Lavinia waiting for us.

'Miss Barnard told us at chapel that Mrs Rivers was dead!' gabbled Kitty, as soon as she saw us. 'Everyone's panicking. And Miss Lappet slipped out halfway through – I think she was looking for you!'

'She found us,' said Daisy grimly. 'She is an enemy of the Detective Society for life. But that is hardly important. You must listen to what we discovered! Hazel and I have examined the scene of the crime more carefully, and we are making headway – we have confirmed that Mr Turnbull could not have killed Mrs Rivers, so we are down to four suspects.'

We explained what we had learned from the Hall, and the Inspector. The others looked impressed.

'But we were stopped before we could carry out a

proper re-creation. We must try again, as soon as possible,' Daisy went on.

'How are we supposed to do that?' asked Lavinia.

'Ooh, I know!' said Beanie. 'We can use lunch, isn't that right? So that we can see if other people notice what we're doing?'

There was a pause.

'Yes, exactly that,' said Daisy. 'Detective Martineau, you have . . . hit upon what I was about to say. Which is very annoying, Beanie – when did you get clever?'

'She's always been clever. You just don't notice,' said Lavinia with a shrug.

'We must use lunch as our opportunity,' said Daisy. 'We will each be one of our remaining suspects. I shall be Mr Thompson-Bates. Lavinia, you be Mr El Maghrabi. Beanie, you be Mr Dow. And Kitty, you be Mr Stone. Hazel can be Mr Turnbull, and watch us. Our aim is to get something into the food or drink of Mrs Rivers – played by someone from the other fourth-form dorm – without anyone but Hazel noticing anything.'

'Why Hazel?' asked Lavinia.

'Because Hazel notices things,' said Daisy, and I blushed. 'Position yourselves as they were sitting at the table on Saturday night, and as soon as everyone has begun eating lunch, we shall begin our play.'

'What are we supposed to be putting in fake Mrs Rivers' food and drink?' asked Lavinia, just as the lunch gong went.

'Not dirt,' said Daisy. 'Nothing they can see – oh, use salt or pepper. It's easiest! Now, hurry in, before the other dorm come down!'

The five of us rushed into the Dining Room and threw ourselves down at the fourth-form table. I was at the far end of the table, with Beanie on my left and Daisy next to her. Kitty was opposite Beanie, and Lavinia was opposite Daisy.

'Give me your pullovers,' whispered Daisy. 'Here, quick!'

I thought she was going to put them in the space between her and Beanie, but instead she piled them all on the chair between her and Lavinia (in violation of House rules, of course – pullovers must be worn, or hung on the back of the chair you are sitting in).

I didn't have time to ask what on earth she was doing before Clementine walked in, with Amina next to her, and saw us all sitting at the table, carefully separated. 'What are you queer fish doing?' she asked. 'Have you rowed?'

'Yes, that's right,' said Daisy, 'we can't bear to be next to each other.'

Clementine eyed her. 'If this is a prank . . .' she said.

'*This* isn't,' said Lavinia. 'But just you wait!'

'Hah, you don't have the brains to think up anything good,' sniffed Clementine (there is no love lost between her and Lavinia).

She pulled out the seat between Daisy and Lavinia, threw the pullovers off, and sat down, smirking. She meant it as a slight, of course, but Lavinia coughed to hide her laugh, and even Daisy let a very small smile flit across her face. I put up my hand to hide my grin. I suddenly realized what Daisy had been playing at – of course, if there is one thing a person like Clementine cannot resist, it is the sight of a pile of pullovers keeping a seat free.

She had just volunteered herself to play the part of Mrs Rivers.

Amina sat down next to Kitty, in the space where her mother, Mrs El Maghrabi, should have been, and Sophie Croke-Finchley sat next to Beanie.

The plates were handed round – it was rarebit (I made a face) – and knives and forks chinked as everyone began to eat. It was time to act.

All I had to do was pay attention. I tried to behave as I would at any ordinary lunch time – passing the salt and pepper and salad cream, leaning over to talk to Beanie and Lavinia, but my eye kept on being drawn to Clementine, and I was not the only one. Kitty got up and bent over her, throwing salt over her shoulder, and Clementine twitched round to look at her. Kitty blinked back at her innocently, and sat back down.

Clementine looked around at the table, scowling. 'Why are you all staring at me?' she snapped at last.

'I think it's a prank,' said Amina. 'They're playing a prank on you, Clem!'

'That's not true. You're just *awful*,' hissed Lavinia.

'Shut up, Lumpvinia,' snarled Clementine.

'Don't be horrid!' cried Beanie. 'Why can't we all be nice to each other?'

'Because that's not how people work, Beans,' said Kitty.

'I KNEW IT!' shrieked Clementine suddenly. 'Which one of you just poured salt all over my food? Look, it's everywhere! Ugh, you're beasts! Sophie, this wasn't you, was it?'

'It wasn't!' gasped Sophie. 'I don't even *like* salt!'

'That's not NICE!' shouted Clementine, and she shoved her chair away from the table and went storming out of the Dining Room. Amina jumped up and rushed after her.

'Clementine's father didn't come to the Anniversary after all, even though he promised to,' whispered Sophie to all of us. 'She's terribly upset.'

I got a shock of guilt. Of course, I had used Clementine's father's absence to rule him out, but I hadn't thought about the consequences. In fact, I had never really thought of Clementine that way at all – as a person who was more than meanness and hockey pitches. But of course she must be feeling as miserably incomplete as Daisy and I were. I knew that Kitty and Lavinia were furiously embarrassed by their parents, and Beanie in an agony of despair over hers, but that was still better than not having them here at all. You can be angry at parents when they are in front of you, disappointing you, but you cannot be angry at parents who do not even bother to be here – so you have to take out your anger on everyone else.

I looked at the other four members of the Detective Society. Daisy nodded at me, and so did Kitty and Lavinia. Then I looked at Beanie. She had not got up at all, and so I was sure she would shake her head. But to my surprise, Beanie beamed back at me and nodded proudly.

I could not understand it. I had been looking at her. She had not done anything unusual at all. How could she possibly have put salt on Clementine's plate?

4

Pudding (sago) went by in a blur. I was thinking as hard as I could – *what on earth had Beanie done?*

At last, chairs squealed backwards as we all stood up.

'QUICK CHANGE FOR THE GARDEN PARTY!' shouted the prefect on duty. 'Go on, go!'

We could not get up to the dorm fast enough. The door slammed behind us, and Daisy barked, 'Lavinia! Lean on it to make sure the other dorm can't come in. And· listen out for anyone breathing suspiciously – I don't trust Amina and Clementine not to listen in on us. Now, the results of our test, if you please. I'll go first. I was being Mr Thompson-Bates, and it was quite easy for me to poison Mrs Rivers, as we thought. I spilled some salt onto her plate as I passed along the salad cream. Lavinia, you're next. You were being Mr El Maghrabi. What did you find?'

'It was easy for me as well,' said Lavinia, shrugging. 'I

just threw some salt on her plate when she looked over at you. Anyone could have done it if they were sitting where I was.'

'I did mine when I stood up and bent over her,' said Kitty. 'You told us Mr Stone got up, after all.'

'I saw you!' I said. 'But I don't think I would have noticed if I hadn't been looking for it.'

'Excellent,' said Daisy. 'Kitty, help me with this button . . . Beanie, why on earth were *you* looking so cheerful? You can't have managed it, even now you have long arms.'

Beanie, her school blouse over her head, made a noise that sounded like 'Bhfflwhd!' Lavinia stepped away from the door for a moment and tugged at her blouse, and it came free, Beanie emerging rather pink in the face.

'But I *did*!' she said. 'I put salt on her plate, just like you said to.'

'*How*?' asked Daisy.

'I *passed* it to her,' said Beanie. 'When Hazel gave the salt and pepper to me, I pretended to put something in the salt cellar while I was pouring it on my food. Then I passed it to my left – to you, Daisy, but I knew you wouldn't take any.'

This was very clever of Beanie, and quite true – Daisy, like Sophie, likes the bland school food we are served, and never salts anything.

'Then *you* passed it to Clementine, Daisy, and she poured it on her food,' said Beanie. 'I knew she would – she loves salt. So I *did* put salt on Clementine's plate.'

I was gaping at Beanie. So was everyone else. Daisy paused her struggle to get into her party dress to stare at her.

'How dare you!' said Lavinia at last. 'You might have poisoned *me* – I got the salt *after* Clementine, after all!'

'Sorry,' said Beanie. 'It – it wasn't really real, you know.'

'I *know*, idiot,' said Lavinia. 'Genius idea, though.'

'But,' said Daisy, 'clever as it was, it won't quite do. Hazel and I have already effectively ruled out the salt as being used to poison Mrs Rivers – and the pepper, for the same reason. Because if something was in the salt cellar, then why *wasn't* anyone else poisoned, as we know they weren't? If Mr Dow *did* do that, then Mr Thompson-Bates would have been poisoned as well – I saw him pouring salt onto his plate with my own eyes! He loves it as much as I do. Mr El Maghrabi would have been all right, because he didn't eat anything, so you would *not* have been poisoned after all, Lavinia. But how would Mr Dow know all that before he put his plan into action? And would he really be able to doctor the salt cellar without anyone else noticing? I should think if Mr Dow had done that, Mrs Thompson-Bates would have asked him what he was playing at.'

'He could have brought it with him and put it in his pocket?' I suggested. 'A second salt cellar?'

'Yes, but it's still too risky! Why did only Mrs Rivers die? Why wasn't anyone else taken ill? It doesn't make sense. No, Beanie – it was a good idea, but it won't wash in this case. Mr Dow must be ruled out.'

'I know,' said Beanie sadly. 'I just thought it was quite clever.'

'It *was* clever!' said Kitty. 'Oh, Beans, that dress is hopelessly the wrong size.'

She fiddled about with Beanie's dress, which was indeed far too short and showed Beanie's white school slip quite obviously, and while she did so, Daisy came over to me.

'Do you really think he couldn't have managed it?' I murmured.

'I'm sure he couldn't,' said Daisy. 'Such a bother, because it really is genius. Disgusting of Beanie to have got tall *and* clever this year.'

'But – is there something in the *idea* of passing something round?' I said. 'We do keep coming back to that.'

'If anyone else had been taken ill, then perhaps. But no one was! There wasn't anything that only Mrs Rivers ate and drank apart from what was on her plate and in her glasses,' said Daisy, shaking her head. 'So it seems as though the only people who could have put poison onto

221

Mrs Rivers' plate are Mr Thompson-Bates, Mr Stone and Mr El Maghrabi.'

I thought about the dinner scene we had witnessed, the candlelit hum of it, the comings and goings – and startled myself with the idea that popped into my head.

'That's not quite true,' I said slowly, thinking it out as I spoke. 'One other person *did* get up. We've been ignoring it because she's not a man, but ... Daisy, *Mrs* Dow went past Mrs Rivers. What if ... what if the Dows are working together somehow? Mr Dow might have been the man Beanie saw on the hill, and Mrs Rivers the woman – but what if the poisoner was *Mrs* Dow? Perhaps ... perhaps they're in it together?'

'Hazel!' gasped Daisy. 'You think – a conspiracy! Why, that's *quite* ingenious. I was ready to rule out Mr Dow as a suspect, but *both* of the Dows ... you're right, they could be working together. Detectives! Listen! Hazel has had a rather genius idea. Mr Dow on his own could not have committed the crime, we've proven that – but the Dows *together* could have, for reasons that we do not yet understand.

'And that means that we still have four suspects – or three individual suspects, and one pair – left to watch at the party this afternoon. And we need to watch them *like hawks*. Pay attention to everything they do and say, and do not let up for even a second, otherwise something terrible may happen.'

'Something terrible?' quavered Beanie. 'But – but do you really think it will?'

'Perhaps!' said Daisy ominously.

'No!' I said. 'What Daisy means is that if you do, you might miss out on vital clues.'

'WE SHALL SEE,' said Daisy. 'Now, Lavinia, you're on Mr Thompson-Bates. Beanie, you watch the Dows. Hazel and I shall watch Mr El Maghrabi. And Kitty – well, you can take Mr Stone.'

Matron stuck her head round the door.

'Girls!' she cried. 'Hurry! You have to be down at school in five minutes, and Miss Barnard has asked me to remind you to look presentable, like ladies, not like little ruffians – brushed hair, clean faces and no slips or petticoats on display, do you hear?'

'Yes, Matron,' we chorused – and the meeting dissolved into ruffles and ribbons and bows.

I felt rather nervous, though this time it was not about detecting. At the party I knew we would be hemmed in by English niceties. Daisy is good at Deportment, and polite etiquette, but it never comes naturally to me. I might have learned how to act at the Rue, but sometimes it only makes me more nervously aware of playing a part.

5

The sun was hot on my face – or perhaps I was only blushing. My good Sunday dress, the one I had not unpacked from my trunk until this week, was pinching under the arms, the pink fabric pulled tight. Rather a lot of my legs seemed on show and, try as I might, my petticoat *would* pop out. Perhaps, after all, I have been growing.

Daisy, of course, looked like an advertisement for a chocolate company, in a white frock with buttons and ruffles, her hair smoothed into plaits. Lavinia was sulky in white with green trim, Kitty fresh and pretty in blue-sprigged cotton, but Beanie looked almost as awkward as I did. She had been too tall for her dress by quite a few inches, so we'd had to put her in one of Kitty's second-choice frocks. It was all right in the leg but all wrong in the chest, for Kitty has bosoms, while Beanie still absolutely does not.

'You look like a stick insect in a ballgown,' said Kitty. 'Poor Beanpole!'

'I think she looks pretty,' I said stubbornly, and Beanie looked at me with huge wet eyes, like a kitten in a rainstorm. I knew she was dreading the garden party as much as I was. It is painfully difficult to focus on being a detective when you feel an idiot, and it is no good people who always look well in clothes telling you that the outside of yourself does not matter. When you are dressed wrong, it is all you can think about. You can almost *smell* the way people are looking at you, and you are too busy shrivelling up inside to be able to think cleverly.

'Never mind clothes!' said Daisy, proving my point. 'We must detect. You must all think of yourselves as sets of eyes and ears, nothing more. Do not be noticeable, do not be obvious. I know this is difficult for *some* of you – Lavinia, I am looking at you for a reason – but in your quest to discover the truth of this case you must be subtle.

'Remember that we have two hours to uncover more about the motives of our remaining suspects, and to narrow them down. After this party, we have only two more events, the play and Leaving Prayers, to solve this case. And we *must.* Not only must we save Nancy and Beryl from suspicion, but now you know the terrible truth: Deepdean itself is at stake! We are under more pressure than ever before, but I am quite convinced that our intellects are equal to this challenge. Detectives – ready?'

'Ready!' we all chorused.

'Detective Society handshake,' said Daisy, 'which is difficult with five of us, I know, but we can at least try.'

We did a very messy, confused handshake, and then looked around at each other seriously.

'Oh, come on, why are we all hanging about?' asked Daisy. 'Let's go and solve a murder!'

6

Through Old Wing entrance we went, part of a crowd of brightly coloured and beautifully ribboned girls. We hushed as we walked through the solemn black-and-white-tiled quiet of Library corridor, for this afternoon Deepdean rules were being strictly enforced.

We trotted along, caught up in the stream – and then we turned left, out of the wide doors onto the lawns.

Daisy and I had not seen it this morning, but a huge white tent had been set up in the very middle of the garden, and it floated like sails above the green of the grass. Its sides were open, and in the cool space inside I could see smooth white tables laid out with beautiful tiny sandwiches and creamy cakes, and rows of sparkling glasses, all attended to by a neat row of black-and-white-clad maids. Nancy and Beryl were missing, of course – and seeing that made me suddenly feel quite ill. We ought to have been able to protect them, I felt, even though I knew that there was little we could do other than catch the real murderer. We ought to be able to protect them, and Deepdean itself. We were failing our school.

I felt that even more as I looked about. Before the tables moved handsomely dressed adults in suits and floral dresses. Wide-brimmed hats bobbed as their owners turned to each other – but they did not seem easy and cheerful, as people at a garden party should. They were tense, afraid – and the crowd was thinner than it ought to have been. There were faces missing, and those who were there were huddled up together like deer afraid of a tiger.

'There's Mum and Dad,' said Kitty. 'Why are they looking so *odd* this weekend?'

'Your mother is so pretty,' said Beanie. 'All plump and happy!'

I was not sure Mrs Freebody *did* look happy. Although there was a smile plastered on her face, her cheeks were tensed behind it, and she was clinging to Mr Freebody's arm as he held a glass of fizz. I thought again about what Daisy and I had overheard in Deepdean Park and felt worry settling over me.

'Kitty, DARLING!' cried Mrs Freebody – and I thought her voice a little shrill. 'How are you? Are you enjoying the party?'

'I'm all right, Mum. Don't fuss,' said Kitty.

'Where is Binny?' asked Mr Freebody. 'Ah, there she is. Kitty, why don't you come with us? Have a little family time!'

Kitty rolled her eyes as she allowed herself to be led away.

Daisy, Beanie, Lavinia and I were left alone.

'Lavinia, Beanie, there's the Thompson-Bateses and the Dows,' said Daisy, pointing to where Mr Thompson-Bates and Mr Dow were in loud conversation. Mrs Dow and Mrs Thompson-Bates were standing watching them, Mrs Dow glancing at Mrs Thompson-Bates fearfully out of the corner of her eye, while Mrs Thompson-Bates, in a gorgeous, sleek, high-necked dress and gloves, pointedly ignored her.

'Remember old Manning, the science master?' Mr Dow was saying.

'I remember I set his coat-tails on fire with a Bunsen burner,' said Mr Thompson-Bates, laughing. 'And you debagged him as he was in the middle of a lesson. Come to think of it, wasn't that the same term we bet you couldn't eat the entire rugby team's tea?'

'And I did!' cried Mr Dow, bellowing with laughter. 'I could have done it twice over. School food – that's one thing that hasn't changed. There's simply nothing to beat school stodge. Sukie will keep on trying to feed me dishes with *spices* in them. I can't abide it!'

Mrs Dow winced.

'Really?' Mrs Thompson-Bates asked her. 'You *cook*? Good grief! Whatever's the point when you can pay someone else to do it?'

'Oh, do I *have* to listen in to their dull conversation?' Lavinia groaned – and then she caught sight of someone behind us. 'Oh heck, there's my father and Awful P . . . All right, I'm off. *Don't* tell them you saw me.'

I had never seen Lavinia move so quickly, but she and Beanie had barely ducked away when Mr Temple and Patricia (wearing a glossy green dress and matching wrap today) appeared next to us.

'I thought I saw Lavinia . . . isn't she with you?' asked Patricia, her pretty face falling. 'I still haven't had the chance to congratulate her on that marvellous game of tennis she played yesterday. I used to be rather good at tennis, in fact, at my secretarial school – Michael was telling me I ought to take it up again, so that Lavinia and I could play together this summer! Did you know that man over there is really *quite* a famous player? My friend Phyllida says she met him in a nightclub last year and—'

'*Patricia!*' said Mr Temple, glaring at her. 'Small pitchers have big ears. And I told you that you might well want to try with the tennis, but Lavinia won't be having any of it. She hates you. Oh, don't look now, there's my cat of an ex-wife over by the tea tent.'

'We must be going!' trilled Daisy. 'We have to be at the other end of the garden *immediately*!'

We scuttled away, the Temples having apparently accepted Daisy's nonsense excuse, as people usually do if you say it in the right tone of voice.

'Wasn't what Patricia was beginning to say interesting?' asked Daisy, once we were alone. 'I wonder what she was going to tell us about Phyllida and Mr Thompson-Bates, before Mr Temple interrupted?'

'Something grown up, from Mr Temple's face,' I said.

'Agreed,' said Daisy, nodding. 'Something fearfully grown up, I should say. Anyway – I'm glad it's just the two us again, if only for a little while, Watson. Managing three other detectives can be quite exhausting.'

'But the others are being helpful!'

'Of course they are, up to a point,' said Daisy. 'Don't you see me letting them detect, Hazel? But can you blame me for preferring the company of someone who is almost as intelligent as me, who does not require me to order her about like one of my informants?'

'I *am* as intelligent as you,' I said.

Daisy waved her hand. 'Now, Hazel, let us go looking for more information!' she cried.

And I know that I am quite past finding her mysterious and fascinating – but, all the same, when Daisy prefers me I still get a warm glow.

7

The sun was heavy on the hats of the crowd, the white peaks of the marquee and the green-ivied walls of Deepdean itself as Daisy and I wormed our way around the garden, through the chattering mass of parents and mistresses and girls. As we went, I got little dashes of conversation.

Have you seen Pippa Daventry's mother? That dress! SO brassy.

You won't believe what I heard about Mr Stone. In love with a married woman – killed his own wife! You'd never think it about an Old Westonian!

No, really? That's why the parents aren't here, then. Poor girl – and it seemed such a good family, but you never can tell. The brother is a bit of an aesthete, you know.

Her father has something to do with the opium trade, I heard.

Keeps her on a short leash, doesn't he? While of course he's been dallying with half the—

She was a mouse then, and she still is. No wonder we all ragged on her! Poor little Emily, she's got no hope . . .

There were hopes for her *career once too – but you know what happens to girls: they fall head over heels for some chap and that's the end of it.*

He's a sheik, or a . . . pasha? Is that the right word? I'm sure he is, though apparently he denies it.

She's pretty – oh yes! But that's hardly enough these days, is it?

She was a real heartbreaker. Had all of Weston School dangling after her, and then she goes and marries that old fogey! Had one chap convinced he should seek his fortune in Egypt to be worthy of her – and then when he got home she'd already tied the knot with someone else! Perhaps he's the one who did it . . .

The school can't hush up another murder, can it . . .?

I heard that he *was the one who killed her last night . . .*

Last night . . .

Last night . . .

Whispers about the fateful dinner seemed to be everywhere. I could feel the uneasiness in the air. The parents who had been on Mrs Rivers' table were all ringed around with something invisible but electric, a charge in the looks thrown at them. They were each being watched out of the corner of a hundred eyes, and they were each the topic of ten hushed conversations.

'Lucky for the Detective Society,' hissed Daisy. 'We'll be less suspicious, now that everyone else is watching them as well.'

'Are you all right?' I asked her, just as quietly. I knew that she had heard the same whispered words I had, and I knew some of them – the ones about her – must have hurt. I am almost used to the lies about what my father does, but at least the events of Hong Kong had not followed me back to Deepdean the way the Trial has followed Daisy. And if people were whispering about Bertie, might those whispers be dangerous for him?

'I am absolutely perfect, Hazel, as always,' snapped Daisy, by which I knew that she was not. I patted her arm, and she twitched away from me.

I was thinking about what we had heard. Some of the rumours were lies – the one about Mr El Maghrabi being a sheik was of course impossible, and the one about my father was simply untrue. But – what if some *were* true? Could we use any of them to build cases against our suspects? For example, he *was the one who killed her last night* . . . I got chills remembering that.

We made a circuit of the garden and at last ducked into the shadow of the marquee. It was half empty, warm with the sun striking through its roof. The people still inside were panting and fanning themselves with their gloves and clutch bags, and the maids all looked distinctly pink in the face.

And there, next to the drinks table, was Mr Stone, picking up a glass of fizz in each hand – and moving towards him were the El Maghrabis.

'Excellent!' gasped Daisy. She glanced around her, and her gaze fell upon a platter of fondant fancies, their icing swooning gently earthwards in the heat. 'What a useful meeting! Come with me, Hazel, and look uninterested!'

Daisy swept up the platter in her hands (I put a fancy in my mouth as discreetly as I could), and together we went sauntering towards Mr and Mrs El Maghrabi and Mr Stone, looking about as though the party bored us, and so did everyone at it.

'Daddy's taking me to St Tropez this summer,' said Daisy, as we approached.

'How dull,' I said.

'Isn't it! Yes, utterly predictable of him.'

We were now close enough to begin to hear snippets of conversation.

'. . . managed to destroy them in time,' Mr El Maghrabi was saying. 'They don't know!'

'I *told* you it was stupid of you to bring them,' said Mrs El Maghrabi. 'I told you the whole thing was stupid. I told you not to talk to her. And now look! She's *dead*!'

'I still can't believe it,' said Mr Stone, circling his hands so the fizz in the glasses he was holding sloshed from side to side like a wave. 'I know you don't like her, Omar, but she didn't deserve it – any of this. I was going to ask – I really thought – she ought to be *here*, dammit!'

I looked at him as he spoke and saw that his eyes were touched with red, and his lips were trembling – and perhaps it was the fizz, or perhaps it was something else. I was still looking when Mr Stone's eyes met mine. He broke off suddenly, and frowned at us.

'Can I help you?' he asked.

'We're supposed to be offering you these,' said Daisy, curling her lip slightly as she held out the fancies, as though the task was utterly beneath her. 'We were told to.'

'We don't want any. *Do* go away!' said Mr Stone.

Miss Dodgson went hurrying by.

'Mamzelle!' she called. Mamzelle was standing next to the tea table, yawning, with a glass of fizz in her hand. 'Mamzelle! I've just seen El Maghrabi and Delacroix going into Big Girls' Wing, and you know it's out of bounds this afternoon. They're up to something! I shall go after them, but I need you to pay attention to the tent while I'm gone. All right?'

She rushed away, and Mamzelle shrugged and took a sip of her drink.

Mr El Maghrabi looked at his wife. 'Nour!' he said. 'Amina's up to something again.'

'After we told her!' said Mrs El Maghrabi. 'That naughty girl! England has changed her.'

They exchanged cross looks, and then Mr El Maghrabi said, 'Excuse us, Tom.' They both turned

236

away from Mr Stone to follow Miss Dodgson into Big Girls' Wing.

'Oh, bother!' said Daisy, backing away. 'But I think we heard some interesting things. Mr Stone and the El Maghrabis appear to know each other. I wonder if Mr Stone was the man who went to Egypt to make his fortune and win Mrs Rivers' hand, and that's how they met? Goodness, there's Lavinia, lurking by that herbaceous border. Lavinia! *Lavinia!*'

8

'Go *away*!' hissed Lavinia. 'I'm *hiding*! Patricia keeps looking for me so that she can pretend to be nice to me. I want to *punch* her.'

'Mightn't she really be nice?' I asked.

'She's a snake. She's marrying my father for his money, that's all. Honestly, it's money that makes people so unhappy. Wealth ought to be redistributed so that everyone has the same amount.'

'Don't let any of the mistresses hear you say that! You sound like a fearful Red,' said Daisy.

'Perhaps I am,' said Lavinia.

'What I would like to know is why you aren't watching Mr Thompson-Bates,' said Daisy.

'I tried!' said Lavinia. 'Only – Patricia, you know. And there was a tray of sandwiches that no one was looking after. I got you some, if you'd like? But don't worry about Mr T-B. Look, he's over there, I haven't lost him.'

I looked where she was pointing, and saw that Mr Stone had wandered over the grass to where Mr and Mrs Thompson-Bates were standing together, looking glamorous as always, he in a well-cut suit, and she with a dash of plum lipstick to match her silk dress. Mr Stone held out one of his full glasses of fizz to Mr Thompson-Bates, and Mr Thompson-Bates took it. Mr and Mrs Dow hovered behind them, her gloved hand pressed in his. They were staring at Mr and Mrs Thompson-Bates – Mrs Dow with a lost, frightened look, and Mr Dow with his brows together, resolute.

'Now, there's Kitty!' hissed Daisy. 'Really, why can't anyone follow a perfectly simple mission? She hasn't been staying on Mr Stone at all. KITTY!'

'Something's up with her,' I said. 'Kitty, are you all right?'

'No!' said Kitty forcefully. Her face was pale and drained, and she did not even look at the napkin full of sandwiches Lavinia held out to her. 'Mum and Dad just told me and Binny that – that they're having another baby.'

I gasped. So *that* was why Mrs Freebody had been acting oddly, and why we had overheard them arguing.

'Oh, what rotten luck!' cried Daisy.

'They didn't want to tell us because they thought we'd be upset,' said Kitty. 'And I am! Really, why anyone would want another baby after Binny, I have no idea. And – ugh! They're *old*! Mum is *thirty-three*.'

'I'm sorry,' I said – for I knew how she was feeling. My father had surprised me in exactly the same way only this spring. 'It's not so bad, really, once you get to know them.'

'*Hazel is lying,*' whispered Daisy. '*It's awful.*'

'It's not! *Daisy!*'

'I must tell Beanie,' said Kitty, staring about distractedly. I caught sight of our suspects again – Mrs Thompson-Bates was sneezing, while Mr Thompson-Bates chivalrously held her glass. Mr Dow leaned over to them, but Mr Thompson-Bates waved him away.

'Oh – there she is,' said Kitty, 'hidden away by the pond. Beanie! Bean— Wait, look – there's something wrong!'

We all looked – and there was Beanie, in tears. And beside her, looking quite as devastated, was her father.

Kitty marched towards the pond, fists clenched as though she was going into battle to protect her best friend. Daisy, Lavinia and I began to wiggle our way through the crowd, Daisy ducking and diving so expertly that she was soon several people in front of us. Lavinia simply shoved everyone aside, and I moved in her wake, as parents tutted at her and Miss Morris cried, 'Lavinia Temple, manners if you please!'

The pond was away from the pavilion and the main crowd, and its chatter faded a little as we approached.

Beanie and her father sat on the pond's stone lip, Mr Martineau's hand resting on Beanie's.

'Beanie!' Kitty cried, reaching her at last. 'What's wrong? What is it?'

Beanie simply sobbed, her face in her hands.

Kitty turned on Mr Martineau with a boldness that I gasped at. 'This is *your* fault!' she said to him. 'This is about Mrs Martineau, isn't it? What *have* you done with her?'

It really is simply not done to speak to a grown-up like that. Mr Martineau towered over us all, even Daisy – it was obvious where Beanie had got her new-found height from. I waited for him to put Kitty in her place.

But he only shook his head gently, and sighed and looked sorry.

'You don't know, of course,' said Mr Martineau. 'I've only told Becky myself now. I've been waiting for the right moment to tell her, but – well, I'm not sure there's ever a right time to tell someone something like this.' His eyes were suddenly shining with tears. 'I'm afraid that it's bad news. The disease – the one her mother had last year – it's come back.'

'But she'll get better?' I asked.

'The doctors don't know,' said Mr Martineau slowly. 'They don't think she will.'

'Then they aren't very good doctors!' cried Kitty. 'Beans, it's all right, it really is – we'll fix this, I promise!'

241

A bird called from somewhere on the roof of the school. A fish stirred the surface of the pond.

Beanie sobbed harder and squeezed her fingers over her eyes.

'I can't say that, pet,' said Mr Martineau. 'I don't know if anyone can make her better.'

We all stared at him, flabbergasted. Daisy and I are used to grown-ups lying, but we had never heard a grown-up admitting something like that.

The bird called again, a low whooping sound. Daisy stiffened.

'What on earth is a male tawny owl doing at Deepdean during the middle of the day?' she whispered.

'Shush, *Daisy*!' I hissed. I was shocked. Did Beanie not matter to her?

'But – but—' stammered Kitty. 'Beans, it'll be all right, I promise!'

Beanie looked up. 'You can't promise that!' she gasped through her tears. 'And anyway – I'm being brave!'

'Oh, BEANS,' said Kitty, and threw her arms round her – and the other three of us put our arms round them, until we were standing in a squashed, sweaty and tear-stained huddle.

The owl called once more.

'But, really – *listen*!' said Daisy, pulling away.

'Daisy!' I cried furiously – and at that very moment a window banged open, far above our heads, and out fell something large and white, like a spill of paint flooding down the side of Big Girls' Wing.

Everyone's heads jerked upwards to see what was happening. It was not paint at all, I realized, but a bedsheet, one of our regulation ones from House. But on its rather muddy grey-whiteness had been daubed the words:

THE EL MAGHRABIS ARE INNOCENT

Someone laughed. Several other people gasped. Miss Lappet made a wordless bellowing noise. Two heads (one fair, one dark) popped up at the window and then rapidly vanished again, as though they had been pulled away by invisible arms. The bedsheet dropped, and fell to the ground like a dying ghost.

'Miss Lappet,' said Miss Barnard, mouth so pinched it was entirely bloodless, 'fetch Amina El Maghrabi at ONCE.'

9

What followed was a confused twenty-five minutes – of the mistresses hunting for Amina, of Amina and Clementine being discovered in the grip of Amina's furious and embarrassed parents, of Miss Barnard more white-hot angry than I had ever seen her before, of Amina and the El Maghrabis being taken to the headmistress's office for a Serious Discussion and Amina coming back with her head held high and her cheeks pink.

'They didn't do it,' she said to everyone crowding round her. 'They didn't, and I wanted to say so.'

I was extremely impressed. It was a bold and dangerous thing to do when she knew how cross the school and her parents would be, and it made me feel warmly towards Amina. After the alarm-clock incident, Amina was on thin ice, and so she must care very deeply about her parents to be willing to put herself in such peril for their sake. And for Clementine to help her – I had to grudgingly admit that *she* could not be entirely unpleasant after all either. I could see that Daisy was struggling too. That one moment had knocked down many of the things she'd thought about Amina, and being wrong about someone makes her awfully itchy and cross.

So, like everyone else, we were distracted. The guests all milled about on the lawn awkwardly, until at last they were brought to order.

A podium had been set up in front of the tea tent, and Miss Barnard stood on it, very slender and delicate-looking with her hair pinned back neatly and her soft blue dress fluttering in the breeze. But her expression, when I focused on it, was sharp and furious – suddenly she looked more like Mrs Rivers than she ever had before.

'Welcome,' she said – and she did not raise her voice, but somehow the word carried. Everyone had turned towards her, glasses were lowered and half-eaten sandwiches put down.

'This Anniversary should be a joyous weekend. There is much to celebrate, for the achievements of our girls both past and present are many and great. This school has nurtured generations of women, and it will raise up generations more.

'But we are also here to remember. Last night, at the gala dinner, Mrs Rivers – a school Council member, and my own dear sister – passed away.

'It has been suggested to me that we should cancel the rest of the Anniversary weekend, but I know that Mrs Rivers would not want that. We will carry on, as all Deepdean girls do, but we will remember the good works Mrs Rivers did for Deepdean. An old Deepdeanite herself, she worked to mould this school, and its girls, in her image. She did this in memory of the time we spent here, and also of her dear husband, who passed away last year. She will not be forgotten. A minute's silence, if you please.'

Miss Barnard bowed her head. She was very calm, as always – but I saw the sheet of paper she was holding tremble, and her lips twist together. I suddenly felt terribly sorry for her. We have solved seven murder mysteries, so it has become almost natural to us to be around death – but somehow it is still odd for me to realize that, even when you are a powerful, sensible, clever grown-up, you cannot stop terrible things happening. You cannot even stop yourself feeling sad about those things when they happen.

I looked round at Mr Martineau. His huge shoulders were hunched, and his teeth were clenched – I could see his jaw working. I suddenly felt sick with dread. If Mr Martineau was telling us that Beanie's mother could not be saved, then what could we do?

On the lawns, the guests drew together, their heads bowed.

'Thank you,' said Miss Barnard from the podium at last. 'And now, a toast. To Mrs Rivers, and to fifty years of this wonderful school. To Deepdean girls, old and new. We shall move forward in the light held up for us by the women of the past. To Deepdean!'

She raised a glass in her hand.

'To Deepdean!' the crowd murmured, and light flashed all around the garden as glasses were held in the air.

'To Deepdean,' everyone muttered.

The grown-ups raised their glasses and drank.

Then I heard a shattering noise, and Mrs Dow screamed.

1

'Help!' screamed Mrs Dow. 'Oh, help! *It's happening again!*'

I thought that she had been hurt – and had a moment when all I could think about was being able to rule her out as a suspect – but it was *Mrs Thompson-Bates* who had fallen to the ground. She was writhing horribly. Next to her lay glass, gleaming in the sun.

'She's been poisoned!' cried Daisy. 'Oh, heavens, we're finally on the spot! Quick, Detectives!'

She dived forward, and the rest of us followed her.

'What on earth are you doing?' boomed Mr Martineau. 'Becky, pet, don't move. Don't look!'

He tried to catch hold of the back of Beanie's dress, but she glared back at him and wiggled out of his grip. Together, the five of us skirted the pond and ran to where a crowd was gathering around Mrs Thompson-Bates.

But we did not get there as quickly as Mrs Minn.

I did not know that someone so comfortably round could move so fast, but she was suddenly there, in a bright yellow dress that made her look like a sherbet lemon, kneeling over Mrs Thompson-Bates and patting at her cheeks.

Mr Thompson-Bates's face was ashen. 'Cordelia!' he cried, almost knocking Mrs Minn aside in his panic. 'You'll be all right!'

Mrs Thompson-Bates reached out to her husband, scrabbling at his jacket pitifully. He caught her hands and held them, tears in his eyes.

'It remains to be seen whether she will be all right,' said Mrs Minn grimly. 'You – and you – lift her up! She needs charcoal, immediately! It's her only chance.'

She had pointed to Mr Martineau, who had rushed after us, and Mr Dow. Mr Dow had been glancing between the sobbing, crumpled Mrs Dow and Mrs Thompson-Bates like a little boy who didn't know where to turn. But at Mrs Minn's words he bent to Mrs Thompson-Bates with Mr Martineau, and they lifted her into the air as easily as a doll. Still writhing, she was carried away towards San between them, Mr Thompson-Bates and Mr Stone racing after them.

'Kitty!' whispered Daisy. 'You follow them! I don't care how you do it, but go after them and listen in to everything you can.'

Kitty, grim-faced, went dashing away after Mrs Thompson-Bates.

'Hazel, observe the scene of the crime! Lavinia, stand guard over her in case of any *outside influences*. Beanie, follow me. We couldn't speak to any suspects after the *last* attack, but we can remedy that now. We need to know everything we can from Mrs Dow. Do you all understand?'

We nodded. There was not much time, and we had to play our parts. And mine was to document everything I could.

In front of me was the place where Mrs Thompson-Bates had fallen. I could see the long scratches of her heels in the grass, tufts torn up from her writhing.

There, next to them, was her smashed champagne glass. It was in shards, quite broken, but a few bright bubbles of fizz still clung to the pieces, with a smear of plum lipstick on the rim. I did not even breathe on it, for I knew the police would want every drop for testing.

Four more unbroken glasses lay on the ground near it. I thought carefully back to what I had seen. Mr and Mrs Dow, Mr and Mrs Thompson-Bates and Mr Stone had been standing together when the toast was raised, all holding a glass. These were the five glasses in front of me. Aside from the smashed one, two were marked with lipstick, one in a soft pink shade and one in plum, and two were still shining and clean.

Two things occurred to me at the same time. Mr Stone – I had seen Mr Stone pass a drink to Mr Thompson-Bates earlier! He had picked up two drinks, one of which he gave to Mr Thompson-Bates, and one of which he kept for himself. But was that important? After all, it wasn't *Mr* Thompson-Bates who had been poisoned, but his wife.

And then there were the El Maghrabis, who had been talking to Mr Stone as he collected those drinks. They had spoken for a little while, but we were watching them all the time they talked. And then they left, to hunt down Amina. They had been gone from the party for at least half an hour before Mrs Thompson-Bates collapsed, and they had gone nowhere near the Thompson-Bateses. I knew that if Mrs Thompson-Bates had been poisoned with arsenic, it would have been around thirty minutes before it took effect. And so, I realized, that left Mr El Maghrabi with no opportunity to poison Mrs Thompson-Bates. Amina's defiant message really *had* proven her parents' innocence – she had given Mr El Maghrabi an alibi, so we could rule him out.

I looked again at the glasses lying on the ground. One smashed, two lipsticked, two clean. I remembered Mrs Thompson-Bates sneezing, while Mr Thompson-Bates held her drink as well as his own.

My heart sped up. Just *one* of the unbroken glasses should be marked with lipstick, from Mrs Dow. But *two* were – *as well as* Mrs Thompson-Bates's smashed glass.

When you are holding two identical glasses, sometimes they become muddled in your hands. What if that was what had happened here? What if, once Mrs Thompson-Bates had finished sneezing, her husband had accidentally given her back *his* glass, instead of hers? And if so … could it be that it was not Mrs Thompson-Bates's glass that had been poisoned, but *her husband's*?

'Daisy!' I gasped. 'Daisy! It's the *wrong victim*!'

2

I turned round to see Daisy and Beanie speaking to Mrs Dow. Daisy widened her eyes at me warningly and pursed her lips in a way that I knew meant *hush*. I closed my mouth, heart beating wildly. What I had to tell them could wait – now I had to listen in to what Mrs Dow was saying.

'I don't know what to do!' Mrs Dow was saying. 'Should I go after them? Oh dear, this is dreadful!'

'No, no, I'm *sure* they'd want you to stay here,' said Daisy soothingly.

'Oh – really?' asked Mrs Dow. 'Well – oh, this is all terrible! I never saw a thing, not a hint! This whole weekend has been a nightmare – I never should have come back, really!'

'I'm sorry,' said Beanie softly, taking her hand and patting it. Daisy glared at her, clearly put out that she was being kind to a suspect, but Mrs Dow let out a stuttering sob and said, 'Thank you, dear. What's your name?'

'Rebecca Martineau,' said Beanie. 'I'm in the fourth form. I've been – I've been talking to Emily. I know how she feels.'

'Oh, have you? Really? Thank you, *thank* you – I can't tell you how much she needs a kind ear . . . how much I wish – well, when I was at Deepdean, the older girls weren't like you, you know.'

She suddenly sounded rather like a shrimp, and when she caught hold of Beanie's hand, I could not tell who was comforting who.

'Gosh, were you at Deepdean?' asked Daisy, chattering breathily away. 'Did you enjoy it?'

Mrs Dow blinked at her and then turned back to Beanie.

'You didn't like it here,' said Beanie, still gentle.

'May I tell you a secret?' whispered Mrs Dow – and now she truly did remind me of a shrimp. She had the same scared, shy look about her that Emily did, as though she was afraid the whole world might bite her. 'I hated every day of it. The bigger girls were awful, and I was so homesick. I remember clinging to my bedframe at home at the end of every holiday, so I wouldn't have to go back. Just seeing Oakeshott Hill from the car still makes me feel sick to my stomach. It's so hard to be back here, with the people who were so horrible to me. Even if – well – *their* lives haven't all been roses, either. Even if *their* husbands . . . well, that's not for me to talk about.

'I didn't want Emily to go away to school, but Godfrey insisted. His schooldays were the happiest of his life – he hasn't been quite the same since. He really has had the most rotten luck – didn't pass the Civil Service exams, and then he was fired from a very promising job, and now he keeps on not being promoted. I don't mind, of course, but *he* does – I think it's rather hard for him too, being here with so many other Old Westonians. Now, they *are* successful. He's been a bear with a sore head all weekend but I haven't wanted to say anything and— Oh, I shouldn't be telling you any of this!'

'But you need to tell someone,' whispered Beanie. '*I* know.'

Mrs Dow laughed shakily. 'This all feels like a dream,' she went on. 'Jean dead, and now Cordelia – it's as though I dreamed it. I did, you know, quite a lot. Dreamed that they were all gone, and they couldn't hurt me any more! I suppose I oughtn't to have wished it – after all— Well, never mind.'

'*Oh!*' said Beanie.

'I really shouldn't be saying any of this,' muttered Mrs Dow. 'I must go and find Godfrey – excuse me – I don't know what I was thinking . . .'

And she pulled back from Beanie and went hurrying away across the lawn, her dress fluttering in the breeze.

Beanie looked stricken, and I could tell she was feeling dreadfully sorry for Mrs Dow. But – could we trust her? Or had Mrs Dow just given herself a motive for both poisonings?

'Girls!' Miss Lappet shouted from Library corridor, waving her hands. 'Get inside immediately! Come on!'

'Come on, everyone,' said Daisy, her head high, and she stalked away towards the doors to Library corridor. We had to follow her. Once again, we were being cut off from the crime scene. But would we be able to put all our facts in order in time to solve the case?

3

With the Hall still out of bounds, and the lawns the scene of yet another poisoning, parents and Council members were led into Big Girls' Wing to be soothed and looked after by the mistresses, while the rest of us were crammed into Old Wing to fend for ourselves until order could be restored.

'They must be calling the police!' Daisy kept on saying. 'Oh, they'll utterly ruin my crime scene, the clodhoppers. I wonder if the Inspector will arrive with them. Oh bother, this is dreadful!'

'I've got a headache,' said Kitty, who was back from her mission to San. She had been stopped at the door by Mrs Minn, and sent away at the same time as Mr Martineau, so hadn't been able to find out anything helpful. 'I keep on thinking about Mum and Dad – and, oh, *Beanie*!'

Beanie began to chew violently on the end of her plait.

'Are you all right?' I whispered to her.

'No,' Beanie whispered back. 'It's all so awful – Mrs Dow and Emily, and poor Mrs Thompson-Bates. I can't bear it. I want to go home – oh, no I don't! I can't – not without Mummy!'

'That's grown-ups for you,' said Daisy. 'You should never rely on them. Now, the only thing for it is a Detective Society meeting, otherwise we shall all keep on moping and go spare. To the cloakroom at *once*!'

The Old Wing cloakroom had once been the scene of a most important detective breakthrough for us. It has a thick, woolly smell, and is not much used in the summer, but, all the same, Lavinia and Beanie went to check the loo cubicles while Kitty and I leaned against the door to make sure no one else could come in.

'Clear,' Lavinia called. 'Clear – ugh, this one's all blocked up.'

'That is not an important detail,' said Daisy, rolling her eyes. 'All right, Detectives, now that we have secured the perimeter, gather round, and let us discuss the developments in the case. The first thing to point out is that it seems we have *another* poisoning. Mrs Thompson-Bates! But *why*? Why has the poisoner struck again? And why was the victim Mrs Thompson-Bates?'

'About that,' I said; 'what I said earlier: I think – I think she was the wrong victim, Daisy.'

I told the Society what I had discovered from looking

at the glasses. 'It wasn't hers that was poisoned!' I explained. 'I think Mr Thompson-Bates was the person who should have died, only he ended up holding both their glasses when she sneezed, and then he accidentally gave her his glass back and kept hers.'

Beanie gasped. Even Daisy looked impressed. 'Good heavens, Watson!' she said. 'What deductive skills you are honing! Well – I can't argue much with that.'

'And, Daisy – it was Mr Stone who gave Mr Thompson-Bates his drink. But I didn't see him drinking from it before Mrs Thompson-Bates sneezed,' I said. 'So Mr Stone's extremely suspicious.'

'Good, Hazel. Very true. Now, what about our other suspects? When Beanie and I interviewed Mrs Dow, she mentioned that her husband felt resentful of his schoolmates' success. The Dows were standing just behind Mr and Mrs Thompson-Bates during the party – what if one of them managed to slip arsenic into Mr Thompson-Bates's drink?'

'They could have,' I said, frowning. 'But I know who couldn't – Mr El Maghrabi. He and Mrs El Maghrabi went off to look for Amina, and before that they were nowhere near the Thompson-Bateses.'

'Unless he gave Mr Stone the poison when they talked earlier, and Mr Stone put it in the glass before he handed it to . . .' Daisy began. Then she shook her head. 'No, the evidence of my own eyes proves that didn't happen. Vice-President Wong is correct. We can rule out Mr El Maghrabi from this second crime. Now, Kitty, what did you overhear?'

'Not much,' said Kitty, 'but enough to know that Minny's sure it's poison, and probably arsenic – that's why she rushed Mrs T-B away. She's hoping she can save her. Mr T-B won't leave her side, he's absolutely distraught.'

'Excellent,' said Daisy, nodding. 'Arsenic, again!'

'They had the same symptoms,' I agreed. 'It fits!'

'Talking of things *fitting*, how on earth does this follow on from Mrs Rivers' murder? Why would the murderer kill again, now? I think Hazel's idea is a clever one – it makes sense that Mr T-B was the intended victim this time, not his wife – but let us be rigorous before we rule her out of being the intended victim. Can we think of any possible reason why anyone would want to kill *Mrs* Thompson-Bates?'

'What if Mrs T-B saw the murderer giving poison to Mrs Rivers at Saturday's dinner?' said Lavinia.

'How?' asked Daisy. 'She wasn't sitting next to Mrs Rivers, was she?'

'All right, then – Mrs Dow might have wanted to kill Mrs Thompson-Bates because she was cruel to her at school.'

'Yes, but that works for Mr Thompson-Bates too. *Mr* Dow is jealous of him because he's doing so much better – he might have wanted to murder him because of that. Really, either victim works equally well, if it was the Dows.'

'What if Mr Thompson-Bates wanted to kill his wife because she's rich and he needs to pay off his gambling debts?' I suggested.

'Very thorough, Hazel! You are right that we must consider everyone at the scene of the crime. But if he is behind this poisoning, how does that explain Mrs Rivers? We've worked out that Mrs Rivers' death couldn't have been random. She *has* to have been the intended victim. And since that is true . . .'

'The most likely answer is that *Mr* Thompson-Bates saw the murderer,' said Beanie. 'He was sitting next to Mrs Rivers, after all.'

'Exactly, Detective Martineau. That is the first really useful thing anyone has said in this meeting so far,' said Daisy.

'Daisy!' I said.

'So if the intended victim this time was Mr Thompson-Bates, that means he's ruled out,' said Lavinia.

'It's all a muddle,' said Kitty, making a face. 'What? It's true! All these victims and suspects . . . and I still don't understand how all the different bits fit together.'

'Well,' said Daisy, 'Hazel, will you summarize the facts of the case so far for us all, so we can consider them?'

'Beanie saw a man choking a woman in Oakeshott Woods on Friday morning,' I said carefully. 'She wasn't close enough to see what either of them looked like, only that they were both quite tall. She saw her fall to the ground, we found a matchbox, an invitation, and a hat with strands of dark hair on its brim in the woods, but no body.

'On Saturday evening, Mr and Mrs El Maghrabi, Mr and Mrs Thompson-Bates, Mr and Mrs Dow, Mr Turnbull and Mr Stone were on Table Four at the gala dinner with Mrs Rivers. Food was served randomly on plates, and drink from bottles and decanters. Mr and Mrs El Maghrabi and Mrs Dow refused their first course, but everyone else was given a plate. Mr Stone and Mrs Dow got up and walked past Mrs Rivers, and Mr Thompson-Bates and Mr El Maghrabi were sitting next to her. During the main course, Mrs Rivers was taken ill and later died, with symptoms that point to arsenic poisoning.

'This afternoon, at the garden party, Mr and Mrs Thompson-Bates, Mr and Mrs Dow and Mr Stone were standing close together during Miss Barnard's speech. At some point, we know that Mr and Mrs Thompson-Bates's glasses became mixed up. Everyone was distracted by Amina El Maghrabi's banner, and later, after the toast, Mrs Thompson-Bates was taken ill with the same symptoms as Mrs Rivers. And that's all we know.'

'Well,' said Daisy, 'that's excellent. Don't you see? Mr and Mrs Dow, or Mr Stone. It must be one of them.'

4

'But how do we prove it? Ah, there's the rub.'

Daisy has got very fond of Shakespeare since our case at the Rue. I stared at her until she sighed and said, 'Is there anything else you think we should consider before we close this meeting?'

'There's one thing that I think is odd, if it was Mr Stone,' said Kitty, butting in.

'*What?*' asked Daisy, frowning at her, for she likes to be the one to make mysterious pronouncements.

'Well, what Beanie saw was so . . . fierce,' said Kitty. 'Choking someone! It's nasty, and it's not like poisoning them.'

'Yes it is,' said Lavinia. 'It's all murder.'

'No, Kitty's right!' I said, for something had been nagging at the back of my mind about that. 'Why, after trying to strangle someone, would you switch to poison the following day? It's a very different sort of way to kill someone. It's . . . more polite. And also, why didn't the killer finish the job in the woods, so that the poison wasn't needed?'

'Perhaps the woods were only supposed to be a threat?' suggested Lavinia. 'If Mrs Rivers didn't do what the killer wanted, he'd really murder her?'

'Perhaps,' said Daisy. 'That is an interesting question.'

'But the arsenic makes it seem as though the plan was to kill her all along,' I said. 'There isn't any arsenic in the Hall, is there? So the poisoner had to know what was going to happen before they arrived that evening.'

Daisy took a deep breath to tell me to stop being so silly, and then she let it out again.

'I do admit that is . . . a point,' she said. 'Not an *important* point, obviously, but . . . well, how did the poisoner get hold of the poison? Did he – they – buy it from a shop? Or did he concoct it himself? It's not hard to do, as we know.

'Now, I have two suggestions for our next steps. First, we must get ourselves into San, to see if we can find out anything else from the people there. And second, we need to recreate the second poisoning to see exactly how it could have been done. It's amazing to me that no one saw the poison go into the glass. But we have to do everything quickly. The play's this evening, and after that the weekend will be over – and so, it is very possible, will Deepdean School.'

SUSPECT LIST

1. *Mr Turnbull.* His wife Artemis . . . She did *not*
   attend! ~~MOTIVE: Possibly worried about Ella's~~
   ~~music scholarship? We must discover more.~~
   ~~NB Where is Mrs Turnbull? He was a suspect~~
   ~~before the poisoning!~~ RULED OUT from the
   strangling! Mrs Turnbull is safe and sound — and she
   has given her husband an alibi for the altercation
   Beanie saw in Oakeshott Woods on Friday morning!

2. *Mr Stone.* According to Uncle Felix, he is a
   smuggler! He has also recently been to Paris.
   ~~MOTIVE: None yet — but he was observed staring~~
   ~~angrily at Mrs Rivers on more than one occasion and~~
   ~~at dinner he got up and spoken to her.~~ We have
   observed him smoking. He was a suspect before the
   poisoning! ~~He seems to have been in love with~~
   ~~Mrs Rivers, but she was trying to rebuff him. Did~~
   ~~he take revenge?~~
   NOTES: He has been to Paris recently!
   MOTIVE for the first poisoning: he loved her, but
   she rejected him, and he is the sort of person who is
   not used to being rejected! OPPORTUNITY
   for the first poisoning: he was at the other end of the
   table to Mrs Rivers, but he did stand up and speak

to her just after the first course was brought in. This is highly irregular behaviour, and could have been a cover for her poisoning.

MOTIVE for the second poisoning: could Mr J–B have seen something at the table on the night of Mrs Rivers' murder? OPPORTUNITY for the second poisoning: he gave a glass to Mr Thompson–Bates, which was swapped with Mrs Thompson–Bates's glass when she sneezed!

3. ~~Mr Thompson–Bates. MOTIVE: Possibly worried about Lattie's tennis scholarship (she seemed upset at her exhibition match) but we must discover more. He has a gambling addiction, he smokes and he also has been on a losing streak in his tennis games. Has he been pawning his wife's jewellery? But how does this fit in with the murder? NOTES: he has been to Paris recently!~~ RULED OUT! We have discovered that HE was the intended target for the second murder, and so must look at him as a victim rather than a potential murderer.

4. Mr ~~(and Mrs)~~ Dow. ~~MOTIVE: Unclear – but Mrs Dow seemed very unhappy at the dinner. He was at Weston at the same time Mrs Rivers was at Deepdean – did they know each other?~~

MOTIVE for the first poisoning: Mrs Dow was bullied at school, and Mrs Rivers seems to have been one of the girls who was cruel to her.

OPPORTUNITY for the first poisoning: Mrs Dow stood up and ran past Mrs Rivers during the first course.

MOTIVE for the second poisoning: Mr Dow bears a grudge against Mr Thompson–Bates for being more successful than him, and Mrs Dow clearly dislikes Mrs Thompson–Bates.

OPPORTUNITY for the second poisoning: they were standing near the Thompson–Bateses at the party, when Amina distracted everyone with her banner. Either of them could have used this as an opportunity to drop poison into Mr Thompson–Bates's glass! NB How does this fit in with the strangling in the woods, though?

5. ~~Mr El Maghrabi. MOTIVE: Possible that he wants to stop Amina from being expelled? He seems to be obsessed with Mrs Rivers' dead husband and his business deals – does he have a vendetta against the Riverses? Did he murder her to get revenge?~~ RULED OUT! Mr and Mrs El Maghrabi were nowhere near Mr and Mrs Thompson–Bates during the party. He could

not have poisoned Mr Thompson-Bates's glass, and so, since the same poison seems to have been used for Mrs Rivers as Mrs Thompson-Bates, it is clear that he cannot be guilty.

PLAN OF ACTION

1. Find out whether Mrs Rivers is truly dead.

2. Find out more about Mrs Rivers! Why would someone want to murder her?

3. Discover more about our five suspects.

4. Discover how the murderer got hold of the arsenic.

5. Stage a reconstruction, to work out how the poison was given to Mrs Rivers.

6. Speak to Inspector Priestley to confirm that the poison was arsenic — and that no one else was affected.

7. Stage a reconstruction of the second poisoning, to work out how it could have happened.

8. Get into San and discover all we can there.

5

'But how are we going to get into San?' I asked, looking at our plan of action. 'We can't use ipecac this time!'

'I could punch you,' offered Lavinia.

'No one is punching anyone,' said Daisy. 'And I am going as well as Hazel.'

'Why is it *you* who gets to go to San, Daisy?' asked Kitty. 'I can pretend to be ill just as well as you can.'

'Yes, but I'm the President,' said Daisy. 'What I say goes, all right? Stop being insubordinate, Detective Freebody. And it's perfectly obvious how we can get into San. It ought to be obvious to all of you.'

We all looked puzzled.

'You have no imaginations!' said Daisy. 'Come on, really, do I have to think of everything? What *one* thing can you say to any mistress to get off lessons and Games? The *only* illness that people don't want to hear more about?'

'*Ohhhh*,' said Lavinia, enlightened.

'I don't understand,' said Beanie.

'Daisy!' I said. 'You can't just—'

'I certainly can,' said Daisy. 'You did it to get out of Deportment last week, Hazel, don't try to pretend you didn't. Now, come on, look after your poor friend in her hour of need!'

I rolled my eyes. But I had to admit that it was one of Daisy's simplest and best plans.

Daisy and I stood outside the door to San. From inside I could hear terrible moans and low, urgent voices. What was happening? Was this like Mr Curtis, all over again? My stomach clenched in sympathy at that thought.

Daisy, of course, was undaunted. 'All right, Hazel,' she said. 'Knock on the door as loudly as you can. If no one comes after ten seconds, we shall just go in, and look terribly apologetic when we're noticed. Are you ready?'

I nodded.

'Go!' said Daisy.

I hammered on the door with my fist, and next to me Daisy doubled up, clutching her stomach.

'OWWWW!' she wailed. 'Oh, help! I'm in DREADFUL AGONY!'

No one answered.

I knocked again, while Daisy made tragic noises.

At last, a very harassed-looking Mrs Minn came running to the door.

'Who's dying now?' she cried, wiping her hands on her apron. 'Fourth formers, what on earth are you doing? Don't you know I'm in the middle of a crisis!'

'Mrs Minn, I'm so terribly ill! Please help me!' gasped Daisy. She had somehow made herself go deathly pale, and her bright blue eyes started out of her face. 'I'm bleeding – it's horrid – I have the CURSE!'

'Good heavens, Miss Wells, if it's the curse then there's nothing in the slightest wrong with you,' said Mrs Minn.

'I think I shall faint,' said Daisy, and she swayed on her feet.

'Now, don't do that – oh, all right, come in, but go straight into that room there and lie down. You can have a cough sweet if you'd like. And, Miss Wong, fetch her a hot-water bottle, will you? I'm very busy right now, so please don't be a bother!'

'I'm so terribly sorry,' I said. 'Poor Mrs Thompson-Bates!'

'Yes, it's dreadful,' said Mrs Minn. 'But thank heavens she seems to be pulling through. She may yet live! Now, go on through, Miss Wells; and, Miss Wong, the kitchen is there.'

And she went puffing away back through the door into the consultation room, leaving us absolutely stunned.

6

'She's not going to die?' gasped Daisy. 'But – but – good grief, *this case*, Hazel!'

'What do we do?' I whispered to her.

'Carry on as planned!' breathed Daisy, setting her chin. 'I *am* dying and you are fetching me a hot-water bottle – which will give you the perfect opportunity to spy on the consultation room. All right?'

'All right!' I said.

'Good,' said Daisy. 'Now, I THINK I AM ABOUT TO FAINT!' She moved loudly across the hallway and into the empty room that Mrs Minn had pointed to. Oddly enough, it was the very one where Daisy and I had been ill last year, during the case of Miss Bell's murder. 'I AM GOING TO FAINT ON THIS BED HERE. *Go on, Hazel, go!*'

'I SHALL GET YOU A HOT-WATER BOTTLE,' I said, nodding at her. Daisy beamed at me and threw herself down on one of the neatly made white beds, making a dreadful groaning noise. Off I went to the kitchen.

While the water for the bottle hummed and burbled and boiled behind me, making a useful little noise, I crept towards the hatch that connects the kitchen to the consultation room where Mrs Thompson-Bates was being looked after. I could hear moans and murmurs – things did not seem to be going entirely well in there, despite what Mrs Minn had said.

Hardly wanting to breathe, I leaned forward until my nose was almost to the closed hatch door and listened.

At first, all I could hear were voices soothing Mrs Thompson-Bates, and Mrs Thompson-Bates herself calling out for water and retching horribly. I wanted to cover my ears and not listen at all.

But then I heard soft footsteps moving towards the other side of the hatch, and Mrs Minn said quietly, 'The worst danger has passed.'

'Are you sure?' said a man – Mr Thompson-Bates. 'She'll live?'

'She'll live,' said Mrs Minn. 'She's had a nasty time of it, though. She needs absolute rest and care ... I understand you'll be leaving for Wimbledon tomorrow, so is there someone else who could watch her while you're gone?'

'There's no thought of that,' said Mr Thompson-Bates. 'I shall pull out. I can't play tennis when my wife's been taken ill. No – rest assured I shall watch her like a hawk. She won't be alone for a minute.'

'You *are* a good husband,' said Mrs Minn. 'How lucky your wife is. Now – you're certain she couldn't have taken this poison in error? Arsenic really is everywhere, you know. Why, only last year I had a stupid girl in here who'd tried to beautify herself by washing her face with water she'd soaked with fly papers previously.'

I had not heard this side of Mrs Minn before. I had always thought of her as just a school nurse – but, of course, school nurses must have to know a fearful lot about illness and the things that cause it.

'My wife is far too intelligent to do something like that,' said Mr Thompson-Bates, and his voice trembled with emotion. 'She isn't the sort to hurt herself, either. No, someone did this to her, and it seems clear to me that it must have been someone near us before she was taken ill. Someone who was at dinner last night. After all, we were all on Mrs Rivers' table, weren't we? Who knows *who* might have seen something important? Someone in this room has a secret, and it won't stay secret for long!'

What was Mr Thompson-Bates trying to hint? Had he seen something – something that the Dows or Mr Stone had tried to cover up by committing murder?

'You're accusing one of us, I suppose?' Another voice – another I had heard recently. Mr Stone.

Mrs Thompson-Bates groaned again and I heard the rustle of her rolling over in her bed.

'Not necessarily,' said Mr Thompson-Bates. 'But, come to think of it – *you* gave us a glass of fizz, didn't you?'

'I say, look here, James – you needed one! You were sharing! I was only doing the chivalrous thing.'

'Please keep your voices *down*,' said Mrs Minn. 'Think of the patient!'

There was a knock on the door.

'May I come in?' called a voice I knew well – Inspector Priestley.

The kettle screamed behind me then and I jumped, stuffing my casebook into the waistband of my dress.

'The kettle must have been left unattended,' said Mrs Minn. 'Excuse me!'

A moment later she was next to me, pushing me gently aside so she could fill up the hot-water bottle with practised hands.

'Take this through to Miss Wells,' she said to me. 'Hurry up!'

I nodded at her and hurried away to Daisy's room, the water bottle hot in my hands and my mind whirling.

7

Daisy was languishing prettily on the bed, one hand on her stomach, but when she saw me come in, she popped upright, her eyes glinting with curiosity.

'What is it? What did you hear?' she whispered. 'Come here and pretend to be . . . plumping my pillows, or holding my hand – whatever invalids need.'

Daisy is dreadful at being ill. I believe she has blocked out her own real illness a few months ago. It has vanished from her mind, because it does not fit with who she is in her own head.

'Mrs Thompson-Bates is going to be all right, Minny says so. But, Daisy, the *Inspector* just arrived next door!' I whispered.

I told Daisy what I had heard, and she nodded along.

'So we've confirmed that Mr Thompson-Bates's glass was given to him by Mr Stone!' she said. 'And it sounds from what Mr Thompson-Bates said about secrets that he *did* see the murderer in action on Saturday night!'

I shuddered.

'What do we do now? You can only keep up being ill for so much longer, before Mrs Minn sends you away. She already thinks you're making it up!'

'Let her think it,' said Daisy. 'Our next step is to go back to House, to recreate the second poisoning and establish a proper plan of action for the play. It's the moment of truth for this investigation. We have only this evening to prove who committed the crimes, and catch them in the act.'

'You think they're going to strike again?' I gasped.

'I don't think, I *know*. Not only is Mr Thompson-Bates still in danger, but the murderer will act as soon as they hear that someone else saw something important during Barny's speech this afternoon.'

'But they didn't!' I said. 'Did they?'

'We have no way of knowing!' said Daisy. 'But when have we ever let that stop us? Hazel, in a moment I'm going to loudly announce to this San that I know who the poisoner is. And then we'll see!'

8

'Come on, Hazel, come on – help me pretend to struggle getting up,' said Daisy to me, before I had even really taken in her words. 'Hurry!'

'Daisy,' I said, 'Daisy, you can't do this – it's terribly dangerous!'

'No more dangerous than the things we usually do in a murder case,' said Daisy, dragging on my arm as she pretended to wince and lever herself up off the bed.

'It absolutely *is* more dangerous!' I whispered furiously. 'This murderer has poison, and they're slipping it into things without anyone noticing. Not even you, Daisy – you didn't see anything, any more than the rest of us did.'

'Well, someone noticed,' said Daisy. 'Mr Thompson-Bates!'

'Yes, Daisy, and someone tried to murder him this afternoon!'

Daisy looked at me levelly, her nose just a few inches from mine. 'Hazel,' she said. 'Sometimes we have to do things we don't want to, to protect things we love. Deepdean is in distress, and we must save the day. We can't let a poisoner just run about dosing people with arsenic, can we? We can't let the school close down, just because we're afraid. We have to do everything, try everything, because Deepdean *matters*. Anyway, if there wasn't any danger, then it wouldn't be so interesting. What's the point of being alive if you mightn't drop dead at any moment?'

'The point is to *stay* alive,' I muttered.

'I will always stay alive,' said Daisy. 'I am the heroine.'

'So am I!' I said.

'An interesting thought,' said Daisy. 'What if you were the heroine all along? No, that wouldn't be anywhere near as good a story. Now, Hazel, we have lingered long enough. Will you help me pretend to have seen a murderer, so that we can provoke the killer into trying to murder me as well?'

She narrowed her eyes at me.

'Yes,' I said at last.

'Excellent, Watson. Detective handshake, if you please.'

We shook, and then Daisy leaned against me, stumbled into the hallway and said very loudly, 'I FEEL QUITE BETTER, HAZEL! I THINK I CAN WALK AGAIN!'

As we had known she would, Mrs Minn popped her head out of the other door and said, 'What a noise! And what a surprise, Miss Wells! Would you like a biscuit before you go?'

'Oh, Minny, I *couldn't* manage one,' said Daisy. 'But – if you insist.'

Mrs Minn brought out the tin of biscuits, and we each took one.

'How IS Mrs Thompson-Bates?' asked Daisy, her voice loud enough to worm into all the nooks and crannies of San.

'She'll live,' said Mrs Minn. 'Thank heavens, we caught her in time.'

'I'm SO glad!' said Daisy. 'YOU KNOW, it's a FUNNY THING, but I could have SWORN that earlier today, during the garden party, in fact, well – well, I saw something a bit ODD, that's all.'

'Odd, Daisy dear?' said Mrs Minn. 'What do you mean, odd?'

'Oh, well, I don't know,' said Daisy. 'I'm sure it was nothing – but I can't quite get it out of my head! POOR Mrs Thompson-Bates!'

Her bait had worked. Mr Thompson-Bates and Mr Stone came striding to the doorway behind Mrs Minn.

'What do you mean?' Mr Thompson-Bates asked, his fists clenched. 'What did you see? Something to do with my wife?'

'Oh, really, I don't know, I'm not *sure*,' said Daisy, darting her eyes from side to side as though she was nervous, and frightened, and rather foolish.

'Come on, spit it out!' said Mr Stone. His arms were folded and he had a sharp, angry look on his foxy face.

Mr Dow came to stand next to him, his jaw set and a vein on his temple pulsing, and I caught sight of the very edge of Mrs Dow's dress – she had come into San and was now hiding just behind her husband.

'Out with it, girl!' he cried.

'Ooh!' squealed Daisy. 'Oh no, I *can't* . . . Hazel, come on, quickly!'

She seized my arm and marched me out into the main corridor, and I could see that she was struggling not to grin. I looked back, and saw the Inspector in the corridor next to our suspects, looking after us with a worried frown on his face, his forehead wrinkled. I felt going-down-in-a-lift, as though we had disappointed him. We should not have put ourselves in danger, I knew that, but – but *Deepdean*.

'Who is that girl?' I heard Mr Dow ask, and Mrs Minn said, 'Oh, that's the Wells child. Poor soul, she's had a bad run of it. *Fallingford*, you know.'

'They've taken the bait!' whispered Daisy to me. She had noticed the Inspector's expression. 'Now we must prepare to set our trap!'

9

Beanie, Kitty and Lavinia were waiting for us in the cloakroom. We told them what had happened, and they all gasped.

'I know!' said Daisy, beaming. 'Wasn't it clever of me?'

'But what if you *die*?' asked Kitty. I flinched.

'What do we do now?' asked Beanie.

'Well,' said Daisy, 'we'll be sent back up to House soon, I'm sure, and then we'll have an hour or so before we have to be down for the play again. It must go ahead, it *must*, despite this afternoon. It wouldn't be – it wouldn't be Deepdean if Miss Barnard just gave up. I move that we use that time to recreate the second crime scene, to see if we can narrow down our final two suspects to one.'

'All right!' piped Beanie. 'We can do it, I'm sure of it!'

But I turned to Daisy while the other three were talking excitedly.

'Do you really think we'll be able to solve it in time?' I asked.

'Of course!' said Daisy. 'We solve impossible cases every few months, Hazel. You ought to have more faith in yourself and me by this time. We are simply brilliant, and we always will be.'

'You don't really mean that,' I said.

Daisy's face fell. 'I don't know that I do,' she said quietly. 'I don't know what to think, Hazel. I feel – I feel *not invincible*. What if we can't save Deepdean? What if we fail?'

She squeezed my hand, and I squeezed back. And I am not sure who was more afraid.

But when we were finally allowed back up to House, we were stopped in the front hall for an announcement. Miss Barnard was standing next to Matron, underneath the big House clock, looking more shaken than I had ever seen her.

'Girls,' she said. 'I want to speak to you about the dreadful event that marred this afternoon's festivities. I am glad to be able to say that Mrs Thompson-Bates will make a full recovery – she is safe, and she will be well. But it seems that her illness may be connected to the tragedy that occurred during Saturday's gala dinner. Because of this, I understand that some of your parents have decided to take you away before tonight's play. I understand, and I – I apologize that I have not been able to keep Deepdean a place of safety for you. I have decided that the play will not be cancelled, but – but I fear that this may be the last anniversary Deepdean has. It is possible that our school will not open again in the autumn. Do you understand?'

There were gasps and sobs.

'But – it can't close, Miss Barnard!' Daisy cried. 'It *can't*!'

'Quiet, Wells, listen to your headmistress,' snapped Matron.

Daisy bowed her head, but I could see her hands clenching at her sides.

'What can we do?' asked one of the Big Girls.

'Nothing, I fear,' said Miss Barnard, 'except be a credit to the school, as you always are. I am proud of you, girls, and I am sorry for everything that has happened this weekend. It is not your fault, and I am sorry that you are being affected by it. You may go now.'

10

We staggered up to the dorm, horrified.

'What do we do? What do we do?' Beanie kept whispering.

'We mustn't give up!' said Daisy fiercely. 'Nothing has ever mattered more than this. We must solve this case – Deepdean itself is at stake!'

'I wouldn't care,' said Lavinia. 'I hate this school!'

'No you don't,' I said, despair sparking in me. 'You *love* to hate it. Imagine if Deepdean wasn't here. What would you do then? You'd have to be at home with Patricia, or at another school. And we might not be there with you! If Deepdean closes, I might have to go home to Hong Kong and never come back. I might never see any of you again. Everything would be *over*. I couldn't – I couldn't . . .'

Tears were stinging my eyes.

'Hazel!' cried Beanie, and she threw her arms around me. Kitty and Lavinia followed suit, but Daisy stood stiffly away from us. Her face was twisted up and her eyes were glittering.

'I won't hear it,' she said. 'I won't have you SAY those things, Hazel! You won't have to go anywhere, none of us will, because *we will triumph*. We have to! Detective Society, stop behaving like wet shrimps and pull yourselves together at once. We have a crime to recreate! Hazel, you – you stop crying and pretend to be Mrs Thompson-Bates at the party. I shall be Mr Thompson-Bates. Kitty can be Mr Dow. Beanie, you be Mrs Dow, and Lavinia can be Mr Stone. Everyone, collect your tooth mugs to be glasses of fizz. I will direct the re-creation. Remember, the goal is for Lavinia, Kitty and Beanie to try to put something in my tooth mug without me noticing. Ready?'

'Ready,' I said, rather shakily.

'Ready,' Kitty, Beanie and Lavinia chorused.

'All right!' said Daisy. 'We are all milling about at the party. What happens first?'

'Lavinia,' I said, thinking. 'Mr Stone gave Mr Thompson-Bates a glass of fizz. I saw him.'

'Good,' said Daisy. 'Lavinia, go.'

'I've poisoned the glass already,' said Lavinia. 'Here, take it, Daisy.'

'Thank you,' Daisy said. 'How kind.'

'And now I sneeze,' I said. '*Atchoo!* I look for my handkerchief in my clutch bag, and—'

'And I hold your glass with mine,' said Daisy. 'I am a chivalrous husband to you, Hazel. Then I give a glass back to you – but it's the wrong one! So, that's easy. If Mr Stone did it, that's how it was done. Next, this is the moment when Amina made her statement. Everyone look up to the left!'

We all looked.

'I ought to put the poison in the glass now,' said Kitty. 'There hasn't been another moment – bother, it's difficult! Are you sure that everyone was standing like this? I can't manage it unless Daisy's on Hazel's left.'

'No!' said Daisy. 'I remember distinctly – Mr Thompson-Bates was on Mrs Thompson-Bates's right. Try it anyway, Kitty, let's see.'

'Well, all right!' said Kitty. 'I'm reaching out my hand, and—'

'But I can see you from the corner of my eye!' I said. 'And I'd have said something, I'm sure of it. And, Beanie, I can see you too – this simply doesn't work!'

'Well,' said Daisy. 'Well! This is interesting. So if we assume that this grouping is correct, then – first of all, Mr and Mrs Dow had no chance to doctor the glass before it was switched over, and second, they had no real chance to doctor it at all. Wait – have we proved that only one of our remaining suspects could have dropped the fatal dose into Mr Thompson-Bates's glass at the right time?'

'I think we have!' I said. My sorrow and fear had almost vanished. All I felt was excitement. 'Daisy! I think we know who the murderer is!'

'Mr Stone!' gasped Daisy. 'Oh – we've DONE it! Now all we have to do is prove it. All right, Detectives! As we know, the play is "walking theatre". It begins on the lawns, moving through the school and ending up on the stage in Hall, where the final scene will be played out. Luckily, I am only in that final scene, and Beanie is in the torchlit parade on the lawns with the rest of the choir. I admit that I was less than pleased to be overlooked for a major role, but now I see that it does have its advantages. I shall be wearing a white dress to play the Spirit of the School, of course, so I shall be quite visible to Mr Stone. My role is to trick him into confessing what he has done. Yours is to keep away from me until the confession has taken place.'

'But . . . shouldn't we stay with you?' asked Beanie.

'Absolutely not!' said Daisy. 'That would entirely defeat the purpose of the exercise. I must appear to be alone and helpless, to encourage him to make his move.'

'What are you going to do when he does?' asked Lavinia. 'Scream?'

'Don't look so sceptical,' said Daisy. 'Screaming is a very useful skill that I have spent a good while practising. But, of course, I shall also hit him.'

I felt concerned. I knew that Daisy thought she had everything under control, but I was not convinced that screaming and hitting a murderer who was both strong and cunning would be enough to stop him. Mr Stone was a large, grown-up man, and Daisy was a fifteen-year-old girl. Could she really stop him hurting her?

As we made our way down to school again, I felt nervous to the depths of my stomach. How could I protect Daisy? And what would I do if something were to happen to her?

1

It was past eight, and shadows were long on the Deepdean lawns, but the sky above was still a clear, soft blue. We stepped out of Library corridor and I saw Daisy at once. She stood out in her white gown. Beanie might have been any of the wood nymphs running about, trailing tree-coloured frills, but Daisy was unmissable, looking tall and beautiful as she whispered to the Big Girl who was playing the Founder. I had a sick pang of worry. We wanted her to be noticeable, of course, that was the plan – but was our plan a good one?

A line of maids stood holding trays of drinks, and among them I saw Beryl and Nancy. I gasped, and squeezed my hands together in delight. Of course, the second poisoning had not only ruled out Mr El Maghrabi and Mr and Mrs Dow; it had proved to the police that the maids could not possibly have done it. One of our problems, at least, was solved.

At that moment I heard a familiar voice behind me, and I turned my head slowly, trying to look ordinary, to see Inspector Priestley talking to a plump old man who I thought must be a Council member.

'But what I think you're *not* understanding, sir,' said the old man in a very carrying tone, 'is that he is doing considerable *good* in his country. Germany was quite done in at the end of the War – he has revived its national spirit, and that must be praised.'

'Warmongering by any name can never be excused, and nationalistic warmongering is the very worst. Now *do* excuse me,' snapped the Inspector, 'I need to be anywhere else but here. Ah, look, there's one of my wards.'

He came striding across the grass, and stood staring down at me, his brow crinkled.

'Why did you call me your ward?' I asked, blushing.

'It's a plausible story,' said the Inspector. 'And while I know that Miss Wells would say that the two of you don't need looking after, that's not entirely true, is it, after what I heard her announce in San?'

'No,' I admitted. 'And – not that we need help, exactly, but . . . this plan does seem *quite* dangerous, even though we know who the murderer is.'

I explained, in whispers, exactly what we had uncovered during our re-creation. The Inspector's eyebrows raised, and his face got even more crumpled-looking than usual.

'Interesting,' he said, 'very interesting. And, knowing Miss Wells, I'm sure nothing I could say could convince her not to go through with her plan?'

I nodded, wincing.

'Well, at least this makes my job somewhat easier. I've done some digging into your Mr Stone – and all your other suspects, though that now seems to have been unnecessary. Although I am inclined to believe that his wife died of natural, if tragic, causes (in a train crash in Leeds, while Mr Stone was out of the country), it's certainly true that he knew Mrs Rivers in her youth, and they were actually engaged for a short while. Mr Stone went to Egypt to make his fortune and Mrs Rivers met Mr Rivers while he was there. They were married before Mr Stone returned, very happily I hear, but after Mr Rivers' death Mr Stone struck up contact with Mrs Rivers again. There are plenty of letters from him at her Kent address – he was quite insistent that they belonged together, a vision she did not seem to share. He became quite enraged in later missives, and I believe that he might have resorted to violence in the face of rejection. If you think that Mr Thompson-Bates may have seen something at the dinner – well, he ought to be watched tonight too. Mr Stone has two targets tonight, and he may strike at either of them, or both. At least the crowd is thinner than it was on Saturday, and those who are left are much less likely to wander off. They're crowded together like sheep.'

I looked around at the crowd on the lawns, and I saw that he was right. The grown-ups were all leaning together as they talked, their hands on their daughters' shoulders, darting their eyes about at the people next to them. No one felt safe, and everyone was under suspicion.

'Sheep or buses,' said the Inspector, 'since I'm a Londoner now. Though being here this weekend has reminded me how much I miss green spaces, even when they are crime scenes. Now, if Miss Wells has the bit between her teeth, I know from experience that I cannot stop her until she has run her course. I can promise you, though, to be on hand to help. I shan't let her or Mr Thompson-Bates out of my sight.'

'Neither will I,' I said firmly.

'Good,' said Inspector Priestley. 'By the way – the station is testing the liquid in the glass Mrs Thompson-Bates drank from, the one that you suggest really belonged to her husband, but I'm sure it'll come back positive for arsenic. Now, remember – keep yourself safe this evening, first and foremost. If you and Daisy put your lives in danger at the same time, I may struggle to save you both. Do you understand?'

'I can save myself,' I said.

'You've been around Daisy too long,' said Inspector Priestley. 'Of course you can, but even the best detectives sometimes need help.'

A violin began to tune up behind us, and the Inspector turned. 'Time for the play,' he murmured. 'Good luck, Hazel.'

2

The violin started up in earnest, and then the choir all began to sing about the Founder walking up through Oakeshott Woods for her first sight of the buildings that would become Deepdean.

It was supposed to be a stirring song, full of bravery and discovery, but the thought of walking through Oakeshott Woods makes me feel nervous now. I imagine it as full of murderers. I shifted uncomfortably, and I saw that, in the choir, Beanie was looking nervous too. She grimaced, and I heard her voice wobble.

The Big Girl playing the Founder appeared, clutching some scholarly books and wearing a pair of horn-rimmed glasses, and began to act out her purchase of the school grounds.

But I was really watching Mr Stone. He yawned and leaned against a wall, just as though nothing at all was going on, and I was amazed at his nerve. Near him,

Mr and Mrs Dow were whispering to each other, Emily looking quite terrified between them, and close to them was Mr Thompson-Bates. I was surprised to see him – Mrs Thompson-Bates was still in San, after all – but I saw how he was hovering protectively over Lallie, his hand heavy on her shoulder, and I understood. I glanced over at Daisy, and she winked at me. In the candlelight she glowed, looking exceedingly spiritual (and rather ladylike), but my heart clenched.

Into Old Wing we went, following the Founder as she argued with various town residents, and mimed welcoming the first form of girls to arrive at the school, and then we went winding through Library corridor, the school being built around us.

Despite my nerves, my mind wandered. It was not a very interesting play – or, rather, it was nothing new to us. It could have been the topic of any Prayers, or any Sunday chapel speech. Faith, hope, striving, intelligence – I had heard it all a hundred times. Instead I thought of the case – the gala dinner, the garden party, and what had happened in those woods.

At least only one person has died, I thought – for we knew that Mrs Thompson-Bates was out of danger and on the mend. At first it was a comforting reminder, but then those words began to sound odd. There had been *three* crimes, we knew that: the incident in the woods, and the poisonings at the gala dinner and the garden party. Yet only one person was dead. Was that odd? *Had* Mr Thompson-Bates been attacked just because he knew something? Was Mrs Rivers supposed to have died in the woods on Friday morning? If so, why hadn't the killer finished the job? But if she was always meant to die at dinner, why throttle her first and give her the chance to tell the police? And the two different methods! They could have made sense when we thought the Dows were behind them, but now we knew that Mr Stone must have done them both, the contrast between strangling and poisoning felt odder than ever.

I felt, suddenly and strongly, that *something did not make sense.*

I looked around. There was Mrs Dow, her round little body tense – I could tell she was remembering horrid things in these corridors – and next to her Mr Dow's face was set. Mr Thompson-Bates was watching the play with a smirk on his face. I had the distinct feeling that he was no more interested in it than I was. And – there, in a blink – Mr Stone was gone. He was leaning against a wall, and then he was not. He had vanished into the shadows. Where was he? Had Daisy seen him go?

We were up in Big Girls' Wing now, and a second former was reciting poetry, Miss Dodgson mouthing along behind her proudly. The lights were off, and an ethereal glow came from the candles we had all been given to hold. The second former motioned forward, and we followed her up the stairs beyond the headmistress's office, stairs that are almost never used – stairs that lead to Deepdean School's observatory tower.

The tower is quite old, and it was built many years ago so that the Big Girls could study astronomy. But it turns out that Deepdean doesn't have many clear nights, and anyway the Big Girls kept on getting up to mischief when they were allowed out of House after lights out. So the observatory has just become a large, disused room with the Deepdean clock built into one side of it, and a sliding shutter in the roof that can be scrolled open to see the stars.

I had never been up there before, but I had heard stories. Now that I was here, I saw that the stories did not match up to the reality. The room was chill, even with our warmth breathing up to the open roof along with our candle flames, and the stars sparked far above us. The candles cast shadows across our faces and spooked hugely on the bare, scratched walls. There were covered objects too, and although my head told me that they were only old boxes and chests, lumber from the school, and a covered telescope, my heart was certain that they were dangers. I felt tightly squeezed in next to too many people, but also quite alone, and quite terrified.

The fifth formers began a scene about the great scientists who'd had their start at Deepdean. They struggled rather, for there didn't seem to be many, apart from an old girl who had discovered a star.

'They're leaving out all the good ones,' breathed Daisy in my ear. 'There's a fabulous lady driver who set the land-speed record, and a woman who looks after the lizards at London Zoo, but neither of them are very ladylike.'

I turned to ask her how she knew these things – although I should not be surprised any more, as Daisy always has unusual facts up her sleeve – but she had gone again, floating gracefully over to the other side of the room.

As she did so, I saw Mr Stone re-emerge from the staircase and turn his head to stare at her. He had a curious look in his eyes, and I did not like it in the slightest.

And then, just as I was noticing that and feeling sick to my stomach, there were several very loud bangs, and the world turned white.

3

Most people screamed. The observatory filled with smoke, and I found myself grabbed and thrown backwards. I saw stars, and I thought with odd clarity that I must be dying – but then I realized that the stars were in the air, not in my head. Rockets were soaring through the open skylight and bursting above us in beautiful rainbow colours, soft against the still-darkening sky. They were, I realized, the fireworks that Miss Runcible had been making for tonight – but surely they ought not have gone off now, while we were all still in the tower?

I pressed myself against the wall – and there in front of me I saw Amina. She was standing in the middle of the room, hands clasped and face lit up. She looked thrilled and terrified, like a person balancing at the edge of an enormously high building. I had to admit that I knew how she felt. Everything was so bright and wild. This is what comes of being friends with Daisy for so long, for the Hazel I used to be would never have enjoyed this chaos so much.

Mr El Maghrabi pushed through the crowd and seized her arm.

'I TOLD YOU TO BE GOOD!' he shouted at her. 'WHY MUST YOU DO THIS?'

'AMINA!' cried Mrs El Maghrabi, next to him. Her hat was singed but her eyes were as bright as her daughter's.

'It wasn't me!' cried Amina. 'I swear! You know I promised not to do anything else after this afternoon.'

Then there was a shriek and a fizz, and a bright jagged ruff of white light spouted from the middle of the room.

'GET BACK!' roared Miss Runcible. 'IT'S A CATHERINE WHEEL!'

More people screamed, and a writhing, fighting scrum of girls and mistresses and parents formed, all surging towards the stairs.

I saw Beanie being swept downstairs, with Kitty following, grabbing at her hand. Lavinia shoved her way after them.

And I crouched down behind a dusty old box at the edge of the room, and hid.

I ought to have got to safety, I knew that. Fireworks were still spinning and bursting around me, and I very much did not want to be hurt. My ears were ringing.

But I did not want to leave Daisy, or ruin her plan. She was standing pressed against one wall of the room, as though she was terribly frightened. Her white dress was singed and her cheeks smutty.

Mr Stone went bounding towards her as the last of the crowd disappeared from the tower room. 'Come here!' he shouted, grabbing at her arm.

I tensed. Was this the moment? Was he about to reveal himself?

'Get away from me!' cried Daisy. 'I warn you!'

Mr Stone raised his hands. 'Excuse me for trying!' he snapped. 'I thought your Uncle M might not want you dead, that's all.'

'What do you know about my uncle?' gasped Daisy – for, at Deepdean, Uncle Felix is rather a deep secret. It was shocking to hear his code name bandied about like that.

'We work together,' said Mr Stone. 'Hush hush, though, eh?'

Daisy gaped at him. 'Work – *together*?' she asked.

'Yes, *work together*. For several years now,' said Mr Stone. 'Hasn't he told you about me? Look, will you get downstairs or won't you? If you die under my watch, Felix is liable to have me killed.'

'I'm sure he would,' said Daisy proudly. 'But I shan't go anywhere with you, because I know the truth. You – murderer!'

She meant it to be dramatic, and it was – but not in the way she was expecting. Mr Stone reeled backwards, staring at her – and then he burst out laughing.

'You mean *this weekend*?' he asked, with some difficulty. 'My dear girl' – and his face changed, and the tears in his eyes were suddenly not mirthful – 'I'm not a *poisoner*. That's a woman's weapon. And I wouldn't kill Jean. I meant to ask her to marry me – look, you idiot!'

He thrust his hand in his pocket – I tensed, and so did Daisy – but when he pulled it out again there was nothing in it but a little velvet box. Mr Stone snapped it open to reveal a thin gold band with a blue stone.

'I was going to offer this to her,' he said, 'not kill her! And why would I hurt that Thompson-Bates woman?'

'It wasn't her. It was *Mr* Thompson-Bates you meant to hurt!' said Daisy, struggling to keep her composure. She was rattled, I could tell. 'He saw what you did to Mrs Rivers!'

'First of all, I didn't do *anything*,' said Mr Stone. 'You ought to ask Mr Thompson-Bates what *he* did, though.'

'What do you mean?' gasped Daisy.

'On Saturday night, when Jean began to fit, he got up and went round the table to her left-hand side. He picked something up and put it in his jacket pocket – I don't know what it was, but I know what it looked like.'

'What?'

'A salt cellar,' said Mr Stone. 'In fact, I've been waiting

308

for the right time to ask him about it. It was odd, wasn't it, James?'

And then there was a sudden movement at the edge of the room.

I froze. Daisy's hand wobbled, though her face remained perfectly still.

A figure unfolded itself from behind the great bulk of the telescope. In the near-dark, with only the light of Daisy's candle casting shadows, the shape looked huge.

Daisy stiffened. I put my hands over my mouth to stifle my gasp.

'What do you mean, Tom?' Mr Thompson-Bates asked. 'What have you got to say to me?'

'That salt cellar,' said Mr Stone. 'You still had it in your pocket at the garden party this afternoon, didn't you? What's in it?'

'None of your business,' said Mr Thompson-Bates. 'And if you know what's good for you, you'll forget you ever saw it.'

'Oh, will I?' asked Mr Stone with a sneer. 'And why would I do that? I've plenty of friends in high places who'll be very interested to hear what's been going on here, you know – proper policemen, not like the clodhoppers out here.'

'Because if you don't, I'll *make* you,' said Mr Thompson-Bates, and without warning he jumped across the room – to *my* hiding place.

4

Mr Thompson-Bates's left hand was squeezing my throat, and his right was over my mouth so that I gasped for breath.

'Leave Hazel alone!' cried Daisy.

'This is dramatic nonsense,' said Mr Stone. 'You can't kill all three of us – and, anyway, it's me you want.'

'Be quiet, I say,' snarled Mr Thompson-Bates. He had begun to shake me as he spoke, and I saw stars again, only this time they were not in the sky above me. My mind was buzzing and scattering with panic. I suddenly knew quite certainly that *this* was the man who Beanie had seen in the woods.

'Really!' said Mr Stone. 'What, will you *serve* me into silence? Shut me up with a lob?'

Mr Thompson-Bates growled. But I felt his fingers clenching against my skin, and I knew that he had no idea what to do next.

'You shan't get away with this!' said Daisy.

'I certainly intend to. If you tell anyone what's happened, who would believe you? You're just a criminal and two silly little girls.'

'WE ARE NOT SILLY!' gasped Daisy. 'And we're hardly little any more. Anyway, we have solved—'

'I'll have you know that I am not a criminal, despite what gossip may suggest,' Mr Stone said. 'I have plenty of friends in high places – and so do these girls. Don't you know who they are?'

Mr Thompson-Bates, confused now, wavered, and the grip around my neck loosened. I pushed myself away from him and ran to Daisy.

'It was you!' I said, with a little difficulty. 'You were the man – I mean, you're the strangler!'

Mr Thompson-Bates flinched. 'Be quiet!' he snarled – and there was the temper of the man Beanie had seen. Why had we not connected Mr Thompson-Bates's rage to the strangler's?

'We've got evidence!' said Daisy. 'We've got someone who saw you do it – and now we know that Mr Stone saw you poison Mrs Rivers!'

'*Someone?*' sneered Mr Thompson-Bates. 'Someone you invented, more like. And Tom saw me pick up a salt cellar on Saturday. So? I was distressed – I didn't know what I was doing. I put it in my pocket for safe-keeping. I noticed it was there this afternoon and put it back in the tea tent. Hardly enough to hang me, is it?'

'You filled the salt cellar with arsenic and gave it to Mrs Rivers to pour on her food!' said Daisy, gabbling now. 'It'll be tested!'

'Oh, Miss Wells, this is stupid stuff,' said Mr Thompson-Bates. 'You don't imagine anyone will find a single fingerprint of mine on that salt cellar, do you? Be quiet, all of you, and let's hear no more about it.'

'We will absolutely *not* be quiet!' cried Daisy – and Mr Thompson-Bates lunged at her.

'STOP!' bellowed a voice – and, suddenly, there was the Inspector, looming up in the doorway like an avenging angel, with Kitty, Beanie and Lavinia behind him.

'He's the murderer!' Daisy cried. 'Arrest him!'

'With what evidence?' asked Mr Thompson-Bates. 'What do you have against me? Nothing at all. Arrest me now and the trial will fall apart in days. You'll be a laughing-stock.'

'Don't listen to him!' I gasped. 'Arrest him! He hurt me!'

'Mr Thompson-Bates, I'm arresting you for assaulting Hazel Wong,' said the Inspector.

'But he's a murderer as well!' I cried.

'Can you prove it?' asked Inspector Priestley.

'They can't,' said Mr Thompson-Bates. 'They're only little girls. Go on, arrest me, I'll be out in a few hours.'

And as Mr Thompson-Bates was led away, we saw a triumphant smile on his lips.

5

'It's all so odd, isn't it?' asked Lavinia, an hour later.

'*You're* odd,' said Kitty.

'Oh, do stop!' said Beanie. 'Don't be nasty!'

Daisy, lying flat on her bed with her eyes closed, did not reply.

We had all been sent up to House after the dramatic fireworks display and Mr Thompson-Bates's arrest. Of course, the arrest had not been the official reason, but Binny – who had been hiding in Big Girls' Wing to watch the reaction to the fireworks that *she* had set off with her candle to impress the third formers' idol Amina – had seen him being led out to Inspector Priestley's car, and the gossip had spread quickly.

Most people thought that he had been arrested for Mrs Rivers' murder, of course. Only we knew the awful, frustrating truth – that he *was* the murderer, but that, without any evidence against him, he'd be released within a few hours. Leaving Prayers tomorrow morning would proceed as normal, but with the poisonings unsolved, the school would have to close as soon as all the prizes had been handed out.

'Why wasn't it enough?' asked Kitty. 'Why didn't the Inspector listen to you?'

'He did!' I said. 'Only – only we don't have all the pieces. We don't have anything that *proves* what happened. The poisoned salt cellar would have done it, but Mr Thompson-Bates all but told us he'd wiped it clean before he put it back!'

'It's all a muddle,' said Daisy. 'Oh, bother, things still don't fit! *Did* Mrs Thompson-Bates take her husband's glass by mistake? Did Mr T-B mean to poison himself, to make himself seem less guilty? Or did *she* see something?'

House, of course, was currently in uproar. Girls were rushing up and down corridors and whispering to each other in corners, and toothbrushes and lights-out were quite ignored. Lallie Thompson-Bates had been sequestered in San in absolute hysterics, a still-recovering Mrs Thompson-Bates at her bedside.

'Wait – d'you think it was Mrs Thompson-Bates he was trying to kill all along? First in the woods, and then at the dinner, and finally at the garden party?' asked Beanie wonderingly. She had Chutney the dormouse in her lap, and she was letting her climb all over her hands and nibble on a bit of old custard cream biscuit.

'Beanie, we *proved* that Mrs Rivers must have been the intended victim of the dinner poisoning,' said Daisy impatiently. 'Mr Thompson-Bates was in an ideal position to do it. And he must have used the salt cellar. If he had an extra one in his pocket, he could have fished it out and handed it to Mrs Rivers. Oh, remember – we saw the pepper and the salt in completely different places on the table, and if you know *anything* about polite society you understand that ought never to happen. They stay together as they travel round the table. But it *might* happen if there was an extra salt cellar being passed about! When Mr Thompson-Bates started the poisoned salt off round the table, he would have sent the original set in the wrong direction – so they would have been split up. There was really not much danger of the poisoned salt being passed on after Mrs Rivers, as Mr El Maghrabi and Mrs Dow didn't eat their starters or much of their mains – and then, when Mrs Rivers became ill, he simply leaped up and pocketed it again.'

'But *why*?' asked Lavinia. 'Mr Stone, Mr El Maghrabi, and Mr and Mrs Dow all made sense. But why should Mr Thompson-Bates want to kill Mrs Rivers? The best motive we had for him was that he was worried Lallie might not get her tennis scholarship, but that's not enough to murder someone over, is it?'

Daisy opened her eyes for a moment and glared at Lavinia.

'What?' asked Lavinia. 'It's a logical question! Now we know that it was Mr Thompson-Bates, it makes far more sense for him to have wanted to murder *Mrs* Thompson-Bates all along than Mrs Rivers.'

I sighed. I did not like to admit it, but I thought that Lavinia had hit on something.

'We know he was a gambler,' I said, trying to think it through. 'Perhaps Mrs Rivers lent him money and wanted it back? Perhaps her husband's company had sponsored him, and she was threatening to pull it since he wasn't doing well in his tennis matches?'

'*And* it's still odd that Mrs Rivers didn't go to the police after what happened in the woods,' Lavinia pressed. 'If she had, she'd still be alive. It makes no sense, this whole thing.'

'Oh, do be quiet!' snapped Daisy at last. 'I am trying to think!'

'So are we all,' said Kitty. 'It's not just you who's a detective, Daisy Wells.'

Daisy let out a groaning noise. Then she leaped off the bed, rushed to the window and clambered up onto the sill in her stocking feet. 'I am going to think. Don't follow me.'

She swung up and out of sight.

'Really!' said Kitty.

'I'll fetch her,' I said, feeling rather apologetic.

'Could you bring her back a bit nicer?' asked Kitty.

I simply shrugged at her.

6

It was funny, but as I hauled myself upwards, I did not feel as wobbly as usual. I found my feet and hands had begun to know the nooks and crannies in House's walls, the place where the drainpipe separates, exactly when to reach up and grip hard.

What if, after all this, we still lose Deepdean? I wondered – and I felt sick with a fear that had nothing to do with heights.

At last I was up among the sharp peaks of the House roof. We had first come here last autumn, during the Bonfire Night case – it had been frightening then, but it felt quite safe now. There were no murderers here, this time. I clambered across the expanse, and finally found Daisy balancing next to a chimney pot and looking miserable.

'Something's wrong,' she said at once.

'I know,' I said. 'I can feel it. What have we missed?'

'It was just too *easy*!' said Daisy – forgetting, of course, that in one evening we had laid a trap for a murderer, almost been set alight by fireworks, and I had nearly been choked. Although I suppose that is the sort of evening that happens to us quite a lot these days. 'The way he denied everything, I mean. He was so sure the Inspector wouldn't have anything on him. And there's something else as well. There was something he said . . . it didn't fit. Or rather, it did, but not with what ought to have been happening. Don't you know that feeling?'

I did. 'Like not remembering which language a word is from!' I said.

'No, not that,' said Daisy, waving her hand. 'It's . . . like doing a puzzle and finding a piece from quite another one. If only I knew the picture on the other puzzle!'

She made a face, wrinkling up her nose, and whispered, 'What was it he said? Something like – yes – *this is stupid stuff. Stupid stuff* . . . no, I've no idea. Bother! I suppose we must just consider what we heard in light of the evidence we've already collected. What did we confirm?'

'I'm sure that Mr Thompson-Bates was the man in the woods,' I said. 'And from what Mr Stone said, Mr Thompson-Bates must have been the poisoner at dinner. He used a salt cellar to give Mrs Rivers the poison, and then later picked it up and put it in his pocket. I suppose that's how he poisoned Mrs Thompson-Bates at the garden party too: he dropped poison in his own glass, and handed it to her.'

'All right, yes. But, Hazel, it's not surprising that there's nothing much to go on. It's all muddled! The victims keep changing! Mrs Turnbull, then Mrs Rivers, then Mr Thompson-Bates, and now *Mrs* Thompson-Bates – we spend ages discovering motives and alibis for the murder of one victim, only to discover that they weren't the right person after all!'

'I know!' I said. 'And – I can't help thinking, Daisy, that Lavinia has a point about Mrs Rivers. Why should Mr Thompson-Bates – who's *famous*, after all, and important – spend so much energy killing Mrs Rivers? You have to be passionately angry with someone to strangle them, but you have to *plan* to get poison and put it in a salt cellar, and bring it out at dinner and simply hope that it only kills the person it's supposed to. It's so *much*!'

'*So much*,' murmured Daisy. 'Yes, Watson. So much *bother*, isn't it. And then to try to kill your own wife too because – because she saw something? But Mrs Thompson-Bates has been absolutely composed all weekend. She gave no indication that she had – had . . .'

Her eyes had gone rather unfocused.

'Daisy?' I said – and Daisy snapped to attention, eyes suddenly blazingly blue.

'HAZEL,' she said. 'What if we've been looking at this wrong, AGAIN?'

'What do you mean?' I asked.

'What if Mr Thompson-Bates *was* passionately angry with his victim, and he'd *also* spent ages plotting exactly how to kill her? We've been ignoring part of what Beanie said about the couple she saw in the woods, because we thought it didn't fit. Remember she said that they were ordinary, *like parents*? But when Mrs Rivers died, we assumed that she was the woman in the woods, and we know that she's not the wife or mother of anyone living. Oh, Hazel, what if Beanie *did* see two parents, a husband and wife? What if the couple in the woods *were* Mr *and Mrs* Thompson-Bates?'

'No!' I said.

'Yes! Listen! What if they went for a walk, he smoked a cigarette using a matchbox he picked up when he was in Paris for the French Open, one of them dropped their invitation to the Anniversary, and then – then they argued about something. Perhaps the gambling, perhaps the other women – but Mr Thompson-Bates became furious with Mrs Thompson-Bates, and he choked her.'

'That's why she never went to the police!' I gasped, shuddering at the thought. 'But – but why didn't he kill her then?'

'Because the evidence would quite obviously point to him,' said Daisy. 'A husband and wife go for a walk in the woods together, and the wife never comes back – the police would look at the husband immediately! Perhaps he realized that and stopped himself, before it was too late. Or perhaps— Oh, Hazel! Perhaps someone *else* saw them in the woods! Someone out for a walk – someone like Mrs Rivers!'

'Just like Lavinia suggested before!' I said.

'Not at *all* like!' said Daisy, typically forgetful about any idea not her own. 'Anyway, he stopped before he killed her, picked her up and carried her back out of the woods, her hat falling off on the way. He might have left it there to punish her – and she might have been too afraid to go back for it . . . But before we go haring off after this fascinating thought any further, can we confirm that it *could* have happened that way?'

'It could,' I said, excitement flowing through me. 'Mrs Thompson-Bates has been wearing high-necked dresses and scarves all weekend. She could have hidden bruises on her neck that way! But oh, Daisy, she behaved so fondly towards him! How creepy – you wouldn't have known that he'd hurt her!'

'You never know what goes on between married people,' said Daisy. 'Look at my parents, and yours! Even the ones who seem to like each other are quite puzzling. However do Aunt Lucy and Uncle Felix cope with each other? And then there's Kitty's people. All sweetness and light in company, but shouting and crying the moment they believe they're alone. No, Hazel, all marriages are essentially two people lying to everyone else.

'Now, let us take the gala dinner. Hazel, I think we now have a way to make sense of the fact that Mrs Rivers *was* the intended victim.'

'Because *Mrs Rivers* was the person who saw them in the woods!' I said.

'Yes!' said Daisy, glowing. 'I think Beanie was not the only witness to the strangling. Perhaps Mrs Rivers was out walking in the woods – we know she was a pupil here once, and loved it, so it stands to reason that she may have wanted to take in the scenery and remember her time here. I expect she shouted something when she saw them – or cried out and ran away. At any rate, if she did see them, and Mr Thompson-Bates saw *her* – well, that finally gives Mr Thompson-Bates a sensible motive to do away with her. And if he had already been preparing to poison his wife with arsenic for some reason, then he could have decided to use some on Mrs Rivers. He was next to her at the dinner, so it would have been quite easy to switch the salt cellars.'

'But not so easy to make sure that the whole table wasn't poisoned!' I said.

'Well, we know that the people on the other side of the table didn't eat their food, so wouldn't want to salt it – but how lucky! Otherwise it might have been like the MacDonalds of Glencoe's feast where everyone died.

'Let's look at the garden party next. We know the poisoned glass was his, and we also know that he was holding both of their glasses while his wife sneezed. But, Hazel – how risky! What if she had refused to take the glass back, or identified hers as the other one! It's an odd plan, I must admit that, but it worked.

'Now, that's the *how*. But we ought to dig deeper into the *why*. What made Mr Thompson-Bates so eager to kill his wife?'

'He's off his game,' I said. 'He's not winning prizes, and he won't get much money because of that. We know he's a gambler too, so he needs lots of it. Mrs Thompson-Bates – her family's rich, aren't they?'

'Indeed they are,' said Daisy. 'Yes, if Mrs T-B dies, Mr T-B stands to inherit. And there's something else! Remember how Lallie used to be a day girl but now she's a boarder? Mrs Thompson-Bates used to stay at home and look after her, so she couldn't travel with her husband. But this year she's left Lallie at Deepdean so she could follow Mr T-B about. I bet that's put a strain on their relationship. Perhaps she discovered the gambling, or – or simply spent enough time with him to hear stories like Patricia's about him and her friend Phyllida! She's angry with him, he's angry with her – after all, there's no one more annoying than the

324

person you spend the most time with. Just look at you and me! Sometimes I think that I could quite cheerfully murder you.'

'Daisy!' I cried. 'Never!'

'Speak for yourself,' said Daisy. 'Of course, I'd never go through with it.'

I ignored that. 'All right,' I said. 'Daisy, it all makes sense. So why do we feel that we've missed something? Lavinia was right earlier – something seems odd. *What is it?*'

7

We sat still and thought. Even though the last tangles of the case refused to clear away, I felt suddenly calm. We were together, after all, perhaps for one last time.

'We've run out of time,' said Daisy, and all my peace vanished. 'He's outwitted us.'

'We've done everything we can!' I said, trying to be grown up and sound more sure than I felt.

'Have we, though?' said Daisy. She sounded quite bleak. 'We've been tricked by this case, Hazel; tricked again and again. My powers of deduction – I must admit, they have been weakened. It's coming back *here* and thinking about school things. It's not good for my detective mind! And now, because we can't solve the case, Deepdean will have to close, and Hazel – Hazel, I *cannot* have you living on another continent to me. That is unacceptable!'

'I'd come back!' I said, my throat tight.

'But what if you couldn't? There'll be no fun in being the world's greatest consulting detective if you're not there to help me!'

'We help each other!' I said, feeling a little spark of crossness through my sorrow. 'And stop it, Daisy. I'm not going anywhere.'

'Not if I can help it!' said Daisy. 'Oh, if only we had proof! Or if I could only remember – *this is stupid stuff, this is stupid stuff, this is stupid*—'

We both froze. We had heard the same thing – soft footsteps on the roof behind us.

'Oh, hello!' said Amina, as though she had come upon us in the common room rather than on top of a roof. Her long dark hair was tied back in a swinging plait, and her regulation pyjamas looked unutterably fashionable.

'What are you doing here?' asked Daisy, astonished and rather put out.

'I come up here sometimes,' said Amina, shrugging. 'To get away from people, you know. And I wanted space to think, after what happened this afternoon. My parents are so cross with me they're threatening to take me away from Deepdean. They don't understand that I did all that for *them*!'

I gasped, but Daisy appeared unmoved.

'So? This is *our* spot, you know. We found it first! You ought to go away and leave us to it.'

Amina narrowed her eyes. 'I won't!' she said. 'Why should I? This is my school too – for the moment, at least.'

'No it isn't!' cried Daisy. 'It – it's *mine*!'

'Is that why you hate me?' asked Amina suddenly. 'I've been wondering. I know you're in the other dorm and we're supposed to hate each other – what a stupid rule, I don't know why you all obey it! – but it's more than that. I keep trying to be nice to you, but it only seems to make you more angry with me. It's not – how I look, is it?'

I felt covered with shame and horror. Did we really seem as though we *hated* Amina? I remembered my own early days at Deepdean, and how difficult it had been. If I hadn't found Daisy to be friends with . . .

'I – I—' Daisy spluttered. 'I don't *hate* you! And I don't *care* how you look. That is – you're beautiful, everyone says so. That's not important. It's only dorm loyalty. It's the *rules*!'

'That won't wash,' said Amina, shaking her head. 'You break plenty of rules when you think no one's looking. Try again.'

There was a pause. Then –

'Deepdean is different this term,' said Daisy, very reluctantly. 'I don't exactly— It has changed. You are part of that, and I don't quite like it. But I don't hate you.'

'Neither do I!' I said. 'I'm sorry if it seemed as though we did. That's horrid of us, and we ought not to have behaved that way. Especially as I know – I know how beastly it can be here at first, when you come from far away.'

'Yes, it can,' said Amina. 'I thought *you'd* understand, and I couldn't work out why you didn't seem to. I thought pulling the alarm-clock prank might finally bring you on side.'

I could feel my face burning, and I was glad it was night. 'I did understand,' I said. 'I ought to have showed it. And – well, the alarm clocks were clever, but I liked what you did today better. The banner, I mean. That was brave.'

'I had to say something! My parents didn't do it, and I won't have any more gossip about them. I love making up stories, but some things are too important to tell stories about. It's – well, it's worth being taken out of school over, if it comes to that.'

'Do you think your parents will do that?' I asked.

'I don't know. They want to, but I've talked them out of worse things. I hope they don't. I like this place.'

We really had been wrong about Amina, I thought. She was determined, and clever, and I wished dreadfully we had not snubbed her this term.

'Here – can we begin again?' I asked. 'Be friends? Whether or not you stay.'

329

'Really?' asked Amina.

'No!' said Daisy.

'YES,' I said, elbowing her. 'She means yes. You're a good person, and so am I, and so is Daisy, even though we haven't been behaving like it.'

'Thank you,' said Amina, her lips quirking into a smile. 'I'll hold you to that. Oh, and by the way – it's poetry.'

'What's poetry?' asked Daisy suspiciously.

'That thing you were saying, over and over. *Stupid stuff.* It's from that composition Miss Dodgson gave us by accident, remember? The poetry by that man with an English name that we didn't know. Home – no, House. House-something.'

'Housman!' shrieked Daisy. 'HOUSMAN! I – you – Amina El Maghrabi, that does it. I forgive you for everything. Friends it is. Hazel, come with me at *once*.'

We scrambled back down the drainpipe into the dorm. We *had* to find a copy of that poem.

'What's up with you?' asked Kitty, astonished at our faces. 'You were miserable just now.'

'We have had an important breakthrough in the case,' said Daisy. 'We need two things from the three of you. First, we need you to remain on high alert during Leaving Prayers tomorrow. We can't stop being detectives yet, do you understand? And second, we urgently need you to help us get into the Library, first thing in the morning.'

8

We had only a few minutes. As we crept through the big doors from Library corridor into the high, leather-bound Library itself on Monday morning, we could hear the rumble of the organ through the walls, and thumps and shuffles as everyone took their seats in the Hall.

Gossip was that Mr Thompson-Bates had been released without charge, and the mood on the way down to school had been sombre. Everyone seemed to be looking about themselves for murderers in the bushes or among the smartly dressed huddles of grown-ups. There is something particularly terrible about imagining a mother or a father as a criminal. They ought to be dull, safe, rather embarrassing and really hardly human, not criminals plotting dreadful murders – but as Daisy and I had discovered in the course of our adventures so far, no one is immune from suspicion, and anyone in the world might be driven to do something awful. But now here we were, and the answer to the mystery was at last almost within our grasp.

We hurried past the bookshelves far too quickly, our feet drumming against the wooden floor. It seemed so rude to disturb the soft library hush – but this was a crucial matter of detection.

'Housman, Housman, Housman,' muttered Daisy. 'Here it is, in Poetry! Well, it must be this *Shropshire Lad* thing. Heavens, there are lots. Hazel, let's both take copies. You begin at the beginning and I'll begin at the end and we'll work towards each other. Scan each page for the *stupid stuff* line and once you've found it keep reading. QUICK!'

I began scrambling through the copy I was holding, the words leaping out at me almost without meaning. It was a strange poem, very long and obscure. But it was Daisy who discovered what we were looking for.

'Here, here!' she cried. '*Terence, this is stupid stuff* – it's poem sixty-two, at the very back.'

As I hurried to catch up with her, she began to read, brow furrowed.

'It's all about being drunk – and then there's some stuff about a dead cow, but . . .'

She trailed off, and then she let out a shriek. 'HAZEL! The last verse! LOOK AT IT!'

My eyes flew down the page, and my heart stopped.

'Read it to me,' said Daisy. 'Read it, so I don't think I'm making it up.'

So I began:

> '*There was a king reigned in the East:*
> *There, when kings will sit to feast,*
> *They get their fill before they think*
> *With poisoned meat and poisoned drink.*
> *He gathered all that springs to birth*
> *From the many-venomed earth;*
> *First a little, thence to more,*
> *He sampled all her killing store . . .*
> *They – they . . . PUT ARSENIC IN HIS*
> *   MEAT*
> *AND STARED AGHAST TO WATCH*
> *   HIM EAT!'*

'Daisy!' My hands were shaking, and I felt short of breath. Daisy and I stared at each other, thrilled and horrified in equal measure.

'Hazel – Watson – this the answer. The king in this poem – he wanted to protect himself against poisoning: he knew that lots of people would want to murder him because he was in power. So he *took poison on purpose*, for *ages*, to build up a tolerance to it. Then, when his subjects put arsenic in his meat, he could eat it up without it affecting him. THIS is why the poisonings didn't make proper sense to us!'

'But – is it really possible?' I asked. 'Wouldn't you just die if you ate poison?'

'Not if you were careful not to have too much, and your body was used to it!' said Daisy. 'I've heard about this before, once, but I wasn't paying proper attention. Oh! This explains *everything*. We couldn't get over how much uncertainty there was in the poisoning plans, could we? Why give your wife a drink when she might refuse it and force you to drink it instead? How could you be sure that poisoned salt would only kill its intended victim? The answer to both of those questions is: you wouldn't. You couldn't.

'No one but Mrs Rivers and Mrs Thompson-Bates felt the effects of the poison, but NOT because they were the only people poisoned. Oh no! Hazel, we know now why Mr Thompson-Bates was quoting Housman at us. He's been taking arsenic *on purpose*!'

'But if – if Mr Thompson-Bates has been dosing himself with arsenic for long enough to build up a tolerance – *why*?'

'As to that,' said Daisy. 'AS TO THAT, it's really rather obvious. Stop thinking just about this weekend, Hazel. We mustn't assume that the murder had to happen *now*. Who would Mr Thompson-Bates be guaranteed to see, again and again? And think, too, about the salt trick. If Mr Thompson-Bates was already sitting right next to Mrs Rivers, why would he need to employ something so risky? We know he could just have scattered arsenic over her plate – he didn't need to complicate things by sending a poisoned salt cellar along the table. But someone else, sitting further away, would need to. Beanie suggested it, remember, only for the wrong person. We ought to have listened to her – it's infuriating how clever she's become!'

'Mr Thompson-Bates picked up the salt from the table when Mrs Rivers collapsed,' I said, thinking through it. 'Mr Stone saw him do it. But that doesn't mean that he was the person who brought it to dinner.'

'Once again, we've been looking at this all wrong,' said Daisy. 'Everything in this case – the woods, and the dinner, and the garden party – they *were* all linked, but not in the way we thought. And Beanie *did* see a couple, a victim and a murderer. But our mistake was that we got them mixed up.'

I nodded, shock and detective excitement thrilling through me.

'We thought that we didn't have the full story,' I said. 'And now we know why.'

'Oh, quick, Hazel, quick, before Prayers begins!'

And together we ran out of the Library – on our way to resolve our eighth murder case.

9

We were just in time. The organ, played by Rev MacLean, was giving one final blare as we slipped through the double doors and into the seats that Kitty had saved for us in the fourth-form row. The mistresses were all on stage, wearing caps and gowns and looking official.

I glanced about, and saw the Inspector nodding at me, his hat low on his head – I wanted desperately to get to him, but several rows separated us. I saw everyone from Table Four: Mr and Mrs El Maghrabi, Mr Turnbull, Mr and Mrs Dow, Mr Stone, Mrs Thompson-Bates, pale and drawn, and rather hunched over in her seat – and next to her, looking triumphant, Mr Thompson-Bates.

I gasped, and nudged Daisy. He *was* already free.

Miss Barnard, in her billowing scholar's gown, stood up, and she looked weakened and sad.

'Good morning,' she said. 'Thank you all for being here. As you know, this has become a weekend of tragedy, not celebration. The police have advised me that the truth of what has happened here may never be fully revealed, and so – and so I have taken the decision to close the school after this morning.'

Her voice trembled as whispers rippled around the room, and her hands gripped the lectern.

'I would also like to stress that these actions have no bearing on this school, or its proud history. Deepdean School for Girls is more than the unfortunate things that have happened within its walls.'

There was a scattering of applause – but I noticed several concerned looks between parents. I saw Mrs Freebody making a face at Mr Freebody behind her hand, and an answering grimace from him. They could not understand what Mr Thompson-Bates was doing back at school.

'But we cannot end this term – end Deepdean – without acknowledging the efforts of our girls,' said Miss Barnard. 'We will begin with the award for first-form singing, which goes to . . .'

I was humming with nerves as Miss Barnard gave out plaques and cups and colours. Deepdean would close unless we revealed the truth. But how were we to manage it before the end of the morning?

I was dragged back to reality when Miss Barnard said, 'And now, the Huckerby-Ostler Tennis Scholarship, for a girl who shows true promise in the sport. This year it is awarded to . . .'

We all swivelled to look at Lallie Thompson-Bates, who was huddled among the other third formers. She looked utterly miserable, and I felt desperately sorry for her. Poor Lallie – and if only she knew what we were intending to say!

'. . . LAVINIA TEMPLE,' said Miss Barnard.

'NO IT ISN'T!' said Lavinia loudly. Kitty let out a squeal and Beanie flung her arms around Lavinia, who had gone rigid with shock.

'I assure you, it is,' said Miss Barnard. 'Please come and collect your award, Miss Temple. Hurry up!'

Lavinia, absolutely scarlet with confusion, staggered out of her seat and onto the stage, almost dropping the small cup as Miss Barnard handed it to her. We whooped and cheered, and I turned round to see Patricia standing up and clapping frantically, as Mr Temple tried to get her to sit down. 'BRAVO, LAVINIA!' she screamed. 'That's my . . . my stepdaughter! She's won a prize!'

'I've had a thought!' Daisy whispered to me under cover of the clapping. 'I would never ordinarily suggest this, but I believe these are desperate times. Hazel, the next time any of us wins a prize, we have to tell the school who the murderer really is when we get up on stage.'

'That's an idiotic idea!' I gasped. It was so dramatic, and it went against all our Deepdean training. A girl could not simply take over the stage and give a speech at the best of times – much less a speech accusing a grown-up of being a cold-blooded murderer. 'And what if no one else wins a prize?'

'Of course we will,' said Daisy, rolling her eyes. 'We're all quite brilliant. And anyway – didn't you hear Barny? She means to close the school after this morning. If we don't speak now, we'll lose our chance of proving to everyone what really happened. It's our last chance!'

I knew she was right.

'But Barny will be furious! It'll look dreadful!' It was my last, weak argument.

'So she will, and so it will, but in this case, solving the crime and saving the school is more important!' said Daisy.

I gave up.

Daisy motioned Kitty, Lavinia and Beanie to her and whispered in their ears. They both gasped at her, and Kitty said, 'We CAN'T!'

'We can!' hissed Daisy. 'We *have* to!'

I sat, tense and nervous, the clapping and cheering ringing in my ears tinnily, as though I was slightly elsewhere. The Inspector was trying to catch my eye, his face worried – of course he could tell that we were up to something.

'. . . And the Fitzgerald Award for Most Improved Girl goes to . . . REBECCA MARTINEAU,' said Miss Barnard.

10

'Oh NO,' said Beanie.

'What is *wrong* with you all today?' grumbled Sophie Croke-Finchley – who, I thought, looked as though she had rather expected to win the award herself. 'Why are you behaving so oddly? Go up and get your award!'

'Go on, Beans, go on!' whispered Kitty, shoving her forwards.

'I don't want to! I can't! Help!' gasped Beanie.

'You *can*,' I said to her. 'I know you can. Just focus above everyone's heads so you can't see them. Go *on*, Beanie!'

Beanie gave us one last despairing look and then went staggering up through the rows of seats to the stage, looking like a lamb going to the slaughter.

'Congratulations, Rebecca,' said Miss Barnard, holding her hand out to Beanie to shake.

'Um,' said Beanie.

'GO ON, BEANIE!' roared Lavinia.

'Um, excuse me,' said Beanie. 'Could I say something?'

'Certainly not, Miss Martineau,' said Miss Barnard. 'Go back and sit down, and well done.'

'But I *do* need to say something,' said Beanie desperately. I could see her hands trembling.

'Sit. Down,' said Miss Barnard, her lips thinning. I could see parents and girls looking about at each other in confusion. Amina was giggling. This was not planned – what was going on?

'No!' said Beanie. 'I'm terribly sorry, Miss Barnard, I will in a moment, but I just need to say that, er – I'm *so* sorry, but I think that *Mrs* Thompson-Bates was the person who killed Mrs Rivers on Saturday.'

The Hall went so still that it seemed under a fairy-tale spell. But Mrs Thompson-Bates twitched, a whole-body involuntary shiver, and Mr Thompson-Bates snapped his head round to stare at her. I saw that, and I knew – I knew we were right.

'This is no time for pranks. *Sit down or I shall have you expelled*,' said Miss Barnard into the pool of silence that had filled the Hall.

Only Daisy was unaffected. She stood, and put up her hand.

'Miss Barnard!' she said. 'It's true!'

'Miss Wells, I am disappointed in you,' said Miss Barnard. 'If you do not sit down and be quiet, I will have to ask you to leave.'

Daisy turned and looked at me, her eyes huge and bright blue – and then I found that I was standing up. My cheeks burned and I could hear my own breath stuttering in my ears. I locked arms with Daisy, and then Kitty was standing too, and Lavinia.

Amina looked at me and Daisy and smiled – and then up she got, dragging Clementine with her.

'Fourth form!' cried Miss Barnard. 'Leave the Hall at once. Miss Martineau, give me back your award. This is too much!'

I saw Miss Lappet shaking her head and tutting, and Mamzelle staring at us, her face puzzled. And then, through a blur of shame, I saw someone else stand up too. I blinked my eyes clear, just as Beanie made a small shrill noise.

The person who was standing was a bird-thin woman with skin so pale it looked quite translucent. Her shoulders were hunched, and she flinched away from herself as though her very clothes hurt her. She was dragging on the arm of the man next to her – and when he stood up as well, I saw that it was Mr Martineau, looking half embarrassed and half stern.

'Mummy!' cried Beanie. 'MUMMY! What are you doing here? What are you *doing*?'

'Excuse me,' said Beanie's mother to Miss Barnard, calling up through the well of the Hall. 'Excuse me! Please ... Becky wouldn't have stood up and said something she didn't believe. Please, could you listen to her?'

'Hear, hear!' said Mr Freebody, and he got up as well. 'Let the girls be heard!'

Kitty went scarlet.

'Ooh, YES!' said Patricia, bouncing to her feet and dragging on Mr Temple's sleeve. 'Get up, darling, let's be supportive.' Mr and Mrs Temple stood up at exactly the same time, and glared at each other.

Miss Barnard gripped the lectern, looking absolutely grey with distress. I could feel the situation slipping away from her, and I knew she could too. The Hall seemed to be half full of standing people now.

'If I may,' said the Inspector, getting to his feet. He spoke quietly, but, all the same, everyone turned to look at him. 'Although I was not here in an official capacity this morning, I am a police officer. Let me take the fourth form – and any other interested parties – into another room to work this problem out. You can continue your ceremony without further disruptions.'

'That,' said Miss Barnard shakily, 'is an excellent idea. Mr and Mrs Thompson-Bates, would you go with them, please?'

As Daisy led us from the Hall like a queen processing before her courtiers, we looked about at each other in amazement. Had we – had we really – taken on Deepdean traditions and *won*?

11

We ended up in Reverend MacLean's cubby – a rather odd sensation, being on the other side of the door for once. But the rules really had shifted today. I remembered our very first mystery, when Daisy and I hid behind the Music Room curtain to listen to the Inspector revealing the solution of the mystery to its suspects. And now here we were, unravelling the case ourselves to a room of concerned grown-ups – and Mr and Mrs Thompson-Bates. He stood up straight, glaring at us, and she was huddled on a chair at the edge of the room, wincing and darting us furious glances. The Inspector stood between them and the door, and I smiled at him gratefully.

There was one thing we had to discuss before we began, and that was the presence of Mrs Martineau. She clung to Mr Martineau, and Beanie clung to her, so they made one lumpy, adoring figure.

'I wanted to surprise you, Becky,' she said. 'I hoped you might win a prize – and look, you did! I *said* you were clever, didn't I?'

'Yes, but – you're ill, Mummy,' said Beanie. 'What if you get worse?'

'Oh, sweetheart, it's a bit past that,' said Mrs Martineau. 'I know your father was against it, but I wanted to see my lovely girl – I couldn't miss the whole weekend, could I? Now, what's all this about you knowing who killed that poor woman?'

'They don't,' said Mr Thompson-Bates.

'Be quiet,' said the Inspector.

'I was the one who found out about it first!' said Beanie, drawing herself up. 'We've been detecting the case all weekend, and now Daisy and Hazel have solved it.'

'That remains to be seen,' said the Inspector drily.

'For your sake, it had better be properly explained,' said Mr Freebody to Kitty. 'What a thing to do to your poor headmistress!'

'Really, darling,' said Mrs Freebody, her face creased up with worry. 'Was this to punish us for – *you* know?'

'It's got nothing to do with you!' hissed Kitty. 'We've *really* solved Mrs Rivers' murder!'

'This all sounds like one of Lavinia's lies,' said Mr Temple.

'Oh, I'm sure it isn't! *Do* tell!' said Patricia.

'I quite agree. Come along, Detectives,' said the Inspector. 'State your case.'

We all looked at Daisy, who beamed, took a deep breath and began.

'It all started because of a poem,' she said. 'That is – I don't suppose it really started there, but that's how Hazel and I discovered the truth.'

'A *poem*!' said Lavinia.

'Yes, *A Shropshire Lad*. You ought to try listening in English lessons sometimes,' said Daisy, as though she had not forgotten all about the poem until Amina reminded us. 'Poetry can be terribly useful – although, as it happens, *this is stupid stuff* is not part of a poem we were ever supposed to be taught. It's on the Big Girls' curriculum, though – and I suppose it must be on the curriculum at Weston School as well.'

'I've never heard of it!' said Mr Thompson-Bates.

'Oh, *do* be quiet!' cried Mrs Thompson-Bates suddenly. 'You own two copies, James.'

'*You* be quiet,' growled Mr Thompson-Bates. 'She's lying.'

'It was actually Beanie who began everything,' I said. '*She* ought to start.'

'I – I saw what I thought was a murder in Oakeshott Woods on Friday morning,' said Beanie, blushing. 'Far off on the ridge, so I couldn't see who it was exactly. But I did see a man and a woman arguing, and the man choking her. She fell to the ground and I thought he'd killed her.'

'Yes, yes, indeed,' said Daisy, waving her hand. 'Beanie told us that, and so we began to investigate the case as a murder. We were looking about for a male guest at the Anniversary who was there without his wife, and our attention became fixed on two people: Mr Turnbull and Mr Stone. So Hazel and I decided to watch them at the gala dinner on Saturday evening, in case they did something that would point to their guilt. What we weren't expecting at *all* was that Mrs Rivers would be murdered during dinner – but when she was, the whole investigation changed.'

'Because of Mrs Rivers' death, we began to suspect that what Beanie had seen had only been *attempted* murder,' I said. 'We thought that a man on Mrs Rivers' table, Table Four, must have tried to kill her in the woods and then finally managed it at dinner. We never did manage to work out why Mrs Rivers didn't go straight to the police about the attack, though – it was a piece of the puzzle that we couldn't make fit.

'Anyway, there were five men on Table Four: Mr Turnbull, Mr El Maghrabi, Mr Dow, Mr Stone and Mr Thompson-Bates. We staged a re-enactment of the crime and ruled out Mr Turnbull, as there was no moment when he got close enough to Mrs Rivers to poison her. We also realized that Mr Dow could only be guilty if he'd used his wife to administer the poison, since only she got up from her seat during dinner.'

'Exactly,' said Daisy. 'Now, you must remember, we thought we were chasing a *man*, or at least a male mastermind. The poisoning of Mrs Thompson-Bates at the garden party, and the evidence of the smashed and poisoned glass – which was Mr Thompson-Bates's, not his wife's, although their glasses were swapped – led us to believe that Mr Thompson-Bates, who had been sitting next to Mrs Rivers at dinner on Saturday night, had seen something important, and was in fact the intended victim of that second poisoning. Mr El Maghrabi never went near enough to Mr Thompson-Bates to have been able to poison his drink, so we were down to two suspects: Mr Stone and the Dows. A further re-creation of the crime showed that only one person – Mr Stone – would have been able to slip poison into Mr Thompson-Bates's glass at the correct time, and so we thought we had our answer.

'We decided to set a trap for the murderer. But it wasn't Mr Stone who was caught by it – it was Mr Thompson-Bates! When he attacked Hazel in the tower, we realized that he had been the man responsible for the attack that Beanie saw in the woods, and so we thought we had found our culprit. But what Hazel and I discovered this morning is that although Mr Thompson-Bates is a brute and a bully, and he *was* the man we saw in the woods that day, he *didn't cause Mrs Rivers' death*. Because— Oh, tell them, Hazel!'

'Because he *was* the intended victim, only not of the second poisoning, of the *first*,' I said.

Several people exclaimed.

'I'm afraid I don't follow,' said the Inspector, quirking his eyebrows at us both.

'This is nonsense,' said Mrs Thompson-Bates, who had gone deathly pale.

'I quite agree,' said Mr Thompson-Bates. 'You ought to look at Tom Stone again. He's a criminal, after all!'

'When you think about it, it's odd,' said Daisy. 'That a man whose first impulse is to strangle a woman – a violent, angry sort of thing to do – should move on to poisoning so soon afterwards. Poisoning is a crime that's about clever concealment and planning – Mrs Rivers' murderer would have had to come to the gala dinner knowing that they were going to kill, since there's no poison to be found on a dinner table!'

'And Mr Stone – who is innocent – gave us a hint that this crime was very well planned,' I said. 'He mentioned Mr Thompson-Bates picking up a salt cellar as everyone crowded around Mrs Rivers, and slipping it in his pocket. We realized that must be how the poison had got into Mrs Rivers' food – a doctored salt cellar! There were two salt cellars going round the table at the same time – not something anyone would particularly notice. We hadn't been able to work it out before, you see.'

'Beanie – who I admit has been rather clever during this investigation – suggested that the murderer might have *passed* Mrs Rivers the poison in the guise of something like salt or pepper,' Daisy put in. 'But we thought that must be nonsense, because of the simple fact that only Mrs Rivers was poisoned. If the poison was in a condiment, travelling all round the table, then why didn't anyone else get ill?'

'Because this is utter fantasy!' said Mrs Thompson-Bates. 'This is nonsense, this is—'

'Because we were looking at it all wrong!' I said, cutting her off. 'We assumed that Mrs Rivers must have been the target, but instead she was simply *extremely unlucky.*'

'And it really *was* luck!' Daisy butted in. 'It was sheer and absolute chance that Mrs Rivers was the only person on the table taken ill. The murderer had absolutely no way of knowing that Mr Dow loved bland school food, and so would refuse salt. They also couldn't know beforehand that Mrs Turnbull would be missing from the table, that Mr and Mrs El Maghrabi would refuse to eat the starter at all, because it contained pork, or that Mrs Dow would leave the table in tears before the meal even began. In fact, they knew only one thing: that Mr Thompson-Bates *would* salt his food. I saw him do it, I remember! The murderer expected him to take the salt cellar and pour enough poison over his food to kill him. It's much cleverer than trying it anywhere else, when you think about it! The murderer could claim that the kitchens had made a mistake. A public dinner would be the perfect place to hide a very personal crime!

'But what happened was – not exactly what was supposed to. Mr T-B *did* dose his food liberally before passing the salt cellar to Mrs Rivers, who did the same. But although she died, he did not, because there was one thing that the poisoner could *not* know: that somehow Mr T-B had already discovered the plan, and had been preparing for it for months. Hazel, recite the poem we found, the one by Housman.'

I cleared my throat. I felt jumpy with excitement, and the words tumbled out of my mouth.

> *They put arsenic in his meat*
> *And stared aghast to watch him eat;*
> *They poured strychnine in his cup*
> *And shook to see him drink it up:*
> *They shook, they stared as white's their shirt:*
> *Them it was their poison hurt.'*

'Don't you see!' said Daisy. 'Mr Thompson-Bates is an arsenic-eater! He's been doing it for *months*. That was why his form suffered, and why he'd been crashing out

12

Mrs Thompson-Bates took a gasping breath.

'The key to this whole mystery is closeness,' said Daisy, nodding. 'We know from Lavinia's tennis magazines that Mrs Thompson-Bates never used to go on tour with her husband before this year – but now she does. Mrs Thompson-Bates might have discovered some rather unpleasant things about her husband – that he gambles, for instance, and goes dancing with other women.'

'You don't know the half of it!' said Mrs Thompson-Bates. 'If you did – you ought to feel sorry for me. He's an unfeeling brute, and he's using *my* money to enjoy himself. When it could have been *my* tennis career, if I hadn't married him! He doesn't know what I've done for him. I've sacrificed so much! So I decided – I decided I wouldn't have it any longer. We Deepdean girls have more respect for ourselves than that! I *did* something about it.'

'I knew months ago,' said Mr Thompson-Bates, sneering. 'I found fly papers soaking in her room. I knew she wasn't intending to use them for her face, and I knew what to do about it. I remembered my Housman! Cordy can't outwit *me*! I know her too well.'

'What about the woods?' Daisy asked. 'Why did you nearly strangle her?'

'Because I told him I'd be going to Wimbledon this year – as a player,' said Mrs Thompson-Bates wildly. She seemed to have decided there was nothing to lose at this point. 'And – and he snapped!'

She reached up and untied the scarf from around her neck, revealing a dark pattern of bruises printed across her skin. 'He's a beast, I tell you! I knew then that it was all over. I had to get rid of him once and for all, I tell you! I thought – I thought the gala dinner that night would be perfect.'

'So Mrs Thompson-Bates put arsenic in a salt cellar,' said Daisy. 'She got it out of her clutch bag and put it on the table when no one was watching – Hazel and I did see her fiddling with her clutch, but we thought nothing of it, because there are plenty of innocent reasons why a lady might need to get something from her bag. Then she passed it to her left, quite innocently. Mr Dow didn't take it, but Mr Thompson-Bates did, and so did Mrs Rivers. Mrs Thompson-Bates then sat there, waiting for her husband to drop dead – only he didn't. It was *Mrs Rivers* who died instead.'

'The other people on the table were only supposed to be ill. No one was supposed to die!' cried Mrs Thompson-Bates. 'I never meant to kill anyone but him!'

'Yes, indeed. Mrs Thompson-Bates was terribly upset on Saturday when her husband wasn't taken ill, but Mrs Rivers was – so upset that she sat frozen for long enough for Mr T-B to rush round the table and snatch up the salt cellar. He must have realized that was how the poison had been given to Mrs Rivers! He slid it into his pocket – and now he had ammunition to hurt his wife. The next day, at the garden party, he played a truly horrid trick on her. He poured poison into the glass they were sharing, and sipped from it without issues. Then he was given another by Mr Stone, and the glasses got mixed up when Mrs Thompson-Bates had a sneezing fit, but it didn't matter – he knew he could safely drink from either. But Mrs T-B, as we know, was poisoned. I saw her grasping at his jacket, just before she was taken away to San – I thought she was just trying to hold onto him, but she must have realized then what he had in his pocket!'

'I had to kill her!' said Mr Thompson-Bates. 'Be reasonable. It was her or me!'

'It was him or me!' cried Mrs Thompson-Bates. 'I had to! He's a beast! He choked me!'

'She's a witch!' said Mr Thompson-Bates. 'She's been poisoning me!'

Patricia said, 'How awful!'

'Very ingenious!' said Inspector Priestley. 'Mr and Mrs Thompson-Bates, I am arresting you both, for murder and attempted murder.'

He led the still-arguing Thompson-Bateses out of the room. The rest of us were left blinking at each other in amazement.

'We *are* ingenious, aren't we?' asked Daisy. 'Hazel and I are really rather clever.'

'It's astonishing!' said Mrs Martineau. She was still clinging to her husband, and her cheeks were pale, but the light of battle was in her eyes – she looked very much like Beanie all of a sudden. 'Becky, I never knew that *this* is what you did at school! And look at all your friends! You seem so happy.'

'I really am, Mummy,' said Beanie. 'I want to stay here next year. I don't want – please don't move me away!'

'I'm afraid we shall have to, if the school closes!' said Mr Martineau.

'But the case is solved!' cried Daisy. 'It can't be closed now!'

'Parents may not see it that way, Daisy,' said Mrs Freebody.

'But there must be something we can do!' said Mrs Martineau.

'Do you know,' said Mrs Freebody, 'I think I have a very good idea. You girls always think that you invented school life, but in fact nothing really changes. Now, what is the thing that makes this school work? How would *you* persuade someone to do something?'

A glimmer came into Daisy's eyes, and Kitty suddenly burst out laughing. 'Mum!' she said. 'That's genius.'

'I know, darling,' said Mrs Freebody. 'Now, will you stop being cross with me?'

'No!' said Kitty. 'That is – of course I will.'

13

Kitty, Beanie and Lavinia's people all slipped away back into the Hall, and we were left alone. We crept through the corridors of Deepdean to Old Wing entrance, where the Inspector was waiting with Mr and Mrs Thompson-Bates, both in handcuffs, their faces set angrily.

We explained what we were hoping to do, and the Inspector frowned. 'We shall have to hope it works,' he said seriously to us.

'Why should you care?' said Daisy. 'It isn't your school in danger, is it?'

'I'm sure I've spent more time here than I ever did in my own school,' said the Inspector. 'And – it would be a grave mistake to break up the Detective Society. Why, we can't let the criminals off so lightly!'

'You're mocking us,' said Daisy, eyes narrowed.

'I may be, Madam Super,' said the Inspector, and his face crinkled up into a smile. 'But I truly believe that the world would lose something if you and Miss Wong were separated.'

'Thank you,' I said to him quietly. Daisy harrumphed, but I could tell she was pleased.

'I have to say, Kitty, that your mother would have been an excellent Detective Society member in her youth.'

'It's annoyingly true!' said Kitty. 'I shall never tell her so.'

We had barely arrived when I heard the doors of the Hall opening, and a hum of people coming towards us along Library corridor. Daisy and the Inspector and I all exchanged glances, and Daisy slipped her hand into mine and squeezed it fiercely.

Then the first parents appeared, and they were all whispering together. *She planned it!* I heard, and *How unladylike! And she went to Deepdean – look at what they're being taught!*

But then I heard one mother say, *Of course, it was the* girls *who worked it out. The Deepdean spirit – we were always taught to be logical!*

Really quite clever, actually . . .

Very naughty, but—

So brave*! Courage has* always *been valued here, of* course *. . .*

And there were other women, I heard – really, it's almost understandable, and she did have her daughter to think of . . .

But with the school so changed – ought we to . . .

Really so many jolly good things about it, though . . .

Perhaps we should give it another chance – after all, I heard that the Freebodys *won't be removing* their *girls . . .*

And do you know what I *heard? Next year, Deepdean may be welcoming a* very *illustrious pupil. She's just about to turn eleven, you know . . .*

You don't mean—

I do! Exactly. *Can you imagine . . . And if we took them out, they'd miss the chance . . .*

The hum built until it was a roar, voices all around us. Would it be enough? Could gossip save Deepdean school?

Everyone caught sight of Mr and Mrs Thompson-Bates at once. The Inspector had one hand on each of their shoulders, leaving their wrists, in their glinting handcuffs, quite clear to see.

They both raised their chins defiantly and glared at the crowd.

'Mummy! Daddy!' said a small voice. Lallie was there, surrounded by the rest of the third form. Binny looked quite furious – but not even she could really blame us for this. I felt dreadfully sorry for poor Lallie. To lose both parents, in less than a day, is more than I think even I could bear. Her face was red with crying.

'Lallie, dear, we may be gone for some time,' said Mr Thompson-Bates.

'You never think of me!' gasped Lallie. 'You're so wrapped up in each other that half the time I don't think you even remember I exist!'

'Of course we do!' said Mr Thompson-Bates.

'I did this for *you*, Lallie!' said Mrs Thompson-Bates. 'You don't know what your father's really like!'

'I know what you're both like. And you did it for *yourselves*,' Lallie hissed, and she turned and fled.

The crowd parted again, and Miss Barnard walked up to the Thompson-Bateses. Her back was very straight and her hands were clenched together, almost as though she was praying.

'I have nothing to say to you, Mr Thompson-Bates. But, Cordelia, I am utterly disappointed in you. You are *nothing* like a Deepdean girl should be. I have made my decision: I will not be closing Deepdean. I appreciate that some parents may feel that they would like to send their daughters elsewhere, but I hope that they will think hard about that decision. Deepdean creates intelligent, brave, sensible young women who dare much to help each other, and I hope it will be doing so for another fifty years at least.

'Inspector, please take these two away. Fourth formers, I would like to speak to you privately.'

And that, as Daisy would say, was that.

14

And now it is Monday afternoon, and House is full of girls rushing about, packing their trunks and shrieking that they can't find their games knickers.

Our meeting with Miss Barnard was short, but surprising.

'I ought to expel you,' she told us calmly. 'Working with the police! Spying and leaving the school grounds and lying to your mistresses!'

'But you won't,' said Daisy.

'Miss Wells! Please! You are on very shaky ground at the moment. Whatever has got into you this term?'

'We're sorry about the lying and the rule-breaking,' I said. 'But – I don't think we're sorry about solving the case.'

Kitty, Beanie and Lavinia shook their heads.

'Miss Barnard, they really ought to be praised,' said Inspector Priestley. 'They outwitted the Deepdean police force as well as the Thompson-Bateses. It's astonishingly good detective work.'

'I certainly can't make a public show of praising them,' said Miss Barnard. 'But – girls, I am grateful to you from the bottom of my heart. Jean's death – I still can hardly comprehend it. But if I had never known what really happened to her, she would feel dead twice over. I want you to promise me – promise not to discuss this with anyone other than the police. No more gossip, if you please!'

'We promise!' we all chorused.

'Well then,' said Miss Barnard. 'Go on, and let me talk to the Inspector.'

We ran away, feeling grateful and surprised and – strange. What we did was no longer a secret at Deepdean, not even from our headmistress.

'It rather takes some of the fun out of it, doesn't it?' said Daisy to me.

'No!' I said. 'Yes. It makes it feel more real, though.'

'That is annoyingly grown up of you,' said Daisy. 'But I think you might be right.'

Kitty and Binny have gone home with their parents – and I can tell that Mrs Freebody's swift and persuasive gossip work impressed both Kitty and Binny, whatever they try to pretend. Beanie has left with hers too, to be with her mother for as long as she can. It feels terribly bitter that we solved a murder, but we could not solve Mrs Martineau's illness. I think we are truly growing up, for we know that there are some things too dreadful to be fixed by a denouement and handcuffs.

Mrs Dow finally got her way: Emily Dow is to be taken out of Deepdean, and educated at home. I saw her leave, and I never knew she could smile so widely. But poor Lallie will stay at House this summer, while her parents' trial takes place. Mr Thompson-Bates will be tried for attempted murder, and Mrs Thompson-Bates for murder – and I cannot free myself of the guilt that we took both parents away from a girl almost our own age. It niggles at me, like a broken tooth. I do know, though, that we had to find out the truth – for Mrs Rivers, and for Deepdean.

Lavinia is downstairs with Patricia and her mother and father, arguing about where she is to be sent for the hols, and Amina is with hers.

She came into our dorm just now, in flagrant violation of the unspoken rules of dorm pride.

'I just wanted to say,' she told us, 'that my parents are letting me come back next year. And – well, if you aren't busy this summer, you're welcome to come and visit me at home.'

'But your home is in—' I began.

'Cairo, I know,' said Amina. 'Far, but worth it. I like you, Daisy Wells and Hazel Wong. You're interesting. And I hope we're friends now.'

'Kind of you,' Daisy said, tilting her chin. 'But – well, Hazel and I already have plans for the hols.'

'Thank you, though!' I added, smiling at her.

'Oh, well, next year then,' said Amina cheerfully, and she stepped back out of the dorm. I glanced at Daisy.

'*Cairo!*' I whispered.

'I know, Hazel!' hissed Daisy. 'It doesn't do to seem too eager – she may still be listening. But just imagine – *Egypt*! Curses and mummies everywhere! How wonderful!'

'Amina is nice, isn't she?' I asked.

'She is all right,' said Daisy. 'I *suppose*.'

Now Daisy and I are sitting back to back on my bed. Some things, at least, do not change.

I am writing this up, and Daisy is whispering poetry to herself. She is terribly taken with the Housman poems, and has found some other gruesome lines which she is very pleased with.

'Do you know,' she has just said, 'we ought to have realized that this case was all about marriage. Couples run all the way through it. It would be the easiest thing in the world to murder *you*, if I wanted to. I know everything about you, after all.'

I turned round and glared at her, and Daisy said, 'But I've already told you I wouldn't! I like you too much. Uncle Felix and Aunt Lucy are motoring down from

London, by the way. Bertie's coming as well, now he's heard about the case. They all want to take us out to dinner and tell us off for getting mixed up in a murder mystery again. Then we'll all go back to London.'

'All?' I asked.

'Of course,' said Daisy. 'I think Felix and Lucy prefer you to me – they certainly wouldn't think of taking me in without you. Oh, we'll be in London again for the summer! How thrilling!'

'And we'll be around Aunt Lucy,' I said, my heart lifting.

'Indeed. After all, if we are going to be the best detectives in the world, we need more training – it's no good hoping that schoolbooks will teach us everything we need. Only three more years of school, and then we can be detectives full time!'

Now I am thinking about training to be a detective. I realize that I rather like the idea.

'But what about university?' I asked.

'You can go if you like,' said Daisy. 'But I don't see the point. Some things, as I say, you can't learn at school, or university.'

'But you have to go!' I said. 'Otherwise I shall be on my own.'

'You might be for a while,' said Daisy. 'But, Hazel, I can promise you this: we shall always end up together, no matter what happens. We are simply at our best around each other, and it would be foolish to ignore that. Even if you married Alexander, I should forgive you and live in your spare room.'

'Is that a promise?' I asked.

'Utterly,' said Daisy. 'And have you ever known me to break a promise? Family is family, and you are mine, Hazel Wong.'

We turned to face each other and did the Detective Society handshake. And I knew then that Daisy was telling the truth.

Daisy's Guide to Deepdean

Really, I think that there can hardly be any words to do with this case and Deepdean that even the most careless readers are not aware of by now, but Hazel insists on my writing this out for posterity. I suppose future generations will thank me.

- **Achilles heel** - a person's fatal flaw, the bit of themselves that always catches them out. It comes from the story of the Greek hero Achilles being dipped in magic water by his mother - only she held him by his heel, and he wasn't protected there.

- **Alumnae** - a way of talking about all the people who used to be at a school, but who are not there any more because they are too old.

- **Aspic** - a sort of savoury jelly, often with meat in it.

- **Atelier** – a French word for a workshop where things are made.

- **Bottled it** – if you bottle something, you fail to do it.

- **The Curse** – a way of talking about a woman's monthlies without actually talking about them at all.

- **Debagged** – if you debag someone you pull their trousers down as a prank.

- **A dish** – an attractive person.

- **Exeat** – this is usually a weekend when we are allowed to leave House and stay with our families. But you can also have exeat mornings, when you are just allowed out for tea or lunch with families.

- **Fondant fancies** – pretty iced cakes.

- **Lob** – a sort of tennis shot.

- **MacDonalds of Glencoe's Feast** – this is a very gruesome and fascinating story about some Scottish people at Glencoe who invited their enemies to a nice dinner and then killed them all.

- **Mary Celeste** – a famous ship that was discovered with all its crew missing, a mystery that has never been solved.

- **Mistress** – our Deepdean word for teacher.

- **Operator** – the person who puts through your telephone calls.

- **Patagonia** – a place in South America.

- **Pash** – a sort of love that one schoolgirl has for another. It is not meant to mean anything or be real, but I think that is silly, because the truth is that sometimes it is.

- **Petticoat** – a sort of underskirt.

- **Pips** – the noise on the telephone line that tells you you're running out of time.

- **A Red** – a slang word for Communist.

- **Rowed** – another word for argued.

- **RSvP** – this is French. It stands for *Répondez s'il vous plaît* and it is how you tell someone that you are coming to their event.

- **Sago pudding** – a sweet starchy pudding. It can be nice, but our House kitchen doesn't make it appealing at all.

- **Shrimps** – the littlest girls in the school, almost babies, really.

- **Slip** – an under-dress, for modesty.

- **Small pitchers have big ears** – a stupid saying that grown-ups use to mean that children are always listening.

- **Stodge** – a slang word for heavy school food.

- **Tuck** – sweets or cakes.

- **Wet** – weak or silly.

Author's Note and Acknowledgements

This is the third time I've taken Daisy and Hazel to Deepdean – and just as they're not quite the girls they were when they discovered Miss Bell's body in the Gym in *Murder Most Unladylike*, I'm not quite the author I was when I first imagined that scene.

I've somehow become ten years older in the time it's taken Daisy and Hazel to age two years. I have to admit to myself that if Daisy and Hazel looked at me these days, they would see an adult the same age as their mothers – so it felt fitting for the third murder mystery at Deepdean to be all about parents and families. (Of course, I completely deny any resemblance to my own marriage or family. My husband and I never argue, and we are marvellous to each other 100 per cent of the time.)

My school friends and I suffered through many gala weekends and Leaving Prayers, which is where Deepdean's Anniversary weekend came from. We also observed and took part in several pranks – not nearly as successful as the ones described in this book, though,

373

and we were very much told off afterwards. So don't get any ideas!

I loved studying poetry at school, primarily because so many old poems are about murders. Notable examples include Wordsworth's *Prelude* (several good bits with dead bodies – eagle-eyed readers will have seen this one pop up already, in *Arsenic For Tea*), Tennyson's *Maud* (many of Tennyson's poems are about murder, actually – he's a man after my own heart) and Keats's *La Belle Dame Sans Merci* (a female serial killer? I loved her at once). The particular poem referred to in this story is both brilliantly creepy and a good reminder that you can find out useful facts anywhere. Never stop paying attention and you'll be amazed at what weird things you can discover . . .

By the way: British schools had a habit of creating offshoot schools across the world in the first part of the twentieth century. The school Amina went to in Cairo would have been one of those – and pupils there would emerge from it using very British idioms, as she does. The Sato that Mrs Thompson-Bates mentions is Jiro Sato, Japanese tennis star, and the two women Daisy refers to in her list of famous Deepdeanites are based on real heroines Dorothy Levitt, one of the first female racing drivers and known as the 'fastest girl on earth', and Joan Procter, Komodo dragon enthusiast and creator of London Zoo's lizard house.

And so, on to the list of heroes and heroines who have made this book what it is.

Thank you to my experts and readers: Derrick Pounder, who told me very kindly that I was wrong about science; Alison Wong and Sarah Warry, who reminded me about nice napkins and the proper way to walk; Clare Rees, who pointed out that etiquette is NOT deportment; Dalia Elashry, Amina Youssef and Sara Sioufi, who helped bring Amina to life; Debora Robertson, who knows how things should be done; Melly Carr, the Inspector's official cheerleader; Charlie Morris, who loves this world almost as much as I do; Wei Ming Kam, whose comments always make me laugh; Anne Miller, the queen of logic; and Kathie Booth Stevens, my most faithful reader.

Thank you to my wonderful fans, who continue to bowl me over with their commitment to the books I write! Ella Turnbull won the right to see herself at Deepdean in the *Death in the Spotlight* pre-order competition. My interpretation of course bears no resemblance to the real Ella or her family, but I hope she enjoys seeing her name in this book. Thanks to fan Aaminah for giving me the idea for Amina's name (it now has a different spelling, but it's still the same one really!). And thanks to my teacher, Mr Dow, who saved my life when I was seven, and who has nothing in common with the Mr Dow in this book apart from his name. Finally, I always enjoy hearing fans' ideas about what the new book's title should be – and I liked Eliza's so much that I made it the title of Part Four.

Thanks to my wonderful Puffin Team Bunbreak, including (but not restricted to) my tireless champion of an editor Nat, my fab publicity team Harriet and Jasmine, my marketing superstar Sonia, my dazzling designer Dom, copyeditor Sarah, proofreader Sophie, editorial ninjas Steph and Wendy, and production controller Emma. Thank you to Nina Tara for another fantastic cover, and thank you to the wonderful Fritha Lindqvist, who has saved my bacon more times this year than I can count. Thanks also to the queen of agents, Gemma Cooper, who I'm so lucky to have on my side.

Thank you to all of my loving, supportive friends, especially my partner in crime Non Pratt, and to my fantastic family. Thanks especially (and again!) to my mother, Kathie Booth Stevens, who I hope I grow up to be half as good as, and to my husband, David Stevens, who absolutely did not have time to listen to me panic about this book, but who always made me feel as though he did. Oh, and one more thing: thank you to Watson the bearded dragon, my prickly little sidekick for the past ten years. I've never thanked her in a book before, but she's always deserved it.

Robin Stevens, Oxford, March 2019

Turn over to discover how it all began in:

1

This is the first murder that the Wells & Wong Detective Society has ever investigated, so it is a good thing Daisy bought me a new casebook. The last one was finished after we solved The Case of Lavinia's Missing Tie. The solution to that, of course, was that Clementine stole it in revenge for Lavinia punching her in the stomach during lacrosse, which was Lavinia's revenge for Clementine telling everyone Lavinia came from a broken home. I suspect that the solution to this new case may be more complex.

I suppose I ought to give some explanation of ourselves, in honour of the new casebook. Daisy Wells is the President of the Detective Society, and I, Hazel Wong, am its Secretary. Daisy says that this makes her Sherlock Holmes, and me Watson. This is probably fair. After all, I am much too short to be the heroine of this story, and who ever heard of a Chinese Sherlock Holmes?

That's why it's so funny that it was me who found Miss Bell's dead body. In fact, I think Daisy is still upset about it, though of course she pretends not to be. You see, Daisy is a heroine-like person, and so it should be her that these things happen to.

Look at Daisy and you think you know exactly the sort of person she is – one of those dainty, absolutely English girls with blue eyes and golden hair; the kind who'll gallop across muddy fields in the rain clutching hockey sticks and then sit down and eat ten iced buns at tea. I, on the other hand, bulge all over like Bibendum the Michelin Man; my cheeks are moony-round and my hair and eyes are stubbornly dark brown.

I arrived from Hong Kong part way through second form, and even then, when we were all still shrimps (*shrimps*, for this new casebook, is what we call the little lower-form girls), Daisy was already famous throughout Deepdean School. She rode horses, was part of the lacrosse team, and was a member of the Drama Society. The Big Girls took notice of her, and by May the entire school knew that the Head Girl herself had called Daisy a 'good sport'.

But that is only the outside of Daisy, the jolly-good-show part that everyone sees. The inside of her is not jolly-good-show at all.

It took me quite a while to discover that.

2

Daisy wants me to explain what happened this term up to the time I found the body. She says that is what proper detectives do – add up the evidence first – so I will. She also says that a good Secretary should keep her casebook on her at all times to be ready to write up important events as they happen. It was no good reminding her that I do that anyway.

The most important thing to happen in those first few weeks of the autumn term was the Detective Society, and it was Daisy who began that. Daisy is all for making up societies for things. Last year we had the Pacifism Society (dull) and then the Spiritualism Society (less dull, but then Lavinia smashed her mug during a séance, Beanie fainted and Matron banned spiritualism altogether).

But that was all last year, when we were still shrimps.

We can't be messing about with silly things like ghosts now that we are grown-up third formers – that was what Daisy said when she came back at the beginning of this term having discovered crime.

I was quite glad. Not that I was ever afraid of ghosts, exactly. Everyone knows there aren't any. Even so, there are enough ghost stories going round our school to horrify anybody. The most famous of our ghosts is Verity Abraham, the girl who committed suicide off the Gym balcony the term before I arrived at Deepdean, but there are also ghosts of an ex-mistress who locked herself into one of the music rooms and starved herself to death, and a little first-form shrimp who drowned in the pond.

As I said, Daisy decided that this year we were going to be detectives. She arrived at House with her tuck box full of books with sinister, shadowy covers and titles like *Peril at End House* and *Mystery Mile*. Matron confiscated them one by one, but Daisy always managed to find more.

We started the Detective Society in the first week of term. The two of us made a deadly secret pact that no one else, not even our dorm mates, Kitty, Beanie and Lavinia, could be told about it. It did make me feel proud, just me and Daisy having a secret. It was awfully fun too, creeping about behind the others' backs and pretending to be ordinary when all the time *we* knew we were detectives on a secret mission to obtain information.

Daisy set all our first detective missions. In that first week we crept into the other third-form dorm and read Clementine's secret journal, and then Daisy chose a first former and set us to find out everything we could about her. This, Daisy told me, was practice – just like memorizing the licences of every motor car we saw.

In our second week there was the case of why King Henry (our name for this year's Head Girl, Henrietta Trilling, because she is so remote and regal, and has such beautiful chestnut curls) wasn't at Prayers one morning. But it only took a few hours before everyone, not just us, knew that she had been sent a telegram saying that her aunt had died suddenly that morning.

'Poor thing,' said Kitty, when we found out. Kitty has the next-door bed to Daisy's in our dorm, and Daisy has designated her a Friend of the Detective Society, even though she is still not allowed to know about it. She has smooth, light brown hair and masses of freckles, and she keeps something hidden in the bottom of her tuck box that I thought at first was a torture device but turned out to be eyelash curlers. She is as mad about gossip as Daisy, though for less scientific reasons. 'Poor old King Henry. She hasn't had much luck. She was Verity Abraham's best friend, after all, and *you* know what happened to Verity. She hasn't been the same since.'

'I don't,' said Beanie, who sleeps next to me. Her real name is Rebecca but we call her Beanie because she is very small, and everything frightens her. Lessons frighten her most of all, though. She says that when she looks at a page all the letters and numbers get up and do a jig until she can't think straight. 'What did happen to Verity?'

'*She killed herself*,' said Kitty in annoyance. 'Jumped off the Gym balcony last year. Come on, Beans.'

'Oh!' said Beanie. 'Of course. I always thought she tripped.'

Sometimes Beanie is quite slow.

Something else happened at the beginning of term that turned out to be very important indeed: The One arrived.